his belly. Maybe the gentle lady would even
slip off Ace's back and choose to walk rather
than share the space with him.

She turned as best she could to peer at his
face. Raindrops hit her skin and dotted it with
liquid freckles. Her mouth formed the same
perfectly amazed circle that he had seen when
he had galloped on by her earlier.

He leaned backward in the saddle, ready to
dismount and walk the rest of the way to
Green Island.

"Truly? A genuine bounty hunter?"
Unbelievably, she broke into a grin that might
have shot the clouds out of the sky.

While in the third grade, **Carol Arens** had a teacher who noted that she ought to spend less time daydreaming and looking out of the window and more time on her sums. Today, Carol spends as little time on sums as possible. Daydreaming about plots and characters is still far more interesting to her.

As a young girl, she read books by the dozen. She dreamed that one day she would write a book of her own. A few years later Carol set her sights on a new dream. She wanted to be the mother of four children. She was blessed with a son, then three daughters. While raising them she never forgot her goal of becoming a writer. When her last child went to high school she purchased a big old clunky word processor and began to type out a story.

She joined Romance Writers of America, where she met generous authors who taught her the craft of writing a romance novel. With the knowledge she gained she sold her first book and saw her life-long dream come true.

Carol lives with her real-life hero husband Rick in Southern California, where she was born and raised. She feels blessed to be doing what she loves, with all her children and a growing number of perfect and delightful grandchildren living only a few miles from her front door.

When she is not writing, reading or playing with her grandchildren, Carol loves making trips to the local nursery. She delights in scanning the rows of flowers, envisaging which pretty plants will best brighten her garden.

She enjoys hearing from readers, and invites you to contact her at carolsarens@yahoo.com

A previous novel by the same author:

RENEGADE MOST WANTED

REBEL WITH
A CAUSE

Carol Arens

MILLS
BOON®

First published in Great Britain 2013
by Mills & Boon, an imprint of Harlequin (UK) Limited.
Harlequin (UK) Limited, Eton House, 18-24 Paradise Road,
Richmond, Surrey TW9 1SR

© Carol Arens 2013

ISBN: 978 0 263 89804 0

Harlequin (UK) policy is to use papers that are natural, renewable and recyclable products and made from wood grown in sustainable forests. The logging and manufacturing process conform to the legal environmental regulations of the country of origin.

Printed and bound in Spain
by Blackprint CPI, Barcelona

AUTHOR NOTE

For me, the idea for a book sometimes comes with a single scene in my head. What if such and such happened? What then?

For REBEL WITH A CAUSE the scene came about because of cows eating newly washed clothes on laundry day. According to my great-grandmother, Rachael, this was not a rare occurrence.

While travelling the preaching circuit, she found it necessary to wash the family's clothing in nearby creeks. This presented her with a dilemma: carry the heavy wet clothes back up the bank, or dry them on the bushes growing beside the creek and risk them being eaten by an errant cow?

Faced with the same choice, my heroine, Missy Devlin, decides to dry her gown on a bush. I hope you enjoy reading about how her life changes because of a hungry cow.

Warm wishes and happy reading.

To my firstborn, John Michael McDonald,
who taught me the strength of a mother's love.

Chapter One

Cedar County, Nebraska, March 30, 1881

Shivering and nearly naked in her damp, lacy underwear, Missy Devlin gazed across a prairie that seemed as big and empty as the universe.

"The Western Adventures of Missy Lenore Devlin and her Intrepid Pup, Muff," she wrote in her brand-new copybook.

She dipped her pen in the ink bottle, wishing there was a quicker way to write down her story. Life unfolded faster than she could scribble words across a page.

On only her first full day in the west, adventure had come upon her as easily as a cat comes to cream.

Mercy if she hadn't fallen bottom-first into a stream rescuing her puppy. Now, here she sat, all alone on God's great prairie in her next-to-nothings waiting for her dress to dry. It was a mishap that would cause any well-bred young lady no end of distress.

Back home, it was well-known that Missy rarely felt distressed. Truly, she could not have daydreamed a better adventure.

She blinked away an image of her older brother's frown, intent on savoring the hint of sunshine teasing her bare shoulders. Poor Edwin would turn as red as a Boston sunset if he could see across the miles.

Her brother had tried, valiantly, she would have to admit, to do his duty and keep her on a socially proper path, but sadly for Edwin, some things were just beyond a sibling's control.

A crisp wind whined through the rotten slats of wood that tacked together the abandoned wagon she sat upon. She licked her lips, certain that she tasted the green of a thousand acres of newly sprouted grass.

The pages of her journal rippled over her scandalously and oh-so-delightfully naked knees. She smoothed the paper flat once more and wrote another line.

"As related to her sister, Suzie," she read out loud.

Writing tales of adventure was what she had been born to do. Tea parties and cotillions were lovely for her friends, but putting words on paper was what made Missy's heart soar.

With each page that she wrote the world of black-and-white became more real than the wind nipping at her petticoat.

Shrill yapping beside the stream nearly disrupted her burst of creativity.

"Quit that barking, Muff, you'll frighten Number Nine!" she called without glancing up from the inspired text.

Number Nine, the horse she had rented this morning in Green Island, whinnied as if he agreed. His hooves splashed in the stream where she had tethered him to a nearby bush.

"Don't make me tie you to the wagon." With no little effort she closed her mind to Muff's racket.

If Suzie were here to entertain the pup, Missy would not have lost the descriptive phrase that had flitted across her mind. She would have read it out loud to her sister and they would both have admired it.

Missy's heart squeezed in a bittersweet knot. She pictured her twin sitting, hour upon hour, on the front porch of their stylish home. In spite of the fact that it was a haven of security, of love, Suzie would be gazing west, wondering about Missy's great adventures.

The telling would be a joy and a burden. She would have to pick brilliant words so that Suzie could live the adventure as though they traveled side by side, the way they had always planned to do.

Early this morning, while gazing out the window of her hotel in Green Island, she had determined to begin her tale with a description of the crisp spring scene spread before her.

Seen from the upper floor, the Missouri River cut across land that looked like an endless pasture of rolling green. The hills rose in easy swells and then sloped down just as gently. Scattered patches of a late snow glittered and melted in the sunshine.

Pristine beauty is what she had intended to relate, but upon closer inspection, the Great American West was dirtier than she had first thought.

In only seconds, Muff had fallen victim to burrs, rascally things that burrowed into his fur with ferociousness. Suzie would laugh her corset loose if she could see his ragged condition.

"Hush, Muff! I can't think of a word with all that barking!" Missy glanced toward the stream. A stern glare would silence him. "Oh, mercy me!"

The splashing in the stream had not been Number Nine. It was a giant cow.

Missy set aside her writing and stood up. Old wood creaked and groaned. She wiped her suddenly damp palms on her corset.

Gently bred eastern cattle had smaller, daintier

mouths than their wild western cousins. Missy made a mental note of the fact, determined to remember how a piece of meadow grass clung to a glittering glob of spittle oozing out of the cow's jowls…while it munched in apparent contentment on the bodice of her dress!

Muff snipped at the cow's hoof. He whirled to yap at the flick and swing of its fat brown tail.

A brass button shaped like a rosebud clicked against the cow's lower tooth then snapped off and plopped in the grass.

"Adversity holds the seeds of adventure" was a motto Missy lived by, but really, that was one of her favorite gowns.

"Hello, cow," she crooned, dismayed to witness a red satin bow disappear between the great hairy jaws. She slid by slow inches off the wagon. "Let go of my dress."

Missy shuffled a step forward. The cow was shorter than she was, but weighed Heaven's-own-guess more.

So far, the beast seemed to care for nothing beyond the lovely red-and-white cloth being crushed in its mouth. It didn't even kick at Muff who resembled a snowball-sized fiend, nipping and yapping at the cow's muddy hooves.

If the creature wasn't annoyed enough at Muff to silence him with a kick, perhaps it would be safe to walk right up to it.

Chances are it was someone's large pet, a creature used to being coddled and fed a daily ration of women's apparel.

With a deep, steadying breath, she left the security of the wagon behind.

"There's a good brown cow." She knelt and gripped the hem of her gown in both fists. "I'll take my dress now."

A tug on the fabric made no impression on the beast's dedicated gnawing.

She glanced about. Perhaps help would come trotting over one of the rolling hills.

Drat! Where was a heroic, handsome cowboy when a girl needed him? Surely the plains must be speckled with them. As far as she could see, though, the only movement was the grass bending under the breeze and a building mass of clouds that darkened the afternoon horizon.

She yanked. The cow yanked back, tossing its head. A seam ripped and a snort from the bovine nose sprayed something unpleasant into the air.

Muff snarled. The heifer's gaze swung sideways at him. One stomp of the cloven hoof and the dog would be done for.

"Come, Muff, come," she commanded.

Muff charged. Missy let go of the dress. She snagged him by the curl of his tail.

The cow snorted and pawed the ground. It lunged.

Missy ran.

She scrambled onto the wagon with the heat of a deep "Moo" raising the hair on her neck.

"Quiet, Muff." She clamped her fingers over his muzzle, her breathing quick with the narrow escape. "Hush or I'll toss you right back down to get stepped on."

The beast butted the wagon. Three slats of wood splintered under the impact. Missy scrambled for balance and nearly toppled overboard.

Apparently pleased at having the last say, the cow turned and waddled off, dragging the remains of Missy's dress through the dirt and across the stream.

Perhaps she ought to mount Number Nine and follow the giant until it became bored with her gown and dropped it. The problem would be keeping Muff out of harm's way.

Missy plunked down on a slat of wood. She huffed out a sigh. Apparently not considering the day lost, Muff attempted to scramble out of her lap. He would, no doubt, pursue the bovine filcher over hill and dale if he had the chance.

Grasping the fringe of grimy fur that had fallen over his eyes, she flipped it back and settled him securely in her lap.

"You've lost your pretty blue ribbon, you little scamp. You won't be able to see a thing now."

At least he wouldn't see how the clouds on the horizon seemed to boil and blacken by the second. The sun shining down on the wagon lost its kiss of warmth.

She tried to tug her own ribbon and curls back to the top of her head but they sagged in a steadfast knot halfway down her scalp.

"Adversity does hold the seeds of adventure," she announced to a crushed flower on the ground. Its remaining petal twisted in the breeze.

It would take a bit of creativity to write this adventure so that Suzie would laugh and Mother not swoon.

Gossip was bound to spread. She knew from some experience that embarrassing stories had an uncanny way of speeding across the miles.

It wouldn't do for Edwin to hear that Missy had come trotting down the public streets of Green Island wearing nothing but a dirty shift and toting a bramble-infested, purebred Maltese.

No sooner had Muff settled into a quiet, filthy ball on her lap than he growled and scrambled to his paws, stretching to look taller than he was.

"Now what?" She glanced across the prairie, peering through an afternoon being steadily dimmed by the heavy-hung clouds.

A man appeared over the rise of a distant hill, walking. He spotted her and waved his arm.

She had wished for a bold cowboy to ride to her aid and was a good bit disappointed.

The man, breaking into a trot and shouting, "Hello," looked like a gentleman, with his cravat neatly tied and his polished shoes winking with the last ray of sunshine. His pale cheeks jiggled with his awkward gait.

He might as well have been plucked from her mother's drawing room.

Zane Coldridge fastened the top button of his coat against the rising wind and tugged his Stetson low on his forehead.

"We've nearly got him, boy," he murmured to his horse.

The criminal, Wesley Wage, had so far been able to outrun the five-hundred-dollar price on his head, but if his behavior of the past two hundred miles held true, Zane would be able to track him to the saloon in Dry Leaf.

From a quarter mile away, Dry Leaf looked like a pass-through town. With any luck the slick bank robber would follow his usual pattern and be settled in at the saloon, belly-up to the bar, without the marshal being any the wiser.

That was often the way it went. Wesley Wage looked like an eastern dandy so folks seldom realized he was the robber who had been terrorizing innocent bank patrons over the greater part of three states.

Zane urged his horse down the main street of Dry Leaf, taking note of the location of the saloon and the marshal's office. The two were far enough apart so that a busy or inattentive lawman might be unaware that his town harbored a criminal.

Zane tied his horse beside a trough of water outside the marshal's office.

"Take a long drink and a short rest, Ace." He stroked away a film of prairie dust on the horse's neck. "We might not be here any longer than the last ten towns we've ridden through."

Zane took the steps to the marshal's office two at a time, swatting a clinging layer of dirt off his wool coat.

A feminine giggle met him when he opened the door. The rustle of a petticoat and a gasp welcomed him inside. A woman, blushing like a summer peach, leaped off the lap of a young man sitting behind a big polished desk. The marshal's badge hung from his shirt as though it was too heavy.

He didn't look to be more than a boy. The sudden blush of red flooding his cheeks didn't age the image.

"Afternoon, Marshal." Zane nodded to the couple. The woman spun away, tugging at the bodice of her dress. "Miss."

"Mrs.," she muttered. She turned again with her clothing restored. "Mrs. Taylor."

"My wife just…" The young man stood up and extended his hand across the desk. Zane shook it. "…she just brought lunch."

The couple must have been quick eaters. Zane

didn't spot a single crumb on anything that might be an eating surface.

"Mind if I have a look at your wanted posters?"

The boy marshal indicated the wall beside the door, the crimson in his cheeks fading to mottled pink.

"Not much to look at," he said. "Don't get a lot of criminal traffic through Dry Leaf."

Not any that the marshal would recognize by the faded posters on the wall, at least. Wesley Wage was there, half hidden under a bright new page with the sketch of a young lady on it.

Zane stared at her likeness for a moment. She had a pretty smile. On top of her head sat a bundle of curls held up by a ribbon. She seemed to stare out at him with eyes all sparkling with humor and curiosity. He'd give up a cold beer to know whether they were blue or brown. Maybe even green?

She didn't look like any criminal he'd ever trailed, but someone wanted her bad enough to offer a two-thousand-dollar reward.

"What's the lady's crime?"

"Oh, there's no crime, mister. She's just a runaway whose family wants her back in the worst way." The marshal walked over to the wall of wanted posters and tapped the likeness on the nose. "If you read the small print down here on the bottom, you'll see that the money's only good if Lenore Devlin is returned in as chaste and un-harmed a condition as she was when she fled the bosom of her family."

"What about this one?" Zane flipped the wom-an's poster up to reveal the faded image of Wes-ley Wage. "Have you seen him?"

"Like I said, wanted men don't pass through Dry Leaf much."

"I've lived here all my life." A sigh shoved the curve of Mrs. Taylor's bosom against the boy's canvas sleeve.

"I can't recall ever seeing anyone notorious."

The marshal glanced down at his wife's chest and hiccupped. Likely, a villainous horde could ride down the main street of Dry Leaf and Mar-shal Taylor would never see it.

"Thank you for your time." Zane opened the door and stepped out onto the boardwalk. "I'll leave the two of you to finish your…lunch."

He hadn't taken two steps toward the saloon before he heard Mrs. Taylor's giggle cut short by the closing of the door.

He ought to feel relieved that the lawman was too occupied with wedded bliss to notice that Wage had passed his way, but instead he felt an odd sorrow tugging at his gut. Being witness to their intimacy set a yearning smack in his heart.

Zane shook himself from the inside out. He didn't want a wife, couldn't have one even if he did. The life of a bounty hunter was a solitary one.

He set his sights on the saloon half a block down. Wage might be able to outrun the law, but that five-hundred-dollar bounty was about to come crashing down on his head.

The only crashing inside the peaceable saloon in Dry Leaf had been Zane's spirits. According to the patrons inside, Wage had, once again, lit out just a rope toss ahead of him.

Zane stood tall in the stirrups and stared out over the greening hills of the Nebraska countryside. He drew his coat closer about himself. There would be rain before nightfall and the wind whistling past his ears promised that it would be plenty cold.

Unless he caught up with the bank robber soon, he'd spend a long shivering night wrapped up in the rain canvas tucked away in his pack.

It was a shame that life hadn't led him to be a shopkeeper or a banker where chilly nights could be spent gathered around a comfortable fire with a friend or two. Bounty-hunting was cold, dirty and occasionally heartless work, but it paid better than any easeful occupation he'd ever heard of. Any occupation that was legal, anyway.

"There'll be a warm stall with extra hay in it for you, Ace, once we collect that five hundred dollars." He tipped the brim of his hat against the wind. Damned if it didn't just smell cold.

The horse whickered, tossed his black mane, then dug his hooves into the turf. He stood still with his nose flaring at the wind.

"What's the problem, fella, smell trouble?" Zane scanned the horizon but saw nothing more amiss than the ink-stained clouds that seemed to darken while he watched.

He listened, straining to hear over the hiss of blowing grass. He recognized the gallop of pounding hooves an instant before a horse burst over the rise a few hundred feet to his left.

"Looks like luck just fell right out of the sky, boy." He stood tall in the stirrups, gazing hard at the horse that flew over the prairie as if it was being carried along by a wicked gust of wind. "Unless I'm wrong, Wage just lost his mount."

Capturing the runaway horse would be wise but would cost a good amount of time. Wage could only have a few miles on him and Zane wasn't about to let that advantage slip away. If it came to Wage walking to the nearest town in mud up over his ankles, tied to the knot end of a rope, the man was only beginning to collect his due.

The criminal couldn't be behind bars soon enough. With one more bank robber put away, it would be safer for younglings to go along with their mothers to the bank. They'd never have to hear a shot crashing through glass. They'd never feel the jerk backward when—

Zane shook his head, scattering the thought. He touched the worn lace ribbon holding his hair in a neat tail at his collar. The sooner Wesley Wage was put away the sooner he'd have his pocket full of money.

"Let's get him, boy." Zane leaned forward. That was all the urging that Ace needed. The horse cared for nothing more than to run, to let his mane and tail fly straight out in the wind.

At the rise of the first hill Zane ripped the ribbon from his nape and let out a shout. He liked the thrill of cold freedom whipping his hair as much as his horse did.

Racing across the little valley made it feel as though Ace had wings instead of hooves. Fresh air filled Zane's lungs and cleared his brain of lingering memories.

Wage ought to be close, likely over the next hilltop. Coming over the ridge, he scanned the land falling away swiftly before him.

"What the hell?"

He almost stopped Ace in his stride to be sure of what he was seeing, but if his eyes weren't playing tricks he'd need to push the horse to its limits.

He blinked...twice, then leaned low and loose beside Ace's great muscular neck.

Wage was no more than a few hundred yards

away, but he wasn't alone. There was a woman dressed in…yes, by heavens…in her underclothes trying to keep Wage from stealing her horse.

She wasn't likely to win that battle, being only three-quarters of Wage's height and half of his weight. Given Wage's meanness he was likely to lean down from his place on the saddle and hit her to break her grip on the horse's bridle.

The woman's petticoat caught in the wind and whipped up to slap her chin. She struggled with it and tried to keep hold of the horse at the same time. Zane figured he must have dust in his eyes. It looked like a piece of her undergarment had come loose and begun to whip and whirl about the horse's hooves all on its own accord.

Damned if the woman didn't let go of the bridle to scramble after the bit of whatever was about to be stepped on by the horse.

Wage, not one for missing an opportunity, took that instant to give the horse a hard kick. The pony lurched forward then galloped double-time toward the west.

With massive clouds dimming the light, Zane nearly missed seeing the woman's mouth form a perfectly pink circle of surprise when Ace galloped past her.

Guilt squirmed in his conscience for hightailing on by like that. It couldn't be noble to leave a lady stranded so far from town in her underwear, not with one hell of a storm ready to strike the earth like a hammer.

He glanced back to see her clutching the odd white bundle that she had been chasing. Setting his sights on Wage again, he noted the outlaw was still a good distance in the lead, but losing some ground to Ace.

One fat, chilly raindrop smacked him on the cheek. It wouldn't be long until this whole area turned into a mud puddle. He could likely reach Wage before that happened. With Ace in his stride, the other horse might as well be walking.

The bit of worn lace that he had yanked from his hair slapped his thumb.

He sighed hard. Heat skimmed his lips. He sat up slow and leaned back in the saddle. Understanding the unspoken command, the horse slowed to an impatient trot.

"Hold up, boy."

Zane watched Wage disappear over the next hill. His whole body and soul itched to be on the run after the outlaw. With a sour lump in his gut, he turned to look once more at the stranded woman.

Damned if she didn't look like an abandoned angel with her petticoat flapping and fluttering. Blue bows on her underwear caught the wind and looked like a passel of butterflies whirling wild.

Through it all, she clung tight to that squirming…
animal?…in her arms.

Zane tied the ribbon in his hair then turned
Ace's head about.

Missy's mouth hung open in disbelief. It was
surely an unbecoming gesture that her mother
would reprimand her for if she could see it.

Suzie would swoon in pure delight, though,
when Missy wrote home, describing the vision
bearing down upon her with his black coat tails
flapping like the wings of some great dreaded
bird.

The hooves of his huge horse pummeled the
ground. Clumps of sod, ripped from the soil,
flew about. The earth trembled, bringing her
hero closer.

He slowed his animal to a trot. She watched
the man's mouth move. He might have spoken a
colorful word. Indeed, he appeared to have uttered a whole string of them. If only she could
have heard over Muff's snarling and snapping.

The coat settled over his thighs when he
stopped in front of her. The horse's dark hooves
danced and pawed as though it longed to keep
running. She managed to snap her mouth shut,
but her eyes popped wide open.

In her whole sheltered eastern life she'd never
seen a man like this. The West rode wild in his
smoky brown eyes. Black eyebrows slashed

across his forehead like fired bullets. This was a man of adventure!

He slid from his horse in a smooth, muscular leap. The tails of his coat rippled and snapped in the wind. Missy's heart felt like a moth battering at a lantern.

Was it her imagination that the blustery gust had ridden in with him? That it whooshed about her as cold and delightfully fearsome as he was?

"Are you all right, miss? Did he harm you?" His words sounded cordial but his jaw pulsed with tension. Stepping closer, the man's worn boots stomped down the rippling grass.

For all that the sight of him made her heart quake, his deep voice, slow and sweet as summer honey, made her insides turn to mush…hot mush. She ought to be shivering in her undergarments like a proper blushing virgin instead of breaking out in a mystifying sweat.

Still, it wasn't until she tipped her head back to peer at his beard-shadowed face, until her gaze locked on lips framed by a dusky slash of mustache, that she felt the need to swoon.

Even she, who considered swooning silly, thought it might be an appropriate course of action at this very point in time. Unfortunately, she hadn't seen a fainting couch since she'd sneaked away from her mother's parlor.

"Ma'am?" His hand, muscular and calloused,

and unlike any gentleman's hand she'd ever seen, reached for her elbow.

She must have swayed, even without a couch at hand. Mother would be pleased at that anyway.

"You're quite fascinat—" Muff growled, he snapped. Oh, gracious, she'd lost all sense of propriety. She pinched her fingers over Muff's muzzle. "Yes—I'm fine…well, not exactly fine."

"Apparently."

His lips pressed together, looking as tight as her corset strings. His eyes darted over her inadequate attire. A flash of mischief turned his somber brown gaze to hot cocoa. Missy settled Muff squarely over her bosom.

"You've got to catch that man!" She nodded toward the horizon. "He's stolen Mr. Goodwin's horse and an article of great importance to me."

Eyes so briefly warmed with humor turned cold. "He'll pay for accosting you, ma'am. I'll see to it."

He glanced west, glowering as though pursuing the cad with his eyes. A strand of ebony hair whipped loose from a ribbon at his nape and blew across his lips. He shoved it under the brim of his hat.

"There's nothing I'd like better than to run him down." He looked at her. The anger flaring across his face faded to polite concern. "But there's one hell of a storm ready to dump on us. There's no time to fret over the garment he stole from you. You'll be dressed quicker if I take you home."

Perhaps she should weep and moan at her state of undress. She supposed that's what a well-brought-up young lady ought to do in this situation. Although, truth be told, she had never known anyone who had gotten into such a fix.

Not a fix, Missy reminded herself, an adventure!

"It was the cow that took my dress, not the man." Missy shot a frown at the darkening prairie. "The man took something of much more value."

As if by reflex, he touched the gun slung in his holster. What a sight the weapon was, riding alongside his hip, so big and ferocious-looking.

"You don't have to say it out loud, miss, but if the outlaw has harmed you…if he's taken… liberties, just nod your head and he'll be dead by morning."

Outlaw? Dead by morning? Missy struggled to remember those exact words. When she got her journal back, with the inspired first chapter, she'd want to share every one of them with Suzie.

"Oh, gracious! My…my virtue is doing quite well." Why on earth were her breasts suddenly prickled with an odd tingle?

His flaring eyebrows lifted, creasing his forehead in confused lines. The expression made him look almost sweet, in a big, bold, black sort of way.

"This whole thing was Muff's fault, actually, for getting muddy. I don't suppose it was his fault that I slipped in the water, but then I don't think you can blame a silly cow for anything."

Like a lightning flash, his mouth twitched up then jerked just as swiftly to a stern line.

"I'm purely sorry for your misadventure, ma'am. I can't say I understand it, but I'd better get you back to where you came from before pure hell breaks out of the sky."

"I came from the hotel in Green Island, but, naturally, I can't go back until well after dark." She tugged Muff in tightly but he was a poor substitute for her missing dress. "It wouldn't be seemly."

"Seemly or not, I don't plan to stay out here and get washed away."

Clearly, the man did not understand her predicament. Mother would perish, Edwin would have heart failure if they got word that Missy had come parading down a public thoroughfare in her soaking underwear...sharing a saddle with a man!

"You are free as a feather to go, Mr...?"

"Zane Coldridge."

What a bold and wonderful name. Her own sounded weak by comparison.

"My name is Missy Devlin." She spoke the name with force but *Missy* still sounded like a pampered, eastern name. "It was kind of you to stop, Mr. Coldridge, but I'm obliged to stay here until well after dark."

He whistled to his horse. It trotted up behind him and nudged his arm. He reached his hand out to her. "Let's go."

She backed up a pace, just out of reach.

"Go along, please, Mr. Coldridge. I'd take it as a kindness if you'd leave me now."

"Leaving a woman to drown in the rain doesn't sound like any sort of kindness I ever heard of."

"Oh, it would be! Being a man, you wouldn't know what becomes of a ladies' undergarments when they get wet. I can assure you, I can't be seen in town that way."

"Ha!" His bark of a laugh nearly unbalanced her. He bent over, bracing his wide hands on his knees.

Muff wiggled to be free. She twisted her fingers in his fur to keep him still. The last thing she needed was to have to defend Mr. Coldridge's boots against attack.

"Hush, Muff, be still!"

At long last her hero straightened up. He shrugged out of his coat and handed it to her.

She put it on, shifting Muff from one arm to the other. The lingering warmth of Zane Coldridge's body wrapped around her.

"Let's go," he repeated and held out his hand once again.

The sleeve of his coat flopped over her fingertips by several inches. She lifted her arm and let the fabric slide over her bare skin. It left a tingle, just as though the cloth might have been the man stroking her flesh.

"Thank you," she murmured and placed her pale hand in his rough palm.

How on earth would she find enough delicious words to describe Zane Coldridge to Suzie?

Chapter Two

The stream had already washed over its boundaries when the first splat of rain hit Zane square in the back.

The icy slap promised to be only the beginning of a miserable night. Somewhere, not too far off, the squall had to be pumping misery from the sky like no storm he'd ever run afoul of before.

He'd been caught out in the elements many times, even seen the Missouri overflow its banks, but he'd never known gullies swell to the size of rivers before the first drop hit the earth.

He'd sure never had to take on the care of a delicate eastern woman and her…whatever that thing squirming in her lap was.

"What is that critter?" he asked, seeking a distraction from the icy trickle racing down his back.

"Surely you've seen a dog before, Mr. Cold-ridge." She turned about and glanced up at him. Even in the gathering dusk, with the storm clouds pressing out the last bit of light from the day, he caught the teasing blue sparkle in her eyes.

"I've seen dogs." A full dozen raindrops driven by a frigid wind bit through his shirt. He tried not to shiver since there wasn't enough space for two people and a questionable animal to ride in the saddle with any extra movement. "I've also seen rats. That's a rat."

"Did you hear that, Muff?" She tucked the animal inside his borrowed coat and held the front closed with fingers that looked like blue porcelain in the cold. "If you'd behaved like a proper Maltese and not gotten all muddy and prickly, our hero would have recognized you as a dog right off."

Hero? He'd grunt out a laugh at that title if there had been room in the cramped saddle. Zane had been called dirty. He'd heard *low down* a few times. He'd felt the curses of mothers and sweethearts follow him for days, even weeks, after he'd collected a fee for a loved one.

"I'm a bounty hunter, ma'am." He'd better set the record straight before the woman got any fancy ideas about him. "Money-hungry cuss is what I've been called more often than not."

He waited to feel her posture stiffen against his belly. Maybe the gentle lady would even slip off

Ace's back and choose to walk rather than share the space with him.

She turned as best she could to peer at his face. Raindrops hit her skin and dotted it with liquid freckles. Her mouth formed the same perfectly amazed circle that he had seen when he had galloped on by her earlier.

He leaned backward in the saddle, ready to dismount and walk the rest of the way to Green Island.

"Truly? A genuine bounty hunter?" Unbelievably, she broke into a grin that might have shot the clouds out of the sky. "You must have been chasing that awful man, earlier... Oh, mercy, was he an in-the-flesh outlaw?"

"Yes, ma'am, he was."

"A treacherous outlaw has stolen our belongings," she murmured down the neckline of the coat to the dog resting, warm and cozy, inside.

She wiped at the water gathering on her face and slicked back her hair. The silky-looking tresses had turned from sunshine to dark gold with the dampness.

"What was his crime? Murder? Kidnapping? Forgery?" Her eyes snapped. They sparkled in apparent delight. "He was a horse thief, I'll bet!"

"He's a horse thief now, but he's wanted for bank robbery."

"I was in mortal battle with a genuine bank

robber? Did you hear that, Muff? Isn't it marvelous?"

A shot rang out from a buried corner of Zane's memory. He heard the blast of shattering glass and the ting of it falling on a hard pine floor. He felt Missy Devlin's gasp when his arm clamped about her ribs.

Thunder, he realized with sudden relief. The boom and crash had only been thunder.

"There's not a thing marvelous about that bank robber, Miss Devlin. He'd have hurt you in a second and felt no remorse for it."

"Surely not!" She frowned, putting a pretty crease between her eyes. "He looked like a gentleman. Why, I'd nearly recovered my horse when Muff interfered."

"Maybe where you come from, he'd have hopped right down and handed you the reins, but this is the West. Gentlemen and ladies last about ten minutes out here." It was the truth. This hothouse flower sitting so sweetly in front of him would wither in no time. "If we don't drown before we reach Green Island, I'd suggest you take the first train back to where you came from."

As if to confirm his prediction of drowning, the sky opened up like a horse trough being dumped from the sky. Rain so cold that it stopped just short of being snow made puddles the size of ponds all over the low-lying area.

There was nothing for it but to get to higher

ground and hope to make it to Green Island before the storm cut the town off.

Even though the great American West was a good bit wetter than Missy had expected, she had no intention of catching a train home. Just because monstrous torrents of water poured down upon her head and washed over her body in an icy bath was no cause for retreat.

She did feel a bit guilty that the horse had some difficulty plucking its hooves from the muck with each step. The weight of two humans must have made each cold squish in the mud a trial for the beast. Still, she had come to tell the tale of the West for Suzie and a storm would not prevent her from doing it.

Her hero, Zane Coldridge, let out an occasional curse, watching the water flood the gullies and low areas of the land. The tops of the distant hills looked like floating islands.

"Come on, Ace," Zane Coldridge muttered. "Green Island is just over the next hill."

That would be a relief! It wasn't a bit prissy to be longing for the shelter of her hotel room. It wasn't weak-spirited to wish for the comfort of dry clothing. Surely even the man behind her wished for the same. Perhaps they could share a dinner by a cozy fire. He could tell her all of his adventures while they listened to the patter of rain on the windows.

Missy peered through the water dripping off the brim of the hat that Mr. Coldridge had long since removed from his own head and placed on hers. The tall steeple of the Congregational Church made a white slash through the low-hung clouds in the distance.

"Look!" She raised her arm and wagged her finger at the welcome sight. "There's Green Island."

Against her back, Zane Coldridge's chest rose and crashed. He uttered the most colorful word she had ever heard.

"Wait here a minute, darlin'."

With a leap, he washed off the horse. He took long mud-sucking strides up to the high point of the ridge. He looked out to where the steeple vanished then appeared again through the rain.

He made to snatch his hat from his head and toss it down in apparent frustration. Naturally, he grabbed wet air since the hat at this moment dripped in a limp heap from her head.

"What's wrong?" she called over the slap of water on mud.

He walked back, slipping then catching his step on the slick downward slope.

"Green Island's surrounded by water." She hoped to hear him call her *darlin'* again, but he only frowned and wiped his sleeve across his forehead. "Looks like we'll be spending the night here."

"Here…where?" She craned her neck right and left but didn't see a shelter.

He pointed to the top of the hill and picked up the horse's reins. "The higher up we are, the better."

"But the hotel is so close by. Surely we can get to it."

"The town's cut off." Zane Coldridge patted the horse's neck to encourage him up the slope. "It will be full dark soon and cold as a witch's… heart. We'd better settle in before things get any worse."

What they were going to settle in to was beyond her imagination. A few bare trees dotted the hill. Not much in the way of shelter there.

It might take some imagination to make this into a lovely tale for Suzie. It would be best to leave out the part about spending the night with a handsome stranger. If her missive ever fell into the wrong hands, well…there would be no end to the scandal. Her most mortifying exploit to date would pale by comparison.

When they reached the top of the hill, Zane helped her down from the horse then went about the task of untying something from behind the saddle.

Luckily, Muff slept soundly under the coat. She hated to think of the mucky consequences of letting him loose to take care of his needs.

"Mr. Coldridge, would you like your coat back

now?" She hated to give it up but her hero looked as frigid as a block of ice. If she wasn't mistaken, his boldly framed shoulders had begun to shiver.

He gave her a slow, silent shake of his head. Rain pelted his hair. The ribbon securing it at the back of his neck sagged like one of cook's overdone noodles.

It was hard to tell through the deepening gloom, but she thought he flashed her an angry glare just before he spread out a tarp on the ground.

"Lay down." He pointed to the middle of the canvas.

The man must be addled by the cold. What possible good could lying out in the rain do? Still, he hadn't taken his coat back, or even his hat, so it was only right to go along with him for the moment.

She knelt on the canvas then lay down with one arm curled around Muff and the other straight and stiff at her side. With her knees locked, the toes of her shoes pointed up to the clouds.

"Like this?"

"That'll do," he mumbled then sat down beside her.

He yanked the tarp this way and that until he lay prone beside her with the canvas tucked and folded in such a way that it kept out the rain.

What an amazing shelter! Even though water soaked her clothing the warmth of two people protected from the pelting fury outside gradually took some of the bite out of the chill. It wasn't warm, as the shivering body beside her attested to, but it was sanctuary from the elements.

What a shame she wouldn't be able to write about how she'd spent the night, as close as pearls on a strand to Zane Coldridge.

The fainting couch would be worn out if mother ever knew.

Missy Devlin's breath beat warm puffs of air against his neck. That was the only inch of Zane's body not taken with shivers. Even though the rain no longer touched him under the canvas wrap, the icy water had done its damage. It might be some time before a pair of bodies, not entwined, would generate any warmth.

"Tell me about your bounty-hunting adventures, Mr. Coldridge." The lady's voice shivered, but it might have been from foolish excitement as much as chill. Apparently, the woman had some pretty, eastern notion of the West that had nothing to do with real life.

"Haven't got any adventure, miss. I make a living, and an ugly one at that."

"Surely your brain must be packed with tales of peril and risk." Rain pounded on the canvas but not so loudly that it drowned her voice. "Ugly or not, they must be thrilling."

"Somehow, Miss Devlin, I don't see life as a

pack of thrilling stories. Just living, some good and some bad."

"Oh, but that's not true!"

He felt her wiggle onto her side. The plump swell of her breast pressed against his arm and warmed it like a hot cushion. The sultry simmer had to be pure imagination since no part of this miserable night was anything close to hot.

"Life is all made up of stories, some wonderful and some not, but it's all adventure in one way or another."

"Fancy notions from a proper eastern lady."

"Wouldn't mother be pleased if that were true?" she mumbled under her breath.

In the dark, he felt her hand brush across his shirt, light and hesitant. Plainly, Missy Devlin fell short of pleasing her mother.

"You're about to shake to pieces, Mr. Coldridge."

It wasn't the manliest of behavior, but still true. He was a shaking mess. With a different kind of woman he'd know how to get warmed up. Mother's opinion or not, this was a respectable young lady and the most he could do was dream of the warmth her plush little body might provide.

She touched him, her palm over his heart, and his imagination sparked to full-blown life. The scent of warm, womanly skin seeped through the soaked coat that wrapped her up in a tempting package.

A gust of wind howled along the ground and snapped the canvas over their heads, but by some mercy, it held.

"You're not your mother's perfect angel, then?" he asked, trying to get the blamed image of a bare hot woman out of his mind.

"On occasion, I fall a bit short."

Was that an icy finger poking under the space between the buttons of his shirt? Not a single finger, but all four and a thumb!

"Suzie, my twin, and I weren't always the socially graceful young ladies that mother longed for... She loved us like the dickens but—I think that if we wrap our arms around each other we might borrow one another's warmth."

Zane fought the urge to tear out of the canvas when she nuzzled her cheek against his neck then snuggled in as close as a wanton woman. His breath left him in a rush when her fingers tiptoed across his wet shirt and curled about his ribs.

"Suzie and I warmed up this way on many a winter's night."

How innocent could a woman be to believe that his reaction was anything close to what her sister's had been?

"There, that's better already, don't you think?"

A grunt was the best answer he could give until he caught his breath.

"How on earth did your mother ever let you out of the house?"

"Oh, she didn't let me out. I ran away in the dead of night."

Missy Devlin sighed and her thumb tripped across the pocket of his shirt. Heat flushed through his chest.

"It's a wonder she didn't tie you to the bed-post."

"If mother had tied me to the post, Suzie would have let me loose. Now, my brother Edwin would have tied us both... Here, put your arms around me just like this."

To illustrate, she squeezed him closer. If he were a stronger man with a lick of sense, he'd go stand in the rain where the only dangers were the sidelong wind and the creeping flood, but her warmth had already begun to ease the shakiness out of his bones, so he turned to face her.

He tucked his chin on top of her hair and smelled damp roses. He laid his arm across her waist then pressed his palm to the middle of her back, drawing her in.

Since he wanted to put his mouth to use in a way that didn't involve tasting the floral-scented warmth that blushed from her cheeks he asked, "Why did you run away from home, Miss Devlin?"

"To write the great American dime novel."

He felt her smile tickle his neck. He wished he could see it, foolish as the reason for the smile was.

"You ought to have stayed home. All those stories are made up. Pure scandalous trash is all they are."

"I'm sure that's not true, Mr. Coldridge!" Her body squirmed in apparent protest. "Why, in one day Muff and I have been assaulted by a bank robber and rescued by a bounty hunter. I've had my dress eaten and my manuscript stolen. If that is not adventure, I can't tell you what is."

"Sounds more like a string of misfortunes to me."

Evidently Missy Devlin lived in a different world than most folks.

"What on God's earth made you leave the safety and comfort of home for a place like this?"

"Can I trust you not to mock me? You seem to be less than admiring of my ambition."

"You can." At least he wouldn't do it out loud.

"I'll take this as the beginning of a friendship, then. Will you call me Missy…and let me call you Zane?"

Since talking was the only honorable way to spend this long, close night, he agreed.

"Well, then, Zane," she said, relaxing against him in a way more friendly than she must realize. "Let me tell you, safe and comfortable are well and good, but also tedious and restricting. Why, the minute a girl kicks up her heels and does something the slightest bit daring, she gets frowns and stares from everyone she meets."

She sighed. Her breath warmed his neck. Between her belly and his, the animal she called a dog began to squirm.

"A sweet little thing like you getting frowns and stares? It baffles the mind."

"And not only me. Suzie, too!" All at once her voice softened, the spark that animated her snuffed out, as though the tarp had suddenly come loose and the rain doused it. "At least, she used to. Suzie's quite subdued these days."

A long silence stretched, filled up with the beating of rain on the tarp. Close at hand, although he didn't know exactly where, he heard Ace snort in wet misery.

Surprisingly, the thought of a person just like Missy subdued didn't set easy on his heart.

"Why is that?" Maybe he was prying, but she was the one who had declared them friends.

"My sister was paralyzed two years ago when our buggy slipped off a bridge in the rain. Papa died…I got a bruised chin. Edwin had to grow up, just like that. One day he was a boy flirting with girls and the next he was raising them."

He drew her in with a squeeze, offering comfort that he knew could not be found. He understood such grief. Even years from now the loss would sting.

"Since Suzie can't come West, I'm sending the West home to her."

"Darlin', this isn't the place for you. It's not

what you think. It's dirty and wild and unpredictable. Listen, do you hear that?" As if on cue, thunder rolled low and threatening overhead. "The weather alone should be warning enough."

The little dog whined. It wiggled out from between them. It crawled to Missy's face, licked her cheek, and then wagged its musty-smelling tail across Zane's nose. He pushed the dog down, toward his knees.

"What I know is that storms don't last forever. Why, under this tarp we are getting as warm as can be."

"What if I hadn't come along? How long would you have lasted out there without even the clothes on your back to protect you?"

"But you did come along."

The dog scrambled over his hip; a nettlesome growl rumbled in its throat.

"Let's say I didn't? What if it was just you and Wage? There's even worse than him out there who'd have taken more than your horse."

"Muff, no!" Missy reached for her dog.

She grabbed for Muff, reaching above her head, then down Zane's neck and over his chest. When she groped for the dog in a place he'd never invited a proper woman, he did a quick flip.

In the scuffle he managed to keep the dog near his feet without opening the canvas to the rain. The trouble was, he'd also gotten Missy pinned underneath him.

In the darkness, the whisper of her shallow breathing filled the canvas. The quick brush of it against his face filled his nose with her rosy scent.

"It's a lucky thing for me that you're the one who came along," she murmured.

Maybe not so lucky. Even under the coat, he felt the curves of her breasts rising and falling beneath the trip and hammer of his heart. The layer of petticoats wasn't thick enough to keep him from noticing a pair of shapely female legs go rigid, then relax beneath his.

Heated breath moistened his mouth. Her lips couldn't be more than an inch away. He nearly groaned into the tiny space of simmering darkness that separated them.

Would she turn her face aside in outrage if he kissed her? Maybe slap him across the cheek with her slender hand?

Or worse, would she welcome it? Would she melt against his mouth then give herself over to him with an eagerness that would singe his mustache?

With the possibility only a searing gasp away, he shouldn't let himself get carried away with the dream of what it might be like to brush his tongue over her lips, to taste them and explore the shape and delicate texture of them.

Missy's heat flashed through him, spun about his insides then settled low and urgent where it shouldn't. It was wrong to allow his imagination to run wild. His brain, ready to boil over, was a thought away from becoming reckless.

Somehow, the little lady had gotten him stirred up inside, and all by lying perfectly still.

How was it that she made him want to run like hell away and dive in headlong all at once?

One thing he was sure of, if he didn't grit his teeth together, take a big bite of bitter reality, this would be one adventure that Missy Devlin would never write to her sister about.

He pressed the canvas on each side of her shoulders then pushed himself up so that he didn't feel the tug of her breath calling him to behave disgracefully. He lifted up as far as he could without dislodging the shelter and letting in the rain.

There must be some remnant of honor left in him.

The close air stirred, fabric shifted, she touched both of his cheeks with her fingertips. They felt like hot butter against the week-old growth of his beard.

"Go to sleep now, Missy." He settled down beside her then kissed her forehead with a quick peck. The dog scratched and plumped the canvas near Missy's feet. "I'll see you safe on the train first thing in the morning."

Chapter Three

〜⁓〜⁓〜

Missy snuggled into the cocoon-like shelter. The rain on the canvas had slowed to a steady splat.

Hours must have passed. It ought to be morning since the absolute black inside the tarp had given way to shadowed gray.

She felt rested…even energized. Such amazing things had happened in twenty-four hours. Her fingers fairly itched to write them down.

Zane's slow, even breathing told her that he was still asleep…with his arms around her and his chin resting on top of her head! She could only hope that Muff would not need to get out. It would be fine to lie here until the rain quit, feeling the slow rise and fall of her hero's chest, heartbeat to heartbeat against her own.

Last night, she had taken his advice and gone to sleep at once. Her emotions and her body had been tumbling in confusion and delight. A few hours' rest to figure them out had been what she needed. Luckily, sleep always came easily, as sweet as a little bird settling into a nest.

Zane didn't know it, but his vow to put her on the first train home had been wasted breath. It was a wonder that he hadn't felt her silent bubble of laughter.

Out here in the West, free of the restrictions that Edwin had put on her behavior, she was an independent woman. Yes, indeed, free as a feather on the breeze. She certainly hadn't come to Nebraska to have Zane Coldridge take Edwin's place.

Suddenly, Zane sat up. The canvas cocoon burst open with a rush of cold, wet air. Missy noticed his hand reach for his gun even before he had come fully alert.

"What's wrong?" she sputtered against the rain tapping on her mouth.

He didn't speak. He touched her lips with two fingers and cocked his head to the left, listening.

She felt a slight rumbling in the ground a second before she heard a great roar and boom pound the air. Muff exploded from the folds of the canvas, trembling and barking.

Zane leaped to his feet and grabbed her hand. He yanked her up and pulled her along toward the rise of the hill.

Through the rain she looked down on the flood that engulfed Green Island.

Water lapped at the front porch of the hotel. While she watched, a wave washed inside the lobby. A man ran out, lifting his feet high in an attempt to clear the water. Luckily, her belongings were on the second floor and likely safe.

"Damn it all to hell," Zane whispered under his breath and this time his curse didn't sound at all colorful.

Missy followed his gaze upriver to see a massive chunk of ice floating on the current.

"The gorge up in the narrows must have burst." He gripped her fingers tighter. "We'll be safe enough up here."

He scooped Muff up from the ground and stuffed him in the big pocket of her borrowed coat.

Upriver, several boulder-sized ice chunks bobbed after the first. The river was jammed with them, jouncing and crashing into one another, piling up on the shoreline then breaking loose with furious screeches and cracks.

Zane glanced backward, toward the flattened shelter of the canvas. He let out a shrill whistle, barely audible over the thunder of the ice. A second later his horse trotted into view with mud caked on his large black hooves.

He gripped the horse's reins tightly in his fist. If it was truly safe on top of this hill, why did

Zane seem to lean toward the horse as though ready to leap upon its great wide back at any second? Why did a silent shiver race through his arm and into hers?

The first of the giant ice floes hit the Congregational Church. Its tall spire shook but the building held…for a moment.

Hit by three more vicious blocks of ice, the structure left its foundation in one piece. It floated gracefully away with the current. A bend in the river took it out of view. Only the white steeple bobbed in and out of sight behind a grove of bare-branched trees.

The snap of shattering wood splintered the air. The church steeple tipped, then vanished.

Even over the rumble and thunder of the river, Missy heard the splitting screech go on and on. The church must have broken, shattered like toothpicks among the trees downriver.

Missy looked back toward the hotel. The man who had run outside had taken refuge on the roof. He called out to a group of men running and waving their arms on the far bank.

A pair of ice floes hit the hotel and sent it floating after the church. The man flopped down on his belly and rode the peak of the roof.

"God protect him," Zane mumbled. Missy barely heard him over the shriek of splitting buildings.

In only a few moments the river had robbed

Green Island of every building but one, and that one looked half caved-in and fully flooded.

Many of the structures floated away whole, only to be shattered to bits around the bend. A few others broke apart before her eyes.

Still, the worst wasn't the ruined homes and businesses. It was the men, women and children clinging to rooftops, floating doors or any other surface to keep from being sucked into the turbulent water or crushed by a random shift of ice.

People from Yankton, the town bordering the north side of the river, ran along the shore, shouting and waving their arms, helpless to do anything more because of the treacherous current.

On the side of the river where Missy and Zane stood, a roof floated past carrying a family of five. They held tight against the violent lurch and sway.

The roof split down the middle when a jag of ice, pushed to the river bottom by a downward wave, suddenly lurched up again. One member of the family, a little girl of no more than three, clung to the separated piece.

The child's mother tried to scramble into the water but her husband prevented her, holding her down with the weight of his body.

In only a moment, the family's screams faded, carried away downriver along with the rooftop. The baby's wail of terror grew louder when the current swirled her fragile section of shingles toward the shoreline not thirty feet below.

"Stay here," Zane ordered.

He placed the horse's reins in her hand then ripped the ribbon from his hair. He placed the worn scrap of lace in her fist then curled her fingers around it.

In the second that it took him to scramble down the bank, the roof snagged on the shoreline. It bucked and heaved against the current. It reminded Missy of a drawing she had seen in a dime novel of a wild horse trying to dislodge its rider.

The little girl held on as well as any broncobuster she had ever read about.

But, Lord have mercy, her strength would be no match for the huge hunk of ice set on a dead aim for her fragile section of roof.

The wood roof pitched upward just as Zane lunged for it. A splinter of wood that felt like a two-by-four stabbed him under his thumbnail. He bit down on the pain and pulled up with straining arms until he got one leg over the rooftop.

A wave from behind washed him up and over. From an arm's reach away the little girl looked at him. Big brown eyes blinked through hair plastered against her face.

"Hold on, baby, I've got you." He hung on to the slippery roof with his injured hand and ignored the gush of crimson washing from his thumb. He stretched his arm out, straining at the shoulder to touch the child.

He'd just grabbed on to her tiny wrist, cold and slick with water, when a wave tossed her up. Her hand slipped out of his grip. She flew up, over his head. He caught a flash of calico skirt and yanked her back by it.

In the instant that he wrapped her to his chest he spotted the hunk of ice carried in the wave's wake.

"Hold on." She looped skinny arms about his neck then squeezed as tight as any binding rope would have. "Good girl."

The jag of ice crashed down on the roof. It tossed him airborne. Turning and twisting, he dug his fingers into the child's dress.

Upside down and spinning, he thought he saw Missy rushing toward the river, towing Ace behind her. That couldn't be since he'd told her to stay put. Surely it was only a jumbled illusion that she wasn't safely on the hilltop.

Hour-like seconds passed before he crashed back down into the water.

The wonder was that he hadn't been hit by a deadly object coming down. The horror was, that he was down, way down under the water, still tumbling and turning and not knowing which way was up.

His hip crashed into something and then his

shoulder. The little girl struggled in his grasp, needing air.

The current dragged him across the river bottom then slammed his back against a solid object. It knocked the breath from his lungs. Bubbles floated in front of his face. He loosened one arm from around the baby to grip the solid thing that he had hit. He pulled upward following the bubbles.

He broke the surface and lifted the child high against his shoulder. Her terrified screech filled his ear. Thank God.

It turned out to be an uprooted tree that he'd collided with. He wrapped one arm around a wide twisted root.

"It's all right, sweetling. Hang on tight."

His words must have sounded confident because the child clung to his neck like a summer vine twined around a post.

The tree, his only lifeline, shifted in the current. It wouldn't be long before it ripped loose or debris racing downriver crashed into it.

More than twenty feet of turbulent river lay between this unstable sanctuary and the shore. If he let go, made a swim for the bank one-armed, he and the child would likely drown.

"Hush now. Everything's going to be fine." Somehow.

"Zane!" He barely heard Missy call his name

over the rumble of river rushing past, carrying its cargo of deadly debris. "Zane!"

"Get back!" The child whimpered against his neck, probably startled by his outburst, but he couldn't believe what his eyes told him. "Get out of here!"

Six feet out from the shore, with the insane tug of the Missouri pressing and heaving, Missy sat atop Ace. She urged him forward against any instinct the animal had of self-preservation.

"Hold on!" she cried. A wave splashed over the toe of her delicate boot. "I'm nearly there."

"You'll get yourself and my horse killed! Get back!"

"Don't let go!"

Rain beat down on her. The coat blew open revealing her white lace corset with its droopy blue bows. Her dog poked his wet head out of the coat pocket, quiet for once.

"Don't be an idiot," he mumbled. But she didn't look like an idiot. She looked brave and beautiful and too fragile to be urging Ace on through the torrent.

After a few more of those hour-long seconds, Ace stood beside the log in belly-deep water, holding steady. Missy reached down. He lifted the little girl into her arms.

"I'll be back." Missy shouted. "Hold on."

"Damn it, no! Get to shore and stay there!" Ace was strong, but it was only luck that he hadn't been knocked down by debris hidden in the current.

He watched Missy's mouth open and close with some words that he guessed meant he'd wasted his breath on insisting she stay put, but a sudden crack of ice close by drowned out the sound.

She turned Ace's head toward shore and whispered something to the little girl. A second later she glanced back, her face set in an expression that would excuse her brother tying her to the bedpost.

She'd come back all right, and probably die trying.

He lunged for Ace's tail. By Heaven's own luck he caught it and tangled his fingers in the thick, wet mass.

The horse's first step toward shore made Zane swing wide into the current. He hung on, wincing against the pain from the splinter lodged in his thumb.

The brave animal didn't protest the weight hanging on his tail even when a slap of water washed over his haunches. He whinnied then pointed his soaking black nose toward the shore.

It was a miracle. Missy had heard the declaration from the mouths of everyone she encountered that morning. Not a human soul had perished. Livestock and buildings had been washed away to their doom, but each and every human had been reunited with friends and loved ones.

Amazingly, the family of the little girl had claimed her a few moments after Zane crawled out of the river. He had barely caught his breath before the child's mother hugged it out of him again.

With each soul accounted for, people now focused on retrieving their lost goods. Along the riverbank, families hunted under rubble and up in tree branches for pieces of their shattered lives.

Missy lifted a splintered scrap of lumber and peeked underneath it. Scattered about in the muck were the remains of the hotel. Surely she would find one or two of her belongings.

A timid finger of sunshine teased her shoulder blades without offering any heat. Muff, napping in the coat pocket, did warm one side of her knee.

"You've been searching for three hours." Zane lifted a window frame and peered underneath it. "You won't find anything."

Maybe not, but it was a day for miracles, even small ones like finding a dress or a matching pair of shoes.

"Did you hear the church bell ring?" Missy asked, stopping for a moment to arch her back against a cramp.

"The church didn't have a bell." Zane tossed a piece of lumber aside and lifted a muddy hat up for Missy to see.

"Not mine." The ache in her back tightened with the stretch. "And yet half the town of Yankton heard it."

Zane placed the hat on a mangled tree branch sticking up from the mud. "Even if there had been a bell, no one could have heard it ringing."

"They could if it had been a special bell… Oh, look at this." She lifted a milk pail and hung it on the branch near the hat. "A natural bell couldn't be heard, but a supernatural one could."

"Darlin', that might happen where you come from, but out here bells are pretty much brass or iron."

It was hard to tell whether he was annoyed or amused since his hat shaded his eyes and his voice gave nothing away.

"Well, there you have it, then," she said.

He straightened, plucking a man's pipe from the mud. He shoved his hat back from his face. The sun shone bright on his expression.

It was not annoyed or amused. His eyebrows arched in bewilderment. "Have what?"

Mercy, what a handsome man! He nearly made her lose her train of thought.

"Proof, of course. If a brass or iron bell couldn't be heard, and there wasn't one to hear, but so many folks swear that they heard it, then what else could it be?"

"Delirium."

"Magic."

Zane turned and wedged the pipe behind the drooping yellow ribbon on the hat. He glanced back at her with a hot-coffee gaze. The simmer nearly made her knees knock together.

"Did you hear the bell?" he asked.

"No, but—"

"There was no bell." He raised his hands, calloused palms out as though to block her words. "You didn't hear it and I didn't hear it."

"In my book there will be a bell."

"That's the trouble with dime novels. For every word of truth there's ten of fancy."

"That's simply not true. Lots of people heard that bell and it wasn't fancy to them, it was hope."

"I'll tell you what's true. Everything you own is spread across half the county. That's a fact and no matter how you try to twist it into some sort of a bell-ringing adventure it all amounts to a hill of trouble."

So true, but she had long believed that trouble was made to be overcome. "No one died and that was a bell-ringing miracle."

"Take a peek around at your miracle, darlin'. This town is gone. Look at your own situation. You've got less than some others. You can't even borrow clothes because no one has any to lend."

"That *is* a challenge." A rather big challenge that nearly made her feel like weeping. She had to remind herself that adversity held the seeds of adventure.

"No need for a tear." He touched his thumb to her cheek. "If the tracks haven't washed out, you can take the afternoon train home. I'll stand by you until then."

"That certainly was not a tear. I was just considering what to do."

"That's wise." He dabbed her other cheek with his finger.

"I've decided to stay with you."

He jumped backward. His brows arched like dark wings. His eyes widened in apparent horror. Quick as a blink he narrowed them in an uncanny reflection of the grim set of his mouth.

"That's not possible." His voice deepened. It sounded calm but a muscle twitched in his jaw. "I've got an outlaw to catch."

"And so do I. That bank robber had my journal tucked under his arm when he managed to escape me!" Missy paused when a thought hit her. The theft was just another of the day's miracles. If she had made it safely back to town the journal would have been washed away. At least now she had a chance of getting it back. "I need to go with you."

"I ride alone."

"It wouldn't be right to leave me here to be a burden to the folks of Green Island. Even Yankton will have its hands full taking care of its own."

"Go home, Missy. At least there, you'll only

be a burden to your brother." Zane whistled for his horse.

"True enough." Missy couldn't blame him for being annoyed. He'd gone through some discomfort during the last day on her account. She heard Ace's hooves snapping scattered twigs. "But all things considered, I'll stay here."

"Suit yourself, then." He grabbed Ace's reins then lifted up into the saddle.

"Thank you for the loan of your coat." She plucked Muff from the pocket and slid it off her shoulders. Chilly air prickled her skin.

"You keep it." He turned the horse toward the open prairie.

"Thank you!" she called out. "I'll return it to you when we meet on the trail of the outlaw."

He stopped Ace midstride, turned and gave her a hard frown. He shook his head then leaned forward in the saddle. The horse bolted away, racing for the horizon.

She tucked the coat tight against the icy breeze. The cloth smelled like campfire, horse and open prairie. The aroma of Zane Coldridge wrapped her up.

What a shame that such a bold and wonderful hero had come and gone like a flash. When she retrieved her journal, she might use up every page writing about one man, alone.

She stared after him. The drum of Ace's hoofbeats faded against the earth. The breeze carried a shout of triumph when someone found a half-buried plow.

Missy watched Zane and his horse become a small dot on the crest of a distant hill and wondered if it would be right to borrow the hat with the yellow ribbon.

She lifted it from the broken branch, removed the pipe then placed the bonnet on her head. It might be someone's favorite. The yellow ribbon, even though it looked defeated and wilted, felt like pure luxury given the circumstances.

Surely, it would be some devastated woman's hope of a new day. Missy took it off and returned it to the branch with the pipe, once again, tucked into the ribbon.

She glanced at the horizon, expecting to see it empty, but the black dot that had been Zane seemed bigger. She watched while it grew to the size of a pea, then an apple.

At last it took the form of a man and horse coming closer across the prairie.

The horse halted two feet in front of her but pawed at a clump of grass as though impatient to be on its way.

Zane reached down, his calloused palm open.

"I'll take you as far as Luminary."

Chapter Four

∞

Zane peered through the noon sun shimmering off Ballico Street. Luminary looked better by night. For the first time he noticed that much of the town's facade consisted of peeling, faded paint.

It was odd that he had never noticed the splintered wood of the sidewalks or the flies spinning around horse manure deposited near half-cocked hitching posts.

Nightfall ought to improve the look. Lanterns would puncture the dark on both sides of the street. Oil lamps would glint a welcome from the windows of business establishments all over town. Pianos, cranking out tinny tunes from open saloon doors, would weave a ripple of gaiety from one bar to the next.

Somehow, during his younger years in Luminary, he hadn't noticed that the town looked run-down. Maybe it was Missy sitting stiff-backed and proper in front of him that made him see it so. The genteel lady from Boston was sure to take note of every broken window over every weed-filled flowerpot. She would notice that the only freshly painted signs in town advertised alcohol and women.

Luminary would give her plenty to write home about.

Missy turned in the saddle. She gazed up at him with blue eyes gone wide.

"Is this a bawdy town?" she asked.

He had been a fool to bring her here, even though it was the most likely place that Wage would have run to. He ought to have put her on a train headed east, tied her to the bench with his own hands if it came to that.

"It's as bawdy as can be." In truth, there wasn't a place much worse. Funny, it hadn't bothered him until now.

A door squeaked open on a second-story balcony. The aroma of freshly brewed coffee filtered down and mingled with the dusty odor of the street. With the day half gone, Luminary was just beginning to stir. A dog barked in the distance. Muff leaped to his feet in Missy's lap. He stretched as tall as his ten inches would allow.

"Zane Coldridge, where have you been?" A

woman's sleep-tumbled voice drifted down from the balcony. "We figured you were dead."

He looked up, past the front door of Maybelle's Place to the sign that declared in bold red letters, Spirits, Gaming, and Dancing Women. On the balcony just over the sign the speaker leaned against the railing with a cup of steaming coffee cupped in her palms.

It was as though he saw her for the first time. The way Missy must be seeing her.

Red hair that he knew was not natural fell in messy curls over bare shoulders. Pale breasts propped up by her forearms seemed ready to spill over the top of her crimson corset. Whatever she had used to make her lashes black had slid while she slept and given her under-eyes a coal shadow. A white feather, limp from a night of hard work, flopped over one eye.

Missy sagged backward against him.

"Is that...?" she whispered. "Is she...?"

"Miss Emily Perkins."

Muff whined. His dirty tail whipped up a cloud of dust.

"Is Miss Perkins a dancing woman?" Missy settled Muff on her lap with quiet fuss and scolding. She must be trying hard not to stare at Emily.

"She knows a step or two."

"You've...danced with her?" It was a bold question from someone who had suddenly blushed the same shade of red as Emily's sleep-smudged rouge.

"We grew up together. Emily is like a sister to me." And she was, but she hadn't always been. There had been that long-ago summer, just before Emily's folks had died of the cholera, when the pair of them had been green sixteen-year-olds. Emily hadn't been like a sister then.

"She's beautiful."

Missy Devlin was a woman of neverending surprise. "You aren't offended by her?"

"Mercy, no! If all the women in Luminary dress like your friend, I can give you back your coat."

He ought to feel relieved by her attitude. Now he wouldn't lose time trailing Wage while he took Missy to a more appropriate town. But he didn't feel relieved, he felt worried. Her eyes shone too brightly. Her smile curved with anticipation. No doubt by sundown she would get a new journal and write to her sister, describing every step that she saw the dancing women of Luminary take.

Zane slid backward off Ace then led him to the hitching post outside Maybelle's.

"Let's go in, I'll introduce you to Maybelle."

He reached up. She leaned down, keeping both arms around Muff. She didn't tense when his fingers closed about her ribs. She fell into his hands with perfect trust. Unease shivered up his spine. A fearless innocent in Luminary equaled a victim.

He'd have to pay Maybelle extra to keep Missy out of trouble until he arranged her way home.

Missy's hands itched. Words trembled at her fingertips, eager to pop out. Everything she had written before would pale against the description of this cherry-red room.

Enchantment in the form of red velvet curtains covered whole walls. Purple couches sat boldly on a gold carpet. Not a finger of daylight strayed through the windows, so six crystal chandeliers were lit, casting fairy lights on ceiling, walls and floor. On the right side of the room was a marble-topped bar that ran the length of the wall. Behind the bar was an endlessly long mirror framed in polished wood. Above that hung a huge painting of a woman lying bare on a couch that looked very much like the couches in this marvelous parlor.

She had been warned often enough that it was rude to stare, but she had never seen a woman so seductively nude. It was difficult to draw her gaze away from the honey-brown eyes and the moist red mouth that seemed to smile with a great secret. Surely, with her arms sprawled languidly over her head and her breasts pointing at the viewer, with her hips turned so that the black shadow between her thighs was right there for all to see, the woman could have no secrets.

The grand room was empty, quiet except for the swish of Muff's tail stirring the air.

"Maybelle?" Zane called out.

A gray bun streaked with brown popped up from behind the polished bar. The woman's head turned, revealing a round face. Laughter spun in honey-brown eyes. Missy glanced at the painting then at the smiling woman. Her eyes still held a secret.

"Welcome home, sugar." The woman, dressed in plain brown wool, swished out from behind the bar. She hopped, sparrow-like, toward him with her arms flapping in welcome. "Where have you been gone to for so long?"

Zane took half a dozen steps across the room, caught the woman's plump embrace and spun her about. Crisp petticoats swished through the air. Crinkling lace flashed past a piano that gleamed like a mirror.

Missy's fingers itched again. What a surprise to find such a fine instrument in this prairie-weathered town. She could hardly think over the words crowding her mind. She would need them all to describe Maybelle and her decadent, opulent and oh-so-delightful establishment.

"Earning a living." Zane set Maybelle on the floor then pecked her cheek with a quick kiss.

The worldly-wise yet down-to-earth-looking woman blushed and touched her cheek.

"You always were a sweet boy. The girls have missed you."

Sweet boy? Missy looked him over with narrowed eyes. His hair glinted midnight-blue in the light of the chandelier, his thighs swelled beneath his jeans, his feet would be long and lean under his well-worn boots. Possibly Maybelle hadn't seen the way his shoulders filled his flannel shirt. Evidently she hadn't taken note of the way his eyes could melt a woman in her shoes. Certainly, the woman could never have felt the scrape of his beard stubble under her fingertips.

It had been some time since Zane Coldridge was a sweet boy.

Throaty giggles erupted at the top of the stairs. Like a swarm of multicolored butterflies, women fluttered down the steps. Bare arms reached, bosoms jiggled over corsets, red mouths puckered for kisses.

Maybelle had been dead-on about the girls missing Zane.

"Have you brought me a new girl, dear?" Maybelle called out over the brightly colored heads of the women surrounding Zane. She wrapped Missy in a soft, quick hug that Muff didn't seem to mind. Then she took a step back, smiling all the while. "Turn around, dear. Let me get a good look at you."

Missy made a pretty pirouette with one hand out, palm up. Muff, wedged against her side, wiggled in apparent delight.

"Very nice," Maybelle crooned. "Take off that old coat, dearie, and let me see if you will appeal to our gentlemen."

The coat hadn't slipped to her waist before Zane had extricated himself from the flock of soiled doves and yanked the lapels back over her bosom.

"I'd like you to meet Missy Devlin." He fastened the top button and tugged to make sure it held. "She's not a professional lady."

The professional ladies made a colorful circle, gazing at her with interest.

"Why, then, is she in her underwear?" Emily asked. Curly heads of red, black and blond nodded all about.

"Yes, dear, what has happened to your clothing?" Maybelle asked, her voice soft with concern. "Zane?" This time her voice had a bite to it.

"I started off yesterday with a lovely dress, white and red with pretty bows and brass buttons shaped like roses, but it was eaten." A multivoiced gasp came from the circle. Six pairs of eyes stared at Zane with disapproval.

"By a cow!" Zane rushed to clarify.

"Ohhh!" The women sighed as one.

Emily nodded her head in apparent understanding, as though gowns were a regular part of bovine diet in the West.

"Missy is trying to get home to her family in Boston," Zane said to Maybelle. "She lost everything that she had in the flood that took out Green Island."

Maybelle touched Missy's elbow. "Oh, you poor lamb. I heard about that. What a mercy that Zane found you. He's brought me many a stray over the years. Not many women, you understand, but puppies and kittens, even a sick old man once. Our Zane just has a knack for bringing home castoffs."

"Can you put Missy up for a while?" Zane asked.

"She can have your old room." To Missy, she said, "It's lovely and quiet at the top of the house so nothing will disturb you."

If only she could stay for a while. Why, the stories she would be able to tell! But first she had to get her journal back and return poor Mr. Goodwin's rental horse. Very likely, the stolen animal would be the only part of his business to have survived the flood.

"Thank you for your kindness, Maybelle, but I can't stay a moment longer. I have business to take care of."

"In that pretty shift?" A blonde with a scar on her chin asked. "I thought you wasn't a whore?"

"Janie, you know we don't use that word here,"

Maybelle admonished. She smoothed her hands on the front of her modest dress. "We are professional ladies, purveyors of pleasure to discriminating gentlemen."

"Janie didn't begin her career at Maybelle's. She came from outside." Emily inclined her head toward the closed door. "She started at Pete's Palace. Life out there is different."

"It's mean," said a woman who touched her shoulder, appearing to rub away some old pain.

"And dirty," added a brunette with shiny curls.

Maybelle scratched Muff behind his mud-crusted ear. "You and your pup will stay with us until you can find your way home, but I have to warn you, Luminary isn't the place for a lady like you."

"You are a prize, Maybelle." Zane kissed her cheek. "I'll be on my way."

"You chasing some outlaw?" Emily asked.

"Hot on his heels, darlin'."

Missy's heart gave a kick when he called the woman *darlin'*. It had been naive to think that he'd meant something personal when he'd called Missy that.

Zane passed quick kisses all around. Except for Missy. He wished her luck then strode out the front door.

"I sure do hope it's not another year before we see that man." Emily took Muff from Missy's arms. "What a sweet little poochie."

"Let me have that dirty old coat, dearie." Maybelle slid it off her, held the coat at arm's length and wrinkled her nose. "Who knows when this was last laundered?"

"I can't stay, really." Missy sprinted toward the door.

Maybe if she offered Zane a huge sum of money he would take her along.

She yanked open the door then remembered that she didn't have a huge amount of money. She had no money. The only way she had to get money was to wire Edwin and beg him for some.

Missy stepped onto the boardwalk. Bright sunlight nearly blinded her. She shaded her eyes with her hand and watched Zane trot away in a haze of dust.

"Hey, chuckie!"

Missy turned to see a man, greasy hair hanging past his shoulders and black spittle oozing from the corner of his mouth, crossing the street. He reached in his pocket and pulled out a small coin. "This'll be all your'n if you let me taste your—"

Whatever revolting thing the man had intended to say was cut short by a gunshot. The coin vanished from between his fingers. He let out a yelp of profanity and chewing tobacco.

Missy spun toward the sound of the shot. Zane sat tall in his saddle with a gun sitting easy as a heartbeat in his steady hand. Wisps of smoke twirled out of the gun barrel. The fury in his eyes made her shiver. It made the greasy man run for cover.

Half a dozen hands from behind grabbed her shift and yanked her back through Maybelle's front door.

An hour before sundown, Zane settled Ace into the Dereton livery. He gave the liveryman an additional coin to make sure the horse had an extra bag of oats and the best stall. At the stable door he paused and glanced back. The extras he had purchased were bare payment for a couple of hard days. He whistled softly in good-bye and got a whickered reply.

Reassured that Ace was well-tended, Zane walked two blocks to the marshal's office.

The marshal, Joseph Tuner, was a family man who would likely be home for supper with his wife and younglings. Unless he had a tenant in a jail cell, his habit was to leave his office unlocked. That would suit Zane fine. If he could skip a drawn-out conversation, he would be able to search the establishments where Wage might be before he had the relief of checking in to the hotel for a dry night's sleep.

As he had expected, the door was unlocked; it swung open with a rusty groan. The last hour of daylight shot across the floor and cast an orange glow on the wanted posters pinned to the wall behind the marshal's desk. Outside, a dog barked, footsteps passed behind Zane, thumping down the boardwalk. A handbill with the ink barely dry stared back at him.

"Blue eyes," he said out loud then rounded the desk. He tapped the likeness of Missy Lenore Devlin on the nose with his finger. He traced the curls winding pertly on top of her head.

He ought to have known who she was from the first. The clothing on the sketch, particularly the collar, standing stiff and prim, must have thrown him off. The tidy loops of hair marked in pen didn't reflect the sun's gleam the way the true tresses did. But strike him silly, he should have recognized those eyes. The artist had captured the spark of whimsy and lurking mischief that he had struggled to put out of his mind on the short ride from Luminary to Dereton.

Damn, he might never forget the look on her face when he shot the coin from the derelict's fingers. She hadn't uttered a word, but her round eyes and sagging jaw had shown her astonishment.

She looked pretty when she was astonished. He shook his head to dispel the image.

There was the poster of Wage. The poster, as usual, had been pinned under another one, newer with a higher reward.

The sum on Missy's poster nearly blinded him. He ought to turn back to Luminary, collect Missy and deliver her to her mother's doorstep. Two thousand dollars would sit pretty in his bank account. Life would be a good deal more comfortable with that sum behind him.

The reward tempted him, to be sure, but it couldn't sway him from his purpose. Catching Wage, and others like him, made him get up in the morning. It made him saddle up Ace, head out to dangerous, ugly places and do dangerous, ugly things.

Maybe when he quit hearing his mother's dying breath in his ear, if the day came when he didn't feel her blood sticky on his young hands, then he would follow a bounty of sky-blue eyes.

Not today, though. For now, he was after Wage, even at only five hundred dollars.

Zane plucked Missy's flyer from the wall, folded it up and put it in his pocket. For an instant, he thought that her eyes flashed with humor. Of course, if he tried to take her back to Boston it would not be humor that flashed in her eyes.

Pity the bounty hunter who tried to bring Miss Devlin home.

Missy followed Maybelle's swaying skirts up a narrow stairway to the only room on the third floor of the brothel.

"Every great while, we have a guest who only wants to sleep." Maybelle jingled a set of keys attached to a chain looped about her waist. She selected a polished brass key and opened the door. "It's mostly quiet up here, if you keep the windows closed. You will do that, won't you, dearie?"

Missy glanced at the window. It was a small dormer with lace curtains tied back with white satin sashes. It looked tasteful, ladylike even.

Maybelle spun about, giving the room a critical glance. Apparently not expecting an answer to the window question, she didn't catch the negative shake of Missy's head. Who knew what mysteries the night would reveal through an open window?

"Please do understand that this is for your good as well as mine." Maybelle rubbed the room key with her thumb. "I wouldn't want any of my gentlemen to get the wrong idea about you. Since you have everything you need for now, I'll say good night."

The wrong idea? A dozen fascinating stories flashed through her mind at once. In that instant Maybelle swished out the door, closed it and turned the key in the lock with a swift snap.

Missy stared at the door that she only now noticed had two locks. One to keep strangers out and one to keep her…locked in!

Arms spread wide she fell backward onto the bed, mentally borrowing some of the colorful words she had heard Zane use. Drat! She wouldn't learn a thing of interest locked in the tower like a fairy-tale princess.

She stared at the ceiling. It sloped at a narrow angle following the line of the roof. The room would be a cozy place to spend a night if one were not a prisoner. Mercy, but the bed did feel like a cloud after sleeping on the ground last night.

As pleasant as the feather cloud felt, the adventure with Zane had been thrilling. She'd never slept in a man's arms before. Ever since, she'd savored that memory, musing over words to preserve the experience in just the right way.

She had never spent the night in a house of sporting ladies either, but the adventure of it was shut away from her by a locked door.

Still, there was the window. Luckily, she hadn't agreed to keep it closed and could relish whatever sounds came through it without feeling guilty.

Missy bounded up from the bed. She pulled a chair to the window and stood on it to get a good view through the deep dormer. She lifted it open, not a crack but all the way. This close to dusk, the air was too nippy for comfort but some things had to be braved in the name of literature.

Below, the street was quiet but, come dark, her head would be so full of things to write about she would never be able to remember them all.

She turned and slid onto the seat of the chair with a thump. How would she manage without paper and an ink pen?

"Adversity holds the seeds of adventure," she recited to the room.

Adversity she had by the bucketful. She couldn't write without supplies. She couldn't obtain the supplies while clad in her underwear and Maybelle surely would not unlock the door until she was decently clothed.

"What I need…" Missy leaped from the chair. The idea was so bold it stole her breath. She pressed her palm to her chest to still her heart. Suzie would be thrilled, neither of them had ever had this thing. None of her acquaintances had ever had it.

"What I need…is a job!"

Chapter Five

Missy leaned out of the dormer window, certain that she could not be seen from the lantern-lit street three stories down. A cold breeze prickled her skin but she didn't dare pop back inside to get Zane's coat. Something interesting might happen which she would not want to miss.

So far, a man had urinated in the alley across the street and a drunk had stumbled into a pole. Things couldn't help but turn livelier.

In the very instant that a woman let out a lusty laugh from an unseen saloon, there was a tap at Missy's door. She slid the window closed then plopped down into the chair.

While the key turned in the lock, she caught a messy curl in her finger, twirled it in a bored fashion and sighed like a proper captive.

"Sorry about the locked door. Maybelle is one

for caution." Emily stepped inside with a swirl of purple petticoats. She toted Muff in one arm, freshly groomed and smelling of roses. "Moe will be along with a bath in a bit."

Emily set Muff on the floor then laid a sparkling crimson dress across the bed.

"Jolene left this behind last year when she went respectable. Maybelle thought it would be a fit for you." Emily looked her over with narrow eyes. "It might be a little tight in the chest. Not that that ever hurt anything."

Missy leaped up and nearly dashed to the bed. The fabric of the dress winked at her. She touched a ruffle of red feathers trimming the low-cut neckline. The tickle under her fingertips was a call to adventure. If she wore this gown in Boston she would be banned from polite society for years.

Muff hopped onto the chair then jumped to the dormer. He looked out the window, barking and waving his tail madly.

"That dog is as sweet as he can be now that he's cleaned up." Emily wrinkled her nose. "Those pretty drawers of yours are a mess. Here…let me have them. We'll give them to Moe when he comes up. He can wash as good as a woman."

Emily gave no indication that she had said anything shocking. Evidently, in Luminary, ladies stripped and handed their clothes to washermen every day. Since she'd been a toddler, the only one to see her in the all-together had been Suzie.

"Honey, you look positively scandalized. I purely forgot you were a lady for a minute, with you in your underwear." Emily settled on the bed. Muff hopped down from the window and found a soft place on her lap. "I guess when you start whoring, modesty is the first thing you forget."

Surely Emily had misread her expression. Missy Lenore Devlin had never been one to be scandalized! Why, ask anyone back home, she was the one creating a scandal.

She stepped out of her petticoat and let it fall in a heap about her feet. Undressing in front of a stranger was about as adventurous as one could get. Pray that she wasn't blushing herself to embarrassment.

When the last of her garments hit the floor, she kicked them into a corner and sat in the chair with her legs crossed at the ankles and her hands folded on her knees. So what if she was naked in front of a semi-clad stranger? She lifted her gaze, determined to meet this challenge with a confident grin.

Emily was not looking in her direction. Instead, she fluffed Muff's fur and spoke softly to him. She glanced up and smiled.

"What a sweet little fellow."

"Yes…sweet. He's been nothing but that for the entire trip. Why, back home that's what everyone calls him, sweet little Muff." Missy knew she was babbling, but what did one say in such a circumstance? *My, isn't it a lovely evening to be sitting in a whorehouse naked?*

"I used to be like you." Emily said.

"I suppose it's all a part of your job."

"What?" Confusion lifted Emily's painted-on eyebrows.

"Bare as a jay?"

"Respectable." She shrugged her shoulders, twirling her fingers in Muff's fur and looking at something in her mind. "Once I had dreams. There was a day when I'd have turned as red as you are now. "

Missy would have protested her blushing condition, but that was not what this conversation was about. To outward appearances, Emily looked like a goddess in satin and feathers, with her breasts peeking through her sheer underwear and her bare calves showing. Somehow, though, she didn't look a bit like the soiled doves of the novels, laughing and flirting and dancing the night away with glasses of something wicked and intoxicating gripped in their gay fingers.

Emily looked beaten-down. Her smile seemed distant...hopeless even.

"Still, if it hadn't been for Zane, I'd probably be dead." With that, her spirits appeared to rally.

"Me, too." Missy pulled the pins from her dirty hair. She fluffed it about her shoulders then frowned at her fingers where grit had lodged under her fingernails. "He also saved a little girl in the flood."

"A lot of folks are indebted to Zane." When Emily looked at her, Missy was sure that she did not see nakedness. "Then too, a lot of folks don't wish him well."

"Why would you be dead?"

"My folks passed when I was sixteen," she said.

"My father died in a buggy accident." How interesting, Missy thought, that the pampered eastern darling and the scorned fallen woman had so much in common.

"Mine died of scarlet fever. We were homesteaders just outside of town. Some others died, too."

"That's a pure tragedy. Did you have someone to go to?" As much as Missy sought freedom from her restrictive family, she knew from some experience that they could be counted on in a crisis.

"Zane was the only one. We were close back then. Really, he's all I had. I tried to support myself by doing laundry, but my hands bled with the lye. My eyes aren't good enough for sewing. There's only one way a woman can support herself around here when her folks are gone."

"Dancing," Missy said with a sigh.

"Sure…dancing. I was so hungry and lonely,

it was easy to tell myself, 'Okay, Emily, you can do it for a little while, till you get back on your feet.' The thing is, this business keeps you mostly off your feet. It's hard to get back up."

"How did Zane save you?"

"I meant to go to Pete's Palace, but Zane wouldn't have it. He said if I meant to take up the…dancing…life it would have to be at Maybelle's."

"He might have taken you to another town. Maybe a better life."

"Oh, he tried. Years back I was so young and proud. I was set on making my own way in the world. Maybelle's was the best he could do for me. Besides, he grew up here, Maybelle was like an auntie to him, it didn't seem so bad back then."

"What about now? You're a grown woman. You could leave the sporting life, surely?"

Emily studied her fingertips making whirls in Muff's fur. "There is one way." She shook her head, staring hard at Missy. "I don't know that I'd feel right about it, though."

A heavy knock beat on the door. The knob turned. Missy dove for Zane's coat and wrapped herself up a second after Moe stepped into the room with two buckets of steaming water.

He didn't seem to take note of her flash of skin, but by heavens, there were some adventures that she did not need to have.

* * *

Missy stared at Herman Meyer of Herman Meyer's Mercantile over a display of canned goods on the counter. He seemed perplexed. Speechless, he stared at the red hat that had been a gift from Emily. His eyes scanned downward over the feathers that tickled her cleavage.

"I said," Missy pronounced loudly in case the man's problem was that he was hard of hearing, "I'm here about your help-wanted sign in the window."

Herman Meyer blinked hard, shook his balding head and opened his eyes wide. "Just what kind of skills might you be offering, miss?"

"I can do most anything." She gave Mr. Meyer her most winning smile. "I can do mathematical calculations."

"Do that myself, can't be any cheating that way."

"I can serve tea." His frown was not encouraging. "I could embroider little flowers on your window curtains to make the place more inviting."

"I understand that Pete is looking for a new girl." His narrow-lipped smile seemed genuine. "You'd make that place more inviting, sure."

"I can also play the piano. Everyone at home says I have a gift for it."

"Lookie, miss, I don't have a piano for you to

play. You go along to Pete, he got a new one just last month. I ordered it for him myself."

The last place she was going was to Pete's! She had vowed to Maybelle on her honor as a lady that she would not go within a block of the place.

That agreement was what had got her released from the locked room. That, and a promise to return by four o'clock in the afternoon and allow Maybelle to lock her in once again for the night. This, Maybelle had assured her, was to keep the gentlemen out more than Missy in. Since Maybelle was the one holding the keys, Missy could only agree to her conditions.

She gave the dusty mercantile a glance all about. At home, she'd seen the housekeeper sweep and dust nearly every day. It didn't appear to be a difficult task. The maid had even hummed a tune while she did it.

"I can sweep a room like nobody you ever saw." That might be the truth. "You don't even have to pay me in cash. All I ask is for a writing tablet, an ink pen and some ink."

Mr. Meyer glanced around the store. He seemed to be surprised at the layer of dirt that had collected on his floor. "I suppose it could use a sweep. Mind, now, I'll only pay up if you do a good job."

"Just point me to your broom," she said with confidence, but when he placed the object in her hand her courage stumbled. The stick with the straw on the end felt a very foreign object. Exactly how was it that the housekeeper managed the sway, push and swish motion?

Within half an hour she had learned the rhythm. After an hour the smirk left Herman Meyer's lips. At the end of two, he smiled, gazed around his store with newfound pride and handed her the writing materials.

Mother would turn pale if she saw what Missy had done, but stepping out into the sunlight, Missy felt proud. Even though the sparkle of her crimson dress had faded with the layer of dust embedded in it, she felt grand. She had gotten a job and earned her pay. Now, if she could do something to earn some actual cash, that would be a story for Suzie.

Business establishments lined Ballico Street on both sides. If she followed the warped wood of the boardwalk she might come across a teahouse that needed a server, or a seamstress that needed embroidery done. Now that she had pen and paper, she might even write letters for those who could not spell. Really, she had more skills than she would have imagined.

One block up, she went into a restaurant. Tea, she discovered, was scorned as a delicate brew. Only coffee as thick as mud would do, and that the proprietor served with her own calloused hands.

By noon, the weather had warmed. Sweat

dampened the feathers on her chest, but her hope remained fresh as morning. Surely the clothier would need her services.

By two o'clock the only clothiers in town had looked her over with a skeptical eye and then informed her that they only sold ready-made items.

That left writing letters.

She spotted a group of cowboys, some sitting on a bench outside the Red Horse Saloon and others standing. She approached them with her writing materials in clear view. Surely, aside from the feathers tickling her low-cut neckline, she looked like a properly educated young lady.

At first they seemed stunned to silence by her offer of letter-writing. A silent stare passed from one sun-worn face to the next. Finally, one of them made an offer that Zane would have shot him for.

She hurried away, made a turn on a street that took her a distance from the cowboys. A block away she could still hear them laughing. She was shocked. Cowboys were honorable men when it came to women. She had read it many times in the dime novels.

At least bounty hunters were true to their reputations. A woman could count on a bounty hunter. All at once Zane's face filled her mind. Her heart squeezed, it spun dizzily when her imagination gave him a smile.

If only he had taken her with him, she would

be miles closer to finding Wesley Wage than she was now. For each moment that she spent earning the money to follow him, the odds grew that he would lose her manuscript. Or worse, he would read it and claim it as his own!

"Floors, then." Missy straightened her posture and her hat. "I'll get rich if I sweep up all the dirt in Luminary."

She walked up a block then over two. She made a turn and walked down a quiet alley. Here in the shade the temperature took a merciful dip. She took off her hat and fanned her neck with it. Weather in the west was a fickle thing, freezing one day and sweltering the next.

"You one of Maybelle's girls?" A woman's voice, hoarse and scratchy, spoke from somewhere that Missy could not see.

She turned and saw a flash of movement from under a flight of stairs leading to a splintered back door.

"Can you help me, please?"

Missy followed the voice and stooped to peer under the stairs. She had been mistaken about the person being a woman. She couldn't be out of her teens. Her rough voice had sounded old, but her face looked even older. Her cheeks hung close to her bones and eyes that should have been luminous appeared shrunken into her skull. They peered out of her face, gray with melancholy.

"What are you doing under the stairs?" Missy

grabbed the frail hand that reached for her. "My word, you look ill."

"I needed a peaceful place for a bit, that's all."

Shadows of decay ate the child's teeth, the teeth that were not missing, that is. "I'm so far past ill, it ain't even funny."

"Here, now, hold on, I'll help you up and get you home to your folks."

"I'm going home to my folks, sure enough." She coughed. "But not in this world."

She did look that ill. A slight breeze would tip her over.

"Where do you live?" Missy stashed her writing tools under the stairs then gathered the girl's weight in her arms and helped her to her feet. "Where should I take you?"

"I belong to Pete, every last wheezing breath of me. Take me there, if you would."

Pete! She had made a vow. She didn't dare set foot in Pete's Palace. Pete was the devil incarnate from all she'd heard!

"Let's go to Maybelle's instead." The girl weighed nothing and Missy helped her along easily.

"Ma'am, I'll go to Pete's or nowhere." She coughed again. Her narrow chest heaved and caved. When she quit her lips were stained with blood. She wiped them on her sleeve. "In any case, I can't walk so far as Maybelle's."

"But why Pete's? What about a boarding house?"

"Like I said, I belong to Pete, we've got a contract." She stumbled but Missy caught her. "I guess he owes me a place to die."

Silent weeping ached in Missy's throat. Harriet Cooper, sixteen years old, lay on a grimy cot facing her coming death with acceptance. What kind of life had led her to this place where she didn't even care to fight for her next breath?

A career at Pete's could have done it to her. The establishment was an ugly, dirty place full of men who looked like images in a tawdry painting. No wonder Zane had delivered Emily to Maybelle's doorstep those many years ago. If only he were here now, he would help young Harriet.

But he wasn't here and it was up to Missy to give what little care she was able to. She knew nothing about medicine or easing pain, but she did know that clean hair felt better than dirty. Freshly scrubbed skin felt sweeter than pasty, sick flesh.

Two hours ago, she had demanded clean water and sweetly scented soap. Pete, standing in the doorway of the shed-like room that Harriet called home, had frowned down at Missy.

"Hell of a way to get out of an honest contract," he grumbled. "Those things will come out of her pay." He uttered an oath and closed the door with a quiet click.

Fifteen minutes later the water and a new bar of perfumed soap was delivered by a scraggly-haired young woman who seemed afraid to look at Harriet lying on the cot.

Missy had bathed her, washed her hair and covered her with a worn but nearly clean sheet.

She brushed Harriet's hair until it dried, but even clean and fresh, it would not shine.

No book that she had ever read had portrayed a soiled dove in this condition.

"I saw Pete's new piano when we came in, Harriet. Would you like me to play for you?"

Harriet smiled. A blush fought to the surface of her skin and left an echo of the happy youth she might have been. "My mother used to play."

"I'll go play and you think of your mother." Missy touched Harriet's forehead then trailed her fingers along the hollow of her cheek. "Close your eyes and let your mind drift back to a better time."

Missy opened the door of the room that Pete had called Harriet's crib. She glanced back and saw Harriet smile and close her eyes.

The crib lay just off the main room of the Palace. A pair of cowboys wearing dusty boots and a man dressed in a suit with ink stains on his fingers sat at a table playing a card game. The bartender spat a glob of chewing tobacco at a spittoon then wiped his mouth on his sleeve.

Missy left the door open enough for the melodies to come through but closed enough to give Harriet a bit of privacy.

Luckily, the piano was alongside the wall of Harriet's room so it would be easy for her to hear every note. Missy sat down and brushed her fingers over the keyboard, testing the sound. Her former employer, Herman Meyer, had been correct about the piano. It was a fine instrument.

"Here now, miss, you can't just sit down there and play!" The bartender rounded the bar with his fat belly leading. He crossed the room with plodding steps.

"Mister, I've got a pair of lungs like you never heard before. I don't think you want to hear me screech." She couldn't recall ever having had an occasion to screech, but screech she would if the man tried to get her off the piano bench.

"Let her be for now, Mitch." Pete's voice drifted out of a room near the bar, along with a trail of cigarette smoke.

The man named Mitch shrugged his shoulders and returned to his position behind the bar, spitting again at the stained spittoon.

She closed her eyes, she didn't need sheet music to play. She had often been told she had a gift for music. Until this moment she hadn't appreciated the value of it. Until Harriet, her gift had seemed a rather dull one, just a step above embroidery and serving tea.

Almost of their own will, her fingers went to Bach. The heavenly notes of *Jesu, Joy of Man's Desiring* rang off the walls of Pete's Palace and spilled out into the street.

Distantly, she heard a pair of footsteps come into the saloon. She heard a chair scrape the floor.

From Bach, she turned to Pachelbel and his *Canon in D*. She didn't notice when her fingers became tired, she had no knowledge of the sun sinking below the horizon outside. She didn't recall who the composers were any longer, only the lovely, gentle melodies that seemed to come from her heart instead of her fingers.

Last, she played a piece called *Meditation* in which a young, sinful man finds God's love. Finally, she lifted her fingers from the keys, folded them in her lap and bowed her head with a deep sigh. She prayed that Harriet had found an hour of relief from her suffering.

Whistles and applause erupted from behind her. Jolted from her peaceful moment, Missy nearly fell off the bench. She turned to see two dozen people or more, some standing and some sitting, clapping and cheering.

Just inside the saloon doors stood Maybelle, accompanied by Moe. It was well past five o'clock and here she was in the forbidden Palace. She would get locked in her room, for sure.

Missy stood, gave her audience a proper curt-sey, and then looked at Maybelle, ready to face her fate. To her amazement, Maybelle did not seem angry. She dabbed a tear from her eye then handed her lacy handkerchief to Moe who blew his nose into it with a snort and a snuffle.

Captivity had taken a turn for the better. Upon seeing Missy safely to her room, Maybelle de-clared that since the whole town had witnessed that Missy was a lady and not a strumpet, it would be safe to leave the door unlocked. Maybelle still asked that she stay in her room as much as pos-sible during the night. If she had occasion to go out of an evening, Moe would accompany her.

Those seemed fair terms since Missy was wholly dependent on Maybelle's generosity. Gain-ful employment seemed more illusive than ever. A full day had passed and she still did not have a nickel to put in a purse, had she had a purse to put it in.

She did have what counted most, though. Set before her on the writing desk of the third-floor room were the pen, ink and paper that she had earned with her own two hands.

First, she wrote about Zane. She wore his coat against her skin while her feathered dress hung on a wall hook airing out over night. With the scent of him for inspiration, pages seemed to write themselves. Surely Suzie would be able to envision his bold carriage as he walked. She'd melt when she read the description of brown eyes that could send a woman to the fainting couch with a single glance her way. Long black hair tied in a mysterious lace ribbon would make Suzie daydream, but the description of muscular arms holding Missy tight all through a long dangerous night would leave her sister sleepless.

The temperature in the third-story room seemed suddenly stifling. She fanned the lapels of the coat over her breasts. The stirred air felt like breath from a mouth too tempting to linger in thought over. It would be best to write about something else for a while.

"Cold evening air drifts in through the window opened fully to the night." A description of Luminary might be a more comfortable subject for now. "Lusty laughter bubbles up from the street below and an argument a block over blends with the tinkle and pound of the lively piano music from any number of bars. Night in Luminary sounds gay…"

It sounded like red and blue bursting with sparks of gold and silver. What she couldn't tell Suzie was that it didn't quite cover the wheeze and gasp of Harriet Cooper's breathing.

The campfire cast amber shadows on the faces of Zane's companions. Beyond the friendly circle, night stretched black as eternity. Coyotes howled and yipped to one another on the moonless prairie.

He had been pleased to come upon the group of cowboys and grateful when they'd offered him a meal of hot stew and biscuits. Three days on the trail without a soul to talk to, besides Ace, had become wearisome. Nights had turned haunted. Not by ghosts, but by visions of Missy Lenore Devlin.

Blamed if the blanket of stars overhead didn't remind him of the sparkle in her eyes. If he watched long enough, a shooting star would bolt across the heaven from east to west like some joyous spirit set free of its paddock, like Missy on her great Western adventure. It disturbed him to think of those stars that reminded him of her. They shot bright and straight for a while but in the end they fizzled out of sight.

Maybe he shouldn't have left her in Luminary. That town could be a rotten place for a woman alone. He trusted Maybelle to do her best, but when it came to someone like Missy, her best might not be good enough. She would try to send Missy home but that bounty presented a problem. What if some bounty hunter grabbed her for the reward? Not all of that breed lived under a high moral code. He knew several who would ignore the clause about returning her in as pure a condition as when she'd fled the bosom of her family.

With some effort, Zane purged Missy from his

mind. He'd be better off planning a way to trap Wesley Wage, who by all accounts was just a day away, in the quiet town of Creekside. Creekside had a small bank where local farmers trusted their funds to be safe.

A log cracked in the fire and shot a spray of sparks into the dark. Quiet cowboy conversation of steers and horses and what each man would do with his next paycheck lent a cozy feel to the night. Zane closed his eyes, listening.

"I'm spending my dime on that new gal at Pete's," said a deep voice.

Zane's stomach soured in pity for any girl unlucky enough to tie in with Pete.

"She's about the prettiest little thing I've ever seen." This voice was young. It dripped with appreciation for the girl. One thing was sure, she wouldn't be pretty for long. "I'd spend a month of dimes for her services."

"Now, her little white dog with that bow in his fur is something to see," a voice from Zane's right declared.

A little white dog? With a bow? Prickly heat crept up Zane's spine. He sat up straight, peering at each golden face around the fire.

"Pete's sure never had a woman like that one." This came from a man with years of sun etched into his face. The feathered lines of his skin caught the firelight and gave him the appearance of a spirit risen from the underworld. "What that lady can do with her fingers is a pure wonder."

"It's almost holy what those two hands can do." Heads nodded all around.

"Pete's gonna get rich, what with the way she can take care of all the gents at once." This voice, from the man to his left, seemed full of admiration.

"Luminary's got a new sweetheart and that's no lie."

"What's her..." Words cracked out of Zane's throat as if they were struggling through a dust storm. "...name?"

"Why, even her name sounds like music," the youngster said. "It's Missy Lenore Devlin. Mister, you must be the only man around who hasn't been to Pete's just to watch the lady ply her trade."

Chapter Six

Pete, Missy judged, while she stared at his closed office door, was a cruel man. His love of a profit and a truly mean disposition made him a despicable guardian for the women in his service.

Early in the afternoon she had waited with him, standing grim vigil at Harriet's bedside when she passed to her Maker. As soon as his employee had breathed her last, Pete snorted into a grimy handkerchief and hastened from the room. A second later his office door slammed with a wooden thud.

"Do you think there's even a heart in that chest, Moe?"

Moe, the human shadow that Maybelle had assigned to follow her, dabbed at the moisture welling in his eyes.

"Don't you be fooled into thinking so, Miss

Devlin." Moe shook his bald head, sad and slow. He brushed a lock of hair behind Harriet's deaf ear with a trembling thumb. "This lamb weren't nothing to him but another dollar. He'll have himself another poor child by week's end, mark my word."

Dressed in the white nightgown Missy had purchased with a night's earnings, Harriet looked peaceful, like an angel who had flown her way home.

"I'm sure you're right, Moe."

"Right as a feather on a sporting woman, Miss Devlin. You was the one who paid for the laudanum to make her passing peaceful, not that dung worm."

Now half a day had passed since the dung worm had slithered into his hole. Harriet grew cold and stiff in her crib without the undertaker having been called.

Missy curled her fist and pounded on the office door. Harriet could no longer force Pete to live up to his obligation to her, but, by heavens, Missy could.

"Go to hell!" the voice behind the door yelled.

There couldn't have been a more appropriate invitation.

She opened the door, swished her red skirt inside, then leaned backward to close it.

Pete sat slumped in a chair with his back to

her. He gazed out a window so crusted with dust that the pink rays of sunset barely penetrated.

"I quit," she announced to the back of his head.

His boots, which had been propped on the windowsill, hit the floor with a slap of leather. He turned in the chair with a slow pivot.

"You think so, Miss Devlin?" Missy couldn't tell which glowed hotter, the glare in his eyes or the burning tip of the cigarette bobbing between his lips. "My women don't quit."

"Harriet proved that, I guess. She had to die to get away from you." Missy wished that the flush coloring his face came from shame but knew it was pure, red-hot greed.

He plucked the cigarette from his mouth and waved it like an ash-dripping flag. "That wasn't any of my doing. She was sick."

"Where I come from people treat their dogs better than you treated Harriet. You owe her a proper burial."

"If that squirrelly pup of yours is anything to go by, dogs get treated better where you come from than any human soul can hope for." Pete dropped the butt of his cigarette into a glass. The inch of whiskey left inside hissed as the hot tip died. "But to the point, that girl was a starving waif when I took her in out of the cold. She'd have died long ago if it hadn't been for me. Can't see that I owe her a damn thing."

"You owed her ten dollars." Harriet, with a

pained breath, had made Missy promise to claim it for her.

"She ain't here to collect. Besides, no undertaker is going to come and bury a whore for ten dollars." Pete picked up the glass of whiskey, noticed the butt in it and set it down with a frown. "And that is where this stands."

"Here is where it stands." Missy leaned away from the door. She peered through the feather flopping over the edge of her hat, returning his stare, will for will. "I'll perform tonight on the condition that you take the evening's earnings and combine it with what you rightfully owed Harriet, then you give her the burial that her folks would have, had they lived."

"The hell you say." Pete propped his boots on the desk. He knocked over the whisky glass but didn't seem to notice. With a grunt, he crossed his arms over his chest. "And why would I do that?"

"Because it's the decent thing to do, and if you don't I'll invite all your customers to join me at Maybelle's."

She expected him to leap from his chair, ranting like a madman, but he went still, his eyes narrowed in calculation. Outright anger would have felt more comfortable than this silence. A tantrum would be easier to deal with than the quiet ticking of his brain.

"You throw in your share of the take and we have a deal," he said at last.

"You make sure it's a fine funeral." Missy grasped the doorknob, eager to get out from under his scrutiny. "And get her buried next to her parents. I'll be watching to see that you do right by her."

He stood up slowly, like Moe's dung worm unwinding from its coil.

"Sweetheart, I'm dealing with you out of the goodness of my heart. You won't be taking my customers anywhere. I told you that my women don't leave. I meant that."

By heavens, the mealy-faced slug of a man had threatened her! Why, Edwin was twice his size and, although decent to the core, had looked every bit as fierce in his attempt to keep her from leaving home. Did he think she had the backbone of a banana?

"I'm sure you did mean it," Missy said, intentionally smiling at his sneer. "Still, I am not one of your women."

She opened the door, stepped through then slammed it behind her, certain that she had put him in his place.

A thud hit the back of the door. Broken glass tinkled on the floor. Edwin, in all his brotherly fury, had never lifted his hand in anger.

To all appearances, everything about the evening was as normal as mud, but Missy felt the difference down to her bones.

She readied the saloon for the nightly performance, the same as always. She dragged the gaming tables to the alcove under the stairs. She set the chairs in neat rows ten wide and ten deep. Muff slept in his basket beside the piano. Moe stood outside on the boardwalk sipping a beer, but all the while keeping a watchful eye on her.

Until tonight, setting up for the concert had been exciting, but this evening she felt watched. Not by the bartender. Mitch was busy stocking the shelves behind the bar. After the night's performance the men tended to drink heavily and make use of Pete's women until nearly dawn.

The source of her agitation seemed to come from Pete's private sanctum. The office door stood a few inches ajar, which was unusual all by itself, but to make that occurrence truly curious, the lamp had been put out.

Without a doubt, Pete watched her through that crack. After their conversation a few hours earlier, he might be dreaming up ways to force her to become one of his girls. On the nights that she performed, his profits doubled. He wouldn't give that up without a fight.

Were secret stares and wicked thoughts through a crack in a doorway what made the girls fear him?

With her back to the door she felt his eyes pricking at the tender spot between her shoulders. She spun about to face the door, feeling trapped, like a butterfly with its wings pinned against a board. She watched the burning end of a cigarette float up and down in the dark.

As unnerving as the unseen stare was, Missy doubted that it would be enough to keep a girl here against her good judgment. The man must have another way, something subtle yet brutal that would not be noticed outright, to keep his doves in submission.

Missy glanced out the front door to see Moe take a big gulp of beer. He laughed with a fellow drinker on the boardwalk but every second or two he peered inside, sometimes at Pete's cracked door and sometimes at her.

It was clear that Maybelle had not sent Moe to be her personal guardian on a whim.

So far on her adventure west, she had braved a giant, gown-eating cow, spent a rainy night snuggled beside a bold bounty hunter, and she had challenged a river gone wild on top of a huge beast of a horse.

Still the bravest act of her journey, and maybe her life, had been to smile and comfort poor Harriet, to assure her that welcome arms waited for her on the other side of life. She had done that with a smile even though the lump in her throat twisted and ached. Even though the unshed tears behind her eyes had burned like a fury.

Missy went to the piano bench and sat down. She tidied the blue bow holding the fur out of

Muff's eyes then straightened the small black feather that Emily had placed in it. She checked under the dog's blanket to make sure that her writing supplies were snug and safe. One never knew when one's path would take a sudden turn. It was best to keep her valuables close at hand.

"I suppose with all we've been through, that sour-faced weasel Pete shouldn't be much of a challenge." For some reason, Zane's brown-sugar gaze popped into her mind. It was a pleasant sight compared to Pete's secret-keeping stare so she let it linger. She closed her eyes and mentally added his smile, then his frown. She summoned his voice and heard him call her *darlin'*.

"Don't you miss him, Muff?" Muff growled in his sleep. "I wonder if he's caught that outlaw yet. He sure has his mind set on it."

"Sometimes, when a man has his mind set on something, hell can crack apart over his head and he won't give it up." Pete's breath, whispering six inches from her ear, smelled sour with alcohol and nicotine. "For instance, what wouldn't you do to keep that little dog from coming to harm? Things you wouldn't ordinarily consider, I expect."

Threats had never had much of an influence on her, but they had been delivered by Edwin who loved her in a way that only a protective brother could. Pete's threat made her long to pack up

Muff's basket and flee to Maybelle's third-floor sanctuary.

Obligation to Harriet and a dash of willfulness kept her derriere planted on the bench. She turned, sliding over a foot to put distance between his mouth and her nose.

Mindy Nightrose, a middle-aged dove with a jiggling bosom more out of her corset than in, stood close by. She peered over Pete's shoulder with wide eyes, clearly warning Missy to be careful.

"I quit." Missy watched Miss Nightrose's hand fly to her mouth, covering her irregular teeth and her surprise. "Tonight is my last performance. Take your threats and your foul breath somewhere else."

Pete's face flushed, a perfect match to Missy's crimson dress.

"Why, that was no threat, Miss Devlin." He sucked in a draw of his cigarette and blew it straight at Missy's face. "Just a bit of friendly conversation."

With a smile as genuine as the watered-down whiskey he sold in the wee hours, he turned and stomped off to his office, giving the door a solid slam.

Mindy spun about in a purple flash and skipped across the room to where Night Lilly waited to receive the latest gossip. Night Lilly ran up the stairs to whisper in the ear of Miss Laime Down who gaped at Missy with nothing less than astonishment.

Evidently, there were some things that could not be left behind in Boston. Causing a stir would be at the top of that list. Missy had a sinking feeling that this evening would find her in as much hot water as the time at Mrs. Charles Henson's tea for young ladies when she and Suzie had stripped to their bloomers and climbed up the great oak tree along with the stable boys. A dare was a dare, after all, and the boys had called them prissy girls.

Missy sighed. What could not be helped could not be helped. She hoped that Pete the worm would stay in his office until the performance was over, and she could leave quietly with Moe and never come back.

Fifteen minutes later Missy's audience began to arrive. There must have been something about the classical melodies she played that transformed the men. As soon as they strode through the door, rowdy cowboys became gentlemen. They greeted each other with friendly nods and Missy with respectful tips of their hats. A few of them even bowed over her hand.

One by one they took their seats, removed their headwear and folded their hands in their laps. She had rarely come across a more appreciative audience, even in the fancy drawing rooms of Boston.

"Gentlemen." Missy stood up after the first

piece of music concluded. She clasped her hands in front of her. "As some of you know, our friend, Harriet, passed to her Maker earlier today."

Many of the men nodded in sadness, having already heard, but others gasped, sorry at the bitter news.

"But in an act of true generosity, your host, Pete, has offered to give all of tonight's profits for her burial." Public pressure should ensure that he lived up to his agreement.

Pete, standing on the balcony and gazing down, lifted his hands in a show of modesty when the group cheered.

"It's the least I can do for one of our own." His gracious smile might have fooled some, but Laime Down, Night Lilly and Mindy Nightrose, standing on ascending stairs and looking like a bouquet of bright flowers, rolled their eyes heavenward.

"The next piece is called 'Clair de lune,' played in honor of Harriet," Missy announced.

Except for an occasional sniffle or honk into a bandana the room grew silent. Many of the men covered their hearts with weatherworn hats.

Let Pete try to wiggle out of the agreement now!

Missy settled in to the music. It was gentle, tender, and she noticed the clatter when several sets of boots walked through the door. They didn't take seats, but stood beside the bar, even though Pete did not serve drinks during her performance.

One of the men coughed. Another banged on the bar for the bartender to give him a drink.

"Gimme one, too, Mitch." A third cowboy said out loud, flicking his hat against his thigh and setting off a cloud of dust.

Missy's audience craned their necks. Harsh frowns warning the men to silence crossed more than a few trail-hardened faces.

Mitch glanced from Pete to the cowboys to Missy's audience.

Pete nodded his head. The smirk at the corner of his mouth all but shouted that he had planned this disruption.

If Pete wanted to stir things up, the gentle "Clair de lune" was far from the only piece of music that she knew.

Missy turned to her gentlemen with a smile and a wink. She attacked the keyboard with *Orpheus in the Underworld.* Mother had never liked it when Missy played Offenbach's wild and wonderful music, but to Missy it was pure energy and joy. Her fingers might be flying over the keyboard, but in her mind, she and Suzie were on a stage tossing their brightly colored skirts over their heads and kicking their legs high in the scandalous Can Can.

Behind her the men leaped from their chairs with hoots and applause. Until now, everything she played had been sweet and inspiring, lifting the listeners up out of the drudgery of their daily lives.

She glanced at Pete up on the balcony and grinned. His gaze shot red fury at her. His hired men tried to create a noisy distraction, but her piano was louder and her gentlemen more boisterous. Even Muff sat up in his little bed and howled.

Later tonight, when she wrote this all down, every word would be delicious.

It was true, what the cowboys had said. Missy could pleasure every man at once, but not, praise the heavens, in the way he had assumed.

Three days of hard, fast travel had brought him to the doorway of Pete's, primed and ready to do battle. He wasn't sure why he should feel responsible for the woman. She was not his sister…not his intended, not his in any way.

His or not, when he'd learned that she was working for Pete, his heart tripped over itself. He'd bounded up from the cozy campfire, mounted Ace and stopped only to let the horse rest. Until he rushed up the front steps of the Palace, he hadn't taken an easy breath.

He leaned against the back wall away from the lamp, hidden in shadow. Listening, he became enchanted, like the other ninety or more men sitting respectfully with their hats off.

Patrons of Pete's sitting in mannerly fashion, like gentlemen, was a sight he'd never expected to see. The cowboys at the bar, getting frowns and hisses, were more the nightly fare.

Throughout the piece, Missy had seemed lost to the room. Caught up in her playing she looked like an angel in satin and feathers. Even with the disruptive cowboys, she hadn't missed a note in the tune.

Now, with the ruckus becoming intrusive, her fingers stilled over the piano keys. She glanced up at Pete with a sugary smile. The man didn't know to run for cover.

She turned toward her audience with a wink. All at once she became a flame. He could have sworn that sparks glinted from her dress and those feathers breathing against her skin had turned to fire. The fire flew to her fingertips and out came a sound to turn the house upside down.

The audience leaped up, they slapped their thighs, they hooted, they drowned out the noisy patrons at the bar.

Zane scooted along the wall so that he could get a look at Missy's face. Again, she became caught up in the music. No angel this time, but a firebrand consuming every heart and making two hundred feet tap and stomp.

On the stairs, Pete's girls flicked their skirts back and forth. Six knees flirted in abandon and long-forgotten joy.

From his perch on the balcony, Pete grinned, but the expression lay on his face as sincere as a brick.

A man leaning against the bar, the one who had demanded a drink, exchanged a glance with Pete. At the saloon owner's nod, he made his way toward the piano.

Missy did not seem to be aware of his approach. She was somewhere with her music, caught up in a world a lifetime away from Pete's Palace.

The cowboy knelt down to Muff and flicked his finger at a small black feather tied in his fur. Muff tried to nip the intrusive digit but caught a mouthful of air. The man plucked him out of his bed and tucked him under his arm. He darted across the room then pounded up the stairs two at a time. He handed the pup over to Pete without Missy even noticing.

Pete stroked Muff's head. To anyone who didn't know better, they'd think the man had a fondness for the little beast.

Zane took a step toward the stairs. Missy stopped playing. She stood, wriggled her fingers then turned to curtsey to her wildly applauding audience.

"Thank you, Miss Devlin!" Pete shouted to be heard above the roar. "Listen up for a minute! You all are going to be pleased to know that the lady has agreed to stay on indefinitely."

This would never happen on Zane's watch, no matter what Missy had promised. A quiet voice in his brain reminded him that he had no watch over her. But damn, the woman was an innocent. Someone had to take on the job.

"Pete, you snake!" Mindy Nightrose yelled up the stairs, waving a fist at him. "She quit!"

Pete turned a cold glare on the woman, one that should have made her shrink into herself. Amazingly, Night Lilly and Laime Down flanked Mindy, joining forces with arms linked.

"She quits!" they affirmed.

"Is that right, Miss Devlin?" Pete circled his fingers around Muff's neck, pretending to scratch the little throat. "Do you quit?"

Missy's face flushed the same color as the little hat pinned to her hair. She curled her fists and took a step toward the stairs. Within a heartbeat, four of the cowboys lounging at the bar had taken a position three steps up to block her way.

In other circumstances, Missy could probably have charmed the men out of her way, but the mood inside the Palace was turning ugly.

"I told you that earlier." Anticipation silenced angry murmurs from the door to the balcony. Heads swiveled from Missy to Pete. "I quit!"

"We all quit!" Laime Down echoed.

Most nights, Zane wouldn't care to take on the four mean cusses standing on the stairs. Tonight was not one of those nights. He rushed forward

but his way became blocked by a dozen men who
had heard the call to a fight.

A tossed chair hit the mirror over the bar.
Glass shattered, men roared, Missy looked like
a red dot in the crush of flying fists. The feathered hat dangled from her head by a single pin.

Zane turned away from the stairs, trying to get
to her before she was trampled. He pushed a man
in a plaid shirt out of his way. He stepped over
one lying belly-up on the ground. He punched
a rock-hard jaw that refused to let him pass. He
watched the red dot pick her way toward the alcove.

On the stairs, the doves kicked the cowboys
in their posteriors and sent them slugging and
kicking into the blows of the men at the bottom.

From a slit in one bruised and swelling eye,
Zane watched Missy pull a table from the alcove.
He knocked aside a wicked-looking swing from
a bony fist. Missy lifted a chair and stacked it on
top of the table.

A blow connected to his middle and knocked
the wind from him. Hell! He must be hallucinating. It looked as if Missy was climbing the fur-
niture like it was some sort of a damned tree.

She clutched her fingers around the banister.
Her flame of a skirt rippled under her kicking
legs. It swayed like a bell when she swung one
delicate boot up to the balcony floor and wedged
it between a pair of spindles.

He shoved three men out of his way and only made a five-foot gain toward the balcony.

"Missy!" He doubted that his shout would carry over the rumble, but just as she levered her weight over the banister she looked toward his shout.

Her mouth dropped open in a surprised circle. Her hair, which a moment before had been a neat arrangement of curls peeking from her hat, sagged in a tangle of knots and pins. The feathers on her dress floated in time with her quick breathing.

Zane jumped over a ruined chair. He heard bottles shattering against the bar. The air smelled like beer and whiskey.

Looking as angry as a swatted hornet, Missy rushed Pete. He stumbled back in surprise. She leaped onto his back and clamped her slender arms around his neck. Without letting go of the dog, he could do nothing but spin to dislodge her.

Hanging on, Missy looked like a blaze whirling in the donnybrook.

Zane punched the last belly blocking his way. He stood below the balcony watching Missy and Pete in their dangerous dance.

Pete half stumbled, apparently shocked when Muff latched onto his hand with small but effective teeth. He stiffened his arm trying to shake the animal off.

After a heroic moment the dog let go of Pete's

hand and plunked on the floor. Missy delivered a blow to Pete's ear then hopped off his back.

"Come, Muff, come!" Zane heard Missy call.

The dog ran toward the battle on the stairs. Missy chased him and swept him up only a heartbeat before he got stepped on. Backing away from the stairs thick with lunging bodies and flailing arms, she inched along the banister. She did manage to put some distance between herself and the hostilities.

What she didn't see was Pete blocking her retreat. His teeth ground together. His hands clenched into white-fisted balls. Zane had no doubt the man would kill her given the chance.

"Watch out behind!" Zane shouted through an aching jaw. Pete rushed forward, one arm swinging. The imprint of ladylike fingers blistered his cheek. "Jump!"

Zane braced his arms, wide and ready. His heart tripped over itself when Missy spent a precious second turning to scowl at her attacker.

In a swish of lace, she lifted her legs over the banister. She leaned forward, one hand around Muff and the other grabbing the rail. Pete scrambled for her fingers and she let go, falling like an autumn leaf into Zane's arms.

She wasn't heavy and his guts were pumped. He dashed for the door where Ace waited, tied to the hitching post.

"Put me down!" She squirmed and twisted in his arms. "I've got to go back for my manuscript."

A bottle whooshed past his head and shattered on the door frame. He heard wood splintering to his right.

"Darlin'," he whispered heavily in her ear, "not a chance in hell of that."

"Oh," she said and became suddenly still.

He stepped over half a chair sliding across the floor.

Out on the boardwalk, cool air bathed his battle-hot body. He lifted Missy and Muff onto Ace's back and leaped up behind.

Ace didn't need any urging. He bolted down Ballico Street, galloping past patrons spilling out of neighboring saloons to join in the ruckus at Pete's.

When things cooled off there wouldn't be much left of the Palace. Come dawn, Pete would be a man out of business and a good thing, too, by Zane's way of thinking.

The problem was, he'd be a dangerous man with a big grudge against a little lady.

Chapter Seven

"A deal is a deal," Missy said, staring at the blob on the ground while Muff sniffed it.

A bargain made was a bargain kept. She gazed across the sweep of land brushed golden by the sunset, watching Zane mount his horse. Confidence marked his posture. His large tan hands held the horse's reins with years of familiarity. He was certain to keep his end of the bargain that she wished she had not agreed to.

Muff scratched at the brown mound, sneezing over bits of dried grass poking out from it.

At first consideration, gathering the fuel for a fire had seemed a better choice than hunting up dinner. Finding a cook on the plains with a warm meal prepared would be as impossible as pressing her knees together.

After a night and a day in the saddle her legs

seemed to be as bowed as a scurvy-plagued sailor's.

When Zane had presented the deal to her she had jumped at the chance to gather wood. A splinter or two didn't seem a high price to pay for a warm meal.

If only it was a splinter ready to pierce her skin! She kicked at the cake-sized thing on the ground and set up a cloud of dust that made Muff bark and leap at it.

In the many novels that she had read on the wild and wonderful West she couldn't recall a single mention of a buffalo chip. Zane had not bothered to hide his mirth when he explained that the dried excrement of a buffalo made excellent fuel for a fire.

"It burns quick and true," he had stated, with a rare smile that charmed the sense out of her. "So you'll need to gather a lot of it."

If he hadn't turned toward his horse at that very moment and broken the spell, he could have suggested that prairie dogs barked hymns and she'd have believed him.

Now, with the setting sun casting the long moving shadow of horse and man across the earth, the time had come to live up to her end of the agreement. Full night would fall fast and hard. She didn't want to face the darkness without a fire.

"Adversity holds the seeds of adventure," she

mumbled, but for an instant the saying didn't ring true. "What other kinds of seeds might be in this chip? Muff…no, don't eat that!"

She shooed the dog away then tested the edge of the dung with her finger. It was drier than she expected and it didn't smell. With a pinch of her thumb and forefinger she lifted it and carried it to the spot near the creek where Zane had indicated they would set up camp for the night.

Three times she carried buffalo chips from their point of deposit to the campsite with the tips of her fingers. At this rate it would be dawn before she had enough chips for a decent fire.

If she used her skirt for a scoop, she would be done in no time at all. Gathers of satin caught a lingering ray of sunshine and shot back flickers of red and gold. What a crime to use the fabric to cart buffalo dung. Back home, the punishment would be severe.

A coyote's howl carried across the dimming land. From somewhere nearby another answered. The fur on Muff's back stood straight up. Missy filled her skirt with the big oval chips.

"Come, Muff, come," Missy ordered and hurried toward the stream.

The dog stood still with his nose sniffing the wind and his ears cocked toward the calling of the coyotes.

Missy dropped her load then hurried back to gather another bunch of chips. With her skirt filled once more, she lifted Muff and set him on top of the dirty collection.

Was it her imagination that the nearby howl had come closer? Perhaps a mere dash and a leap away?

"Well, I'll be hanged." Zane peered at the campsite from a hundred feet away. A fair-sized fire snapped at the edges of a pitch-black night. "She did it."

He hadn't expected that. Even some prairie-hardened women balked at the task of collecting buffalo piles. Missy Lenore Devlin was a woman of constant surprise.

With the evening so deep, he didn't believe she was aware of his presence. But he was aware of her. His heart tightened, his breathing cramped as he watched the champion of the campsite battling the perils of the night with her blaze.

Firelight shadowed fine lines at the corners of her eyes while she gazed past the circle of light. She seemed uneasy. A shiver rolled over her bare arms. It didn't take much to imagine the chilly bumps that she tried to rub away with a brisk rub of her palms. He ought to have stopped at Maybelle's on the mad dash out of town to get her some kind of a wrap, but his only concern had been to get her as far from Pete as possible.

Missy turned her back to the fire, staring this way and that into the darkness. She lifted her hands to her hair and plucked the pins from it, one after another. Bit by golden bit the strands tumbled and snaked between her shoulders. Her hair looked like a waterfall sparkling with amber light. If he touched those tresses they might feel like mist.

With both hands at the top of her head she skimmed her scalp, sifting the strands through her fingers. He shouldn't stare like a green boy, but by damn, he couldn't yank his gaze to the bleakness beyond her fire-warmed circle.

Her fingers caressed a twining path to her neck, then suddenly she clenched them in apparent vexation. She grabbed a fistful of hair with both hands and pulled it. She kicked at a dirt clod while she tugged the tangle this way and that.

So much for enchantment by firelight. The prairie was what it was, hard and merciless. A day in the saddle would cause a woman's hair no end of trouble.

At last, she gave up on wrenching and tugging. She knotted her fists and slammed them on her hips, her annoyance clear even at this distance. After a moment her shoulders relaxed. He thought he heard her say something but from this distance couldn't tell what it was.

She bent over and gathered up her skirt. One peek at her stocking-clad calves and his heart kicked up a notch. The red glow of the skirt shimmied past her knees and he reminded himself to look away.

His gaze, contrary as a mule having a stubborn fit, only sharpened.

With a wiggle of her hips, she lifted the skirt hem over her thighs then tucked the fabric across her arm. Zane nearly fell off his horse watching the way the garment caressed her round little behind like a lover's hand.

Slowly, she turned around and around, warming her legs. Blamed if she didn't look like dinner on the barbecue spit. Impossibly, the fire's heat seemed to sizzle across the night to singe him. The pair of garters circling her thighs winked a welcome that made his belly simmer.

Had it only been a thought ago that he had dismissed the notion of prairie enchantment? The dark and the fire might hold more magic than he had ever suspected.

The enchantment ended abruptly when Muff barked. Like a pin-pricked bubble the vision burst and the skirt plunked to the cold earth.

Zane remained silent, gazing out over the bleak, dark land for five cold minutes before he dismounted and led Ace toward the campsite. He didn't want Missy to know that he had been peeping at her. That had not been honorable behavior by any standard, but damned if she hadn't touched him in a way he would never have imag-

ined. In a way that made him feel like a man
coming home.

"Nice fire," he announced, stepping into view.
The heat warmed his face when he walked past,
leading Ace toward the stream.

"Nice...bunny," she replied, frowning at the
carcass swaying limply from the saddle pack.

While Ace sucked up a long drink, Zane removed the saddle and propped it against the broken limb of a cottonwood.

"This is dinner, darlin'. Out here it doesn't
come out of a kitchen on a silver platter."

The pup approached the rabbit, tucking his tail
between his legs. He sniffed then scurried behind
Missy's skirt to cower. Evidently the dog was just
as citified as its mistress.

"I'm grateful for the dinner, Zane, truly."
Missy gazed at the game like it was a lost friend.
She reached her fingers toward it but stopped and
curled them in a fist. "It's just that I have a bunny
back home. I found him abandoned in the peonies
when he wasn't bigger than a minute."

Zane lifted the carcass from the saddle and
carried it toward the stream. He knelt down, listening to the water lap against the bank. Without a doubt, he'd be the one to skin and clean
tonight's meal.

Silk whispered and petticoats crinkled. Missy
crouched beside him, nearly thigh-to-thigh.

"It's certain that this rabbit never saw a peony

in his life. He was born to be food, either for us or some coyote," he said.

"It took me for a minute, that's all. My Achilles has the same brown markings."

"Achilles?"

"When he hops about the yard he springs up like he's got wings on his feet."

He looked down at the brown-and-white creature half-skinned in his hands. Next time he'd be sure to bring down a wild turkey. Chances are she wouldn't have made a pet of one of those lanky birds.

"I didn't come adventuring with the expectation of honey-glazed ham and chocolate cake with raspberry sauce for supper every night."

She sucked in a breath and held it for an instant. She flipped a tangled mass of hair from her shoulder to her back.

"I'll cook it." She pointed to the skinned rabbit then looked Zane full in the eyes. "If you'll show me how."

"Exactly how much experience have you had in the kitchen?" He'd spent an hour or more finding a rabbit big enough for both of them to eat. He'd be hanged if he was going to let her burn it.

"Oh, hours upon hours!" Her face brightened with a smile. "Mother insisted that a lady should know how her kitchen runs. Suzie and I spent many a rainy afternoon watching cook take pastries out of the oven."

"The thing about pastries is that they don't have to be gutted."

"Gutted?" she gasped. "Adversity holds…"

She held her hand open waiting for the knife he held.

"Tell me what to do." She squeezed her eyes shut, creasing the corners in spidery lines. Her face blanched as though she was the one about to be gutted.

"I'll need some salt. It's over there in my saddle pack in a leather pouch, if you'd get that for me."

Settlers at the homestead five miles back might have heard her sigh of relief when she closed her fist.

She leaped up and rushed for the salt.

"If you have tea and cups in here, I'm your woman," she called out. "Edwin swears that I excel at serving tea."

Missy watched Zane's throat move, swallowing a steaming sip of coffee. He passed the hot tin cup to her.

The consumption of coffee seemed to have no apparent ceremony to it. Unlike tea that had to be poured in the proper way and sipped with the fingers held just so, coffee could be taken sitting or standing. It could be savored alone or even shared, as now. At a tea party she would never have imagined putting her lips on the same cup rim as a gentleman had.

Now, with the tin warming her palms, she sought the very spot where Zane had put his mouth.

"Dinner was delicious," she said, then took another unsweetened swallow of the dark brew and handed the cup to Zane. "After the second or third bite I didn't give Achilles a thought."

"Looks like the mutt forgot old ties easy enough."

Steam floated up from the mug, tracing a swirling vapor across Zane's face. In the dark it was hard to see the color of his eyes but they were sure to be a reflection of the simmering drink they shared.

"Muff is not a mutt, he's bred as pure as can be." She glanced at the dog, watching his pure-bred fur turn yellow with the grease from the leftover rabbit he devoured. "Back home, heads would turn if he were anything but pure."

"He sure has caused a few heads to turn out here." Zane passed the cup. "What made you bring the runt along?"

"If I wasn't home to keep him in hand, I'm afraid Edwin might give him to a neighbor." Missy snuggled the tin in her palms to gather the warmth. The bite in the night air threatened to snuff out the heat of the little campfire. "For some reason, he has no patience with Muff. No matter how many times I explain that he's just a puppy, Edwin can't forget about his ermine slippers."

"When I was a kid my mother gave me a pup." His eyebrows lifted in apparent surprise, as though a forgotten memory had been restored. "Its teeth were as sharp as a new pencil."

"If only Muff had taken to the slippers with his teeth. Edwin wouldn't have judged innocent chewing to be an insult. As it was, the slippers never did dry right."

Zane rolled his neck, probably easing the aches of a day in the saddle out of the muscles. "Dogs are pretty much of one mind on that, no matter how pure."

Muff, finished with picking the bones of the rabbit, carried the carcass to a nearby bush and began to dig. Dirt stuck to the grease in his beard. It turned his paws brown and his nose a mucky orange. He didn't look a thing like the white puff who had stolen away from home in her satchel.

Zane stretched and tipped the soles of his boots toward the fire. He folded his arms across his flat belly, lounged back against the fallen cottonwood log and closed his eyes. With his face in repose and the fire reflecting off it, the injury to his left eye was plain to see.

"I'm sorry about your eye." The swelling had gone down since they had fled Luminary, but the puffiness had left a sickly purple-green ring that made her feel blameworthy.

"That wasn't your fault."

"I'm sorry about your thumb." A jagged red line sliced through the center of his thumbnail where he had pulled out the splinter with his teeth.

"Not your fault either."

The flood was not her fault, to be sure, but the fact that he was in the position to be injured was no one's fault but hers.

She refilled the coffee tin and thought to offer Zane the first sip but he seemed so peaceful with his feet toasting by the fire. Just as well, the heat in her palms was a comfort she hated to give up. "I'm sorry that your coat got left behind at May-belle's."

"That might be your fault." A smile nipped the corners of his mouth. With his eyes closed she was free to stare directly at his face. *Handsome* was a weak word when it came to describing Zane Coldridge. Mercy forgive her, she wanted to crawl over on hands and knees and kiss that mouth even though it curled with the barest trace of a smirk.

His eyes cracked open and his gaze slid her way as though he had read her wicked thoughts.

"I suppose that if I'd been more careful with my dress, you'd have captured your bank robber by now," she said with a quick glance at the fire to hide any lingering expression of longing.

"Hard to imagine losing your gown to a cow."

She looked back and saw a smile that carried right up to his eyes. She couldn't help but stare openly now.

"If I had imagined it I would have put it out of reach of the beast's jaws."

If a body could know ahead of time the misadventures that might occur, she could be at least prepared to meet them.

For instance, if she had imagined the flood, she would have done any number of things differently. For one she'd have brought along her hairbrush when she rode away from the Green Island Hotel. The past twenty-four hours had made her head feel as messy as an abandoned bird's nest.

As if, once more, sensing her thoughts, Zane untied his lace ribbon. For an instant she hoped he meant to lend it to her but he smoothed the strip with his fingertips, made four precise folds then tucked it in the pocket of his shirt. He gave the pocket a pat, pressing the lace close to his heart.

"That must be a very special ribbon," she said, hoping to hear the story behind it. Flame-burnished hair freed from its confinement sifted across his brow, hiding the tale that his eyes might tell.

An uneasy wind moaned over the land and caught the mournful howl of something rather larger than a coyote. Muff growled but snuggled his grease-and-mud-smeared self deep into the safe folds of her skirt.

"Wolf," Zane muttered, then fed a buffalo chip to the flames.

"Wolves aren't common in Boston." She peered into the darkness, relieved that she did not spot a pair of ferocious yellow eyes. The wind must have carried the cry from miles away. In spite of that, she shivered.

"Scoot on over, darlin'. Sit here between my legs."

The scandalous invitation drew the blood from her face straight to her belly. How curious.

He had seen her shiver and might think she was frightened of the wolf, or cold to the bone. Both of those things were true. But she had noticed his gaze dip a time or two to the peekaboo feathers adorning the low-cut bodice of her harlot's gown. Her shiver came from somewhere else.

"I'm not a bit cold," she made up. "Or scared."

Reflections of flame played across his eyes. His winged eyebrows called like a summons from Lucifer.

"It's this dress, isn't it?" She yanked up the low décolletage. "I'm not really a—"

"I don't have a hairbrush, but I think I can get at those tangles with my fingers."

"Oh." She let go of her bodice. Evidently, he

was not tempted by the chill-prickled flesh swelling out of it. That was a relief...most certainly.

Zane pointed to the space between his knees and, like a magnet drawn to an attracting force, she scooted backward into the V-shape that his thighs presented. Thank the stars that he couldn't see her humiliation when his fingers slipped through her hair and encountered a knot the size of a tumbleweed.

Even though her body had been closer to his a few times, back-to-belly in the saddle or tucked up tight in the tarp, this was more intimate. Those times had been forced by circumstance. This time, he had invited her into his personal space and she had wiggled her derriere right in.

For an instant Edwin's frown flashed in her mind, but she snuffed the vision out like a tiny flame between her fingers.

"Wolves travel in packs, I've read." She continued to scan the dark beyond the fire's reach but the threat seemed diminished with a pair of muscled legs braced about her.

"Wolves sound like the devil, but they're not much of a threat to us. You'd best keep the dog close, though."

The only thing visible of Muff was his nose. It poked out of a fold of her skirt to sniff this way and that.

"The truth is, with a few exceptions, I'd rather face the beasts of the night than many a man."

Zane's voice whispering warmly past her ear sounded relaxed, but even in repose she noticed that he scanned the night for danger.

"Or a tangle," she mumbled, apologizing for the messy challenge he had taken on. "You seem to have a way with hair, though."

She'd had her hair brushed before, pampered by hands that knew just what a lady needed, but never by hands hard with calluses, never by strong, suntanned fingers that sifted through tangles like a spoon stirring honey.

"Along with learning my ABCs I learned to get the knots out of the sporting ladies' hair." He plucked at an especially stubborn knot.

"There is surely an interesting story behind that." How much of it would he be willing to tell?

He hesitated the duration of a wolf's howl and its mate's answer before speaking.

"Maybelle took me in when no one else would; she was like a doting aunt. There weren't a lot of ways to pay her back, but I did learn that after a night's work, the girls sometimes needed help with their hair. Some of them could read so while I worked on their hair they taught me what they could."

He must have learned more than his letters growing up in a brothel. "Why did Maybelle take you in? What happened to your folks?"

"Look at that moon," he said with a neat side-step to her question.

"As slivers go, it's exceptional." Something horrid must have happened to his folks for him to close up at the mention of them, but talking was a balm. "Sometimes, Zane, my heart aches for my father so much that I cry my eyes dry."

His fingers went still in her hair. The night wind tiptoed across her face.

She missed her mother and her brother, as well, but her heart ached for Suzie. Without her twin, there had been no one for her soul to speak to.

Writing her manuscript gave solace, but every time she wrote something down, it was stolen or heartlessly abandoned.

"Have you ever seen a butterfly moon?" she asked. Suzie was not here, but Zane was.

A soft snort whispered past her ear. For a man with gentle hands, he was amazingly cynical.

"I was born under one," she persisted. The world was full of wonder, if a body knew how to look for it. Zane Coldridge would be a happier man if he tried to.

"There can't be such a thing, darlin', since the moon is shining at the exact time that butterflies are down for the night."

"Most of the time that's true."

"I suppose you're going to tell me all about the times it isn't true." Another grisly knot fell victim to his experienced fingers.

"We have a lot of hours with nothing else to

do." She felt the quick catch of his breath then the slow hiss of its release.

"Don't spin me any dime-novel yarns. I told you that the things you read in those books are mostly untrue."

"This is a story from my own dear father's lips. I'm sure it's gospel."

"You can talk until dawn and I guarantee that I won't see a butterfly near the moon."

"Of course you wouldn't, not on a normal night." She took a quick glance at the sickle moon. His fingers felt like warm stones sliding through her hair. This was far from a normal night. "As my father told it, and Papa never told a lie, a butterfly moon happened on the night that Suzie and I were born."

A wolf howled, closer now. The hands in her hair didn't falter, making the mournful wail no more frightening than a puppy whining in the dark.

"It happened at midnight. Mother had been in labor for two days. We didn't come into the world easily, the way my brother had. The doctor told my father to prepare for the worst. Papa was in a state, so fearful of a loss he couldn't bear.

"After listening to the doctor's bad news, he ran out the kitchen door, into the herb garden. He fell on his knees, begging God for a miracle. It was right then that he felt a touch on his shoulder. He said it was so light it might have been a brush of wings."

Zane's rough-knuckled fingers stroked a section of hair that he had smoothed moments before.

"When Papa opened his eyes and looked around, no one was there. From the upstairs window, he heard mother cry out as though it were her last breath.

"Then he looked at the big fat full moon. Even through his tears he saw them."

"Butterflies?" While Zane's voice didn't sound convinced, it didn't sound mocking either.

"Thousands of them. By the light of that moon Papa saw them glow orange and blue and yellow. He likened it to a rainbow cut up into bits and tossed about the sky. Then he heard a baby cry. That was me. He shouted for joy and ran for the house. When he was halfway up the stairs, he heard another cry. That was Suzie. He heard us both wailing away at the same time. He twisted his ankle on a toy ship that Edwin had left on the stairs but he hobbled up to us in a flash. Papa liked to say that since the night of the butterfly moon the house hadn't known a moment's peace and quiet. Papa wasn't a big fan of peace and quiet anyway."

"I'd bet a thief's reward that you take after your pa."

"Mother used to say so before…" Words stuck

in her throat like dry crackers. Before Papa died and the world turned over, she tried to say. Before, when her mother would laugh at the things that she and Suzie did because they reminded her of Papa.

"Gracious, it seems that you've gotten every knot from my hair," she murmured through the brittle crumbs lingering in her throat.

She leaned forward and gathered up Muff to scoot toward the far side of the fire. With her hair finished, there was no seemly reason to remain snuggled between the safehold of his thighs.

Zane's hands closed about her elbows, pressing heat into her cool flesh. "Sit here for a while."

She shouldn't. The proper thing would be to remove to her own side of the fire and shiver, or to be respectably devoured by a foraging wolf.

Evidently, taking the silence of her inner battle as consent, he leaned forward, wrapped his arms around her ribs then slid her backward. His chest rose and fell against her back with his even breathing. His heart pumped half a beat slower than hers did. Heat bubbled around her like a simmering pot.

This side of the fire or that, hot or cold, she shivered.

"When I was fourteen, I turned my uncle in for a fifty-dollar bounty."

Chapter Eight

∽∾∿

What on God's green plain had made him confess that? Had he been distracted by star-kissed hair and the scent of a woman? It might have been her spell-weaving voice that brought him to the brink of believing that hokey butterfly-moon tale.

The hell if he'd told her because he hoped that she might understand why he had betrayed his own kin.

"Oh, mercy, I can't count the times I've yearned to do that to Edwin." Her exasperated sigh pressed against his chest.

"Yearning and doing aren't half the same thing." This was one conversation he needed to get out of. He had said too much already.

"I only yearn it for a minute, anyway. Poor Edwin became a man before his time, taking on the household after Papa died and dealing with me and Suzie." She was quiet, looking at the fire and likely seeing things from her past. Flames and a quiet prairie night could do that to a person. "In some ways you and my brother are alike."

"About as alike as that wolf out there and your little white pup."

To his surprise, Missy laughed. Her voice tinkled across the dark land.

"Something like that," she said. "But what I meant was that you both became men when you were still children. You each gave up your youth for the good of others."

"What makes you so sure I turned in the old crook for anything noble? Maybe I just wanted the reward."

"You make me sure, Zane."

He grappled for a cynical reply to that. How was he to keep the woman at arm's length when she was wiggling a path from between his knees straight into his heart? Hell, when had he reached down and taken hold of her hands and begun stroking her cold, slender fingers like a smitten schoolboy?

"He was planning to rob a bank and I was tired of being hungry. I never agonized over the right or wrong of betraying kin. Afterward, I got a clean hotel room, ate a fat meal and slept warm and full with a smile on my face."

"I admire you for that." She turned her heart-shaped face up to look at him. He couldn't detect a single mocking or accusing thought behind those round blue eyes. "He must have been a horrible man."

"He was a greedy son of a gun. I never understood how that weak-principled cuss could be related to my mother."

"There are some things that just don't make any sense." Missy glanced back at the fire and sighed.

"He was the only kin I had after my mother died." Mentioning his mother's death cut him to the quick. He never spoke of her passing, not even to Maybelle. He didn't recall his father's death, he'd been too young, but at six years old, the loss of his mother had left its mark.

"I do love Edwin, even though I complain at times." He was thankful she did not press him about his mother since he seemed to be unable to keep from spilling his soul to a woman who viewed life as a story to be written down for the country's entertainment.

"My uncle was unprincipled and greedy, but he did take me in." Once again, Missy did not press him about his mother even though he knew she must be yearning to hear the story. He didn't know why, but it seemed natural to tell her about his past. Someday, he might find every word written in a dime novel, embellished ten times over, but for tonight, it felt right to talk.

"For eight years he dragged me around the

countryside committing petty crimes to get us by. Now and then I wonder if I ought to be grateful, but then I remember what hungry times those were… Sometimes, he'd be gone for nights on end."

"He ought to have been whipped for that," Missy whispered and squeezed his fingers.

"Maybe, but those were the good nights."

He couldn't tell her why. It was pitiable to think back on when he used to watch other kids through their windows at night. He'd hide in a shadow and peer through the glass, pretending to be the kid who sat on his father's knee or got patted on the head. He'd taste the sugar when the boy inside got fed a treat then trundled off to bed. Later, when he lurched off into the night he would hold tight to a vision of the goodnight kiss that the kid had gotten from his ma.

"The old man was lousy company," was as much of the truth that he was willing to admit.

Missy plucked her hand from his and reached back to stroke his cheek with the backs of her fingers. The brush of her smooth skin reminded him that he hadn't shaved in days. Compared to the beaus she would have known in the East, he must seem like a heathen.

"Sometimes the heart aches so that a body can't speak of it." She turned, kneeling between his legs to look at him. Her hand brushed aside the mess of hair that had fallen across his eye. "If you ever want to, though, I swear on the butterfly moon that I will never tell a soul…and lightning strike me if I write it down."

His mind had to stretch to recall a time when someone, other than Maybelle, had touched him with tenderness. Memory stretched so thin that it nearly broke before he recalled the time with Emily, before she turned to the sporting life. Too many years had passed.

The intimacy of fingertips against his cheek and the graze of Missy's hand through his hair made his heart ache. She offered a human bond that had been long lacking in his life.

He'd be a fool to believe in a promise vowed by someone who believed in butterfly moons. What she offered was not for him. A man on the hunt, chasing his demons, could not afford the bond that her touch hinted at.

He'd be wise to treat Missy Lenore Devlin the way he had treated every other woman in life, touch her body but never her heart.

"Words can come hard, Zane, but once they're said, for some reason heartaches aren't as sharp." She slid her palm along the line of his scratchy jaw then turned and stretched. She plopped her round bottom on the ground, staring deeply into the fire. "For instance, if I say to you, 'Papa died, Suzie was paralyzed and all I got was a bruise on my chin,' the truth of it hurts like anything, but saying it makes me feel better. Who knows why? Maybe if I think you feel what I feel, that makes it easier."

"You could get hurt, being so trusting. What if I laughed at you?" What if he kissed her?

"You are a better man than you give yourself credit for. I trust you." What if he laid her down in front of the fire?

"There are a lot of folks who wouldn't say that." He drew the hair away from the back of her neck. The chilly air puckered the tender skin he had exposed.

"Do you think I'd go into the wilderness with a man I didn't trust?" He nipped at the curve between her neck and shoulder and felt her flesh turn smooth under the warmth of his mouth.

"As I recall, you didn't have a choice." He curled his fingers around her ribs, high up so that his thumbs grazed the weight of her breasts. The thrum of her blood pulsed under his fingertips.

"Just because you picked me up and set me on your horse doesn't mean I didn't make a choice."

Missy's head tipped to the right, exposing more of her throat to his mouth. Her pulse quickened under his tongue. He slid his hands up and the full weight of her breasts warmed his palms.

The woman was a delicacy, like a bottle of golden whiskey that he might sip in glorious delirium and never feel the consequence of until dawn.

"You never do what you don't want to do?" he asked. She couldn't know what he had in mind.

He rose to his knees then crawled in front of her, over her. The night narrowed to the crackle of the fire and the beating of her heart. It made him feel like a predatory cat. He crept forward until his knees braced her hips. He pressed her shoulders back against the log and gazed into eyes so round that they looked like a pair of blue moons.

"Just ask Edwin," she whispered.

It tickled his conscience that she had spoken her guardian's name, but not enough to make him turn back. Her lips glistened with a reflection of stars. The wind caught a lock of her hair and blew it across her mouth.

"I don't think I will," he murmured close to her lips.

He brushed aside her windblown hair and saw her smile the instant before he kissed her, as though she was the one who had gotten what she wanted. Who was the hunter and who was the prey?

Missy touched his hair, she cupped his ear with the palm of her hand. She sighed his name against his lips. He knew this kiss was different, clear to his soul. Her touch and his response was not at all what he had imagined. He would never be content to touch this woman's body and not her heart.

Dear Lord, he felt as if he'd guzzled that bottle

of spirits and seen a thing that looked like forever floating at the bottom of it.

Someone needed to stuff the cork back in the jug. Judging by the way Missy seemed unwilling to give up his mouth, it was not going to be her.

"You're playing on dangerous ground, darlin'," he managed to pant over the free tumble of his heart and the breathless condition of his lungs. "Anything could happen when you kiss a man like that."

"Probably something I could never write down."

He touched his forehead to hers. Missy's skin simmered but his steamed like a screaming teakettle. Her quick, shallow breathing mingled with his heavy sigh.

A pack of coyotes yipped in the distance and Muff, tossed from the fold of Missy's skirt, answered with a puppy howl.

Night air nipped at his back, but Missy's body sizzled an invitation more welcome than the campfire.

A quiet voice inside urged him to meet with Edwin, suitor to guardian. And then what? a louder voice roared. Drag her around the countryside where she would grow tough as hide while he made his ugly living? Or leave her alone in a fine little house while she wondered if he'd make it home at all?

"Darlin', someday, a man from your own world will be lucky to have you as his wife."

He was relieved when she didn't speak. Her silence, along with a shift of her eyebrows, must mean that she didn't take the kiss and the touching as a permanent commitment.

Then she smiled.

Damn! Thinking on it, the woman did seem to get everything she wanted, in one way or another. Heaven help them both if that pretty curl of her lips meant she had felt the kiss as deeply as he had.

Sixteen hours and twenty miles later the promise in Zane's kiss lingered on Missy's lips.

She stood beside the second-story window of her room in the Dewton Hotel waiting for her bath to be delivered. Even though she gazed at the tidy street below, her mind saw last night's campfire reflecting the promise of something forbidden on Zane's wickedly handsome face.

In the end, he had spun her heart into turmoil by declaring the kiss to be ordinary. Like volcanic eruptions and shooting stars were ordinary, she had whispered back. At that he had scrambled up, dropped the only blanket over her and gone to shiver the night away on the far side of the fire.

The contrary bounty hunter could deny the attraction from now until the Fourth of July, but she knew when a man's touch meant forever. If it hadn't, she would be a compromised woman by now.

"I'd bet the last chapter of my novel that his lips are as blistered as mine are," she announced to Muff. The puppy, curled in an exhausted heap in the middle of a blue gingham bedspread, didn't wiggle an ear.

For a man who didn't care, he had gone to some expense to rent her this room for a week. She had insisted that she could manage very well on her own, but he had given her a ferocious scowl and all but yanked her inside.

In the way of physical comfort, Zane had been more than generous. If only he hadn't closed up his heart like a sea anemone poked with a stick.

"Truth to tell, Muff, I might not have gotten us this nice room on my own. A bath and a nap in a real bed seem only a cloud away from heaven." Muff would hate it, but as soon as she finished her long soak she would give him a thorough scrub. Keeping a white pup up to purebred standards out here in the glorious West was a bigger challenge than she had expected.

Through the open window, the aroma of baking bread and roasting beef floated up from the hotel kitchen.

Anticipation tumbled her stomach, or maybe it was nerves. Zane had invited her to join him for dinner and she knew that he meant to tell her goodbye.

"He has said that to us before, twice," she called over her shoulder. She tapped her fingers on the windowsill.

"Who was the one to have even mentioned marriage?" She spun about to see Muff's feet twitch, chasing something in a dream. "For a fact, that man has a way of filling a girl's head with possibilities."

Missy walked to the bed and plucked a leaf from behind Muff's ear. She crumpled it in her hand then returned to the window to toss it out. Down below, a boy ran after a barking dog. A young couple strolling hand in hand swung out of his way. In the distance a thundercloud blocked the sun. A humid breeze sifted the hair at her temples.

"Before, all I wanted was adventure," she whispered to the changing afternoon. "Now, let's just see if I don't catch a bounty hunter as well."

By tomorrow morning Zane's life would be back on track. He would leave Missy in the respectable town of Dewton and then finally be free to track Wage.

A glance around the hotel dining room assured him that Missy would feel at home with the folks of the growing town. Women, respectable in every way, wore dresses with bodices buttoned modestly beneath their chins. Men, speaking to their ladies with cordial voices, wore wool suits and polished boots.

Even though he had shaved, combed his hair slick to his head and tied it with the freshly washed ribbon, it would be a stretch to mistake him for a gentleman. He had tried to leave his gun upstairs in his room but he felt vulnerable, like a bull missing its horns, so he strapped it back on.

Heads had turned when he entered the dining room, giving him a wary eye. Once he had settled down at a table in the center of the room, the patrons' attention quickly returned to eating and conversing.

He sipped a beer, waiting for Missy. It was good to know that he would be able to enjoy her company without feeling she needed looking after. Dewton was a quiet town, a peaceful place to live, where days rolled along in quiet predictability.

Close at hand, a fork clattered on a plate. A glass of wine tipped and dribbled on the floor. Three feminine gasps whooshed though the suddenly silent dining room. Outside, thunder rumbled over the roof while lightning flickered at the windows.

Zane glanced up from his drink to see Missy in a glory of red satin and bosom-kissing feathers standing in the doorway. Her flirty hat tipped across a halo of golden curls and whirls. A tinge of embarrassment pinked her cheeks.

Standing, he scraped his chair backward, defying anyone to say a word against her. By habit, he had begun to reach for his gun, but Missy smiled and his fingers relaxed.

With the proud posture of a queen, she nodded to the room at large.

"Good evening, everyone." She shifted her engaging smile from the astonished diners to him. "Good evening, Zane."

Missy Devlin looked like an angel spat from the underworld. She approached the waiter, speaking to him in hushed tones. The blushing man nodded his head when she pointed to an old but well-polished piano in the corner of the dining room.

Zane felt like the worst kind of a heel. He ought to have thought of providing Missy with respectable clothing. The Dewton diners would not have been more shocked to see her striding through the doorway wearing her fancy blue-bowed underwear.

"What a lovely hat," Missy commented, passing by a woman whose thick eyebrows met in a frown. "Maybe you'll tell me where you purchased it?"

The woman glanced away, but to Zane's surprise her expression had softened.

Missy sat down on the piano bench, settling her skirt in a flounce of crimson. She glanced back at him with a wink that nearly buckled his knees.

He thumped down on the chair then lifted his beer in a salute to her. If the divine Miss Devlin could tame the wild men at Pete's, this group would ooze like honey between her fingertips.

Music washed from one end of the room to the other in a melodious wave. Diners set down forks. Glasses plunked on tables. The woman whom Missy had complimented, wearing the ugly bird's-nest hat, plumped it with pride.

When the elegant piece ended, gentlemen stood up in applause while properly dressed ladies eyed the scandalous sparkle of Missy's gown with, of all things, an apparent stirring of envy.

Missy, after a nod and a curtsey, returned to her seat, flushed with satisfaction.

"Darlin', you are a wonder," he said, and meant it to the bone.

Day by day the lady showed her resourcefulness. So far, he hadn't seen the problem that she had not turned to her advantage. It might take longer than a few days to put the vision of her easy smile behind him. Bidding her goodbye might not be the relief he had anticipated.

"Well, adversity does hold the seeds of adventure." She took a sip of water then returned the nods of the folks sitting nearby, still clapping in delight. "Besides, it's hardly the first time I've landed in a fix. I discovered long ago that it's a

simple thing to win a woman over with a com-
pliment to her hat or her shoes. Even the stiffest
souls will soften to dear Ludwig van Beethoven."

"Come morning, you'll be famous in Dewton."
A twinge of apprehension twisted Zane's gut.

The eyes of the town would be on the scarlet
angel, for sure, and possibly the eyes of a bounty
hunter. A woman like Missy did not fade into
the scenery. It couldn't be long before a man of
questionable scruples matched the wanted poster
to her.

"That's bound to be helpful when I look for a
job." Missy took another sip of water and blinked
at him. Her eyes grew round. Something was
brewing in that adventure-loving brain of hers.
If he had the sense of a prairie dog he'd run for
the door before he knew what it was. "Is there a
place like Pete's in Dewton, do you know?"

Blood flooded Zane's face. He viewed the waiter's approach through a red haze. He slammed
his fist on the table and the waiter backed away.

"There is no place in Dewton like Pete's,"
he ground out through clenched teeth, striving
for patience, but the bruise under his eye still
throbbed from Missy's misadventure in Luminary.

"That is a shame." She waved the waiter forward and the man advanced with a wary eye
on Zane's hand, open flat against the table but

still tense. "Well, there is always sweeping. I've picked up a talent for that, did you know?"

He couldn't see Missy sweeping floors any more than he could see her playing piano in a low-life saloon.

The waiter stood beside the table with his arms crossed over his apron glancing from Missy to Zane.

"Two steaks," he stated and the man hurried away. "You could go home where you wouldn't have to sweep at all. I'll pay your way."

Lightning blanched the room into a scene from a daguerreotype. An instant later thunder rattled the dining-room windows.

"Zane Coldridge." She folded her hands in her lap and fixed him with a narrow stare, the teasing gone from her eyes from one heartbeat to the next. "When I go home it will be because I choose to. I came to write an adventure for my sister and that is what I am going to do."

She lifted the cloth napkin off the table, opened it with a snap and settled it on her lap.

"What lovely shoes," she stated, flashing an admiring smile to a woman walking by.

The lady paused beside the table and seemed unable to take her eyes off the feathers ruffling with Missy's breathing.

"I've never heard the piano played so well," she said. "If you and your husband will be in town for a while, would you consider playing for the

Ladies of the Afternoon Society? All the ladies would be delighted to hear you."

Husband! Silence hissed like an irritated rattler in the instant before Missy flashed him a bright smile.

"That would be a decision for my husband to make." Missy reached across the table and linked her fingers through his. "What do you say, darling?"

Had he stepped into another world? If he let go of reality for an instant, he could feel Missy as his wife. His insides warmed to the notion of friends and family. If he were a butterfly-moon type of man he would step right into her game.

Since he was not that kind of man, he mumbled that their plans were unclear. The woman nodded and walked away with a flick of her toe, smiling at the tips of her plain brown shoes.

Zane stared at the slender fingers linked with his. They lay in his hand like delicate petals in need of protection. Yet there was something about Missy that made folks do her bidding. No doubt, by week's end every lady in town would be her bosom friend, enamored of their hats and shoes and likely sporting a red feather or two.

"What is it that scares you so, Zane?" Her whisper sounded like honey.

"You scare me, darlin'," he murmured, letting go of her hand. He had to leave before he told her the whole truth of it. She had a way of seeing past the shadows in his heart. "You run into danger with your arms wide open and never give the consequences a thought. I'll say it again, go home to your family."

This was not the amiable way he had meant to bid her goodbye. He had planned a lingering handshake or maybe a friendly peck on her cheek. He stood up, offering neither.

"Folks will talk if you don't give your wife a proper kiss goodnight."

She was toying with him, playing with a fire that she didn't understand. The woman needed a lesson in caution.

He seized her slender wrist and swallowed it with his fist. He drew his arm around her back and hauled her out of her chair, up tight against his chest.

"Goodbye, my love," he murmured then kissed her hard. He opened her mouth with his tongue and tasted her surprise. He slipped his hand to the curve of her round derriere and squeezed.

That should teach the imprudent woman not to play with flame. He let go and she fluttered into the chair, looking at him with great doe eyes. For once she didn't seem to have a thing to say.

The waiter stood behind her with a plate of steaming beef in each hand and his jaw hanging open. The dining room boomed with silence. The report of his boots across the oak floor was not muted by the thunder rolling overhead.

* * *

At noon the next day, Zane stood outside the general store loading supplies into his saddlebags and watching Missy from across the street.

As it turned out, it did not take a week for her to win over the ladies of the town.

Gathered like pale chicks about a bright-red hen, six women ushered her up a flowered walkway and through the front door of a white clapboard house.

That was that, then. His responsibility for Missy had been handed over to the tittering ladies of Dewton. He watched her pass in front of one lace-curtained window then another before she disappeared into the depths of the house.

He shoved a tin of beans on top of a bag of coffee then cinched the saddlebag closed. This was one episode of his life he would never forget. The days he'd spent with Missy would stand out like flowers in a patch of weeds. Too bad he wasn't a different sort of man; settling down with a woman like her would never be dull.

"Hold up, Ace, we'll be on our way in a minute."

He stroked the horse's mane then walked three doors west to the marshal's office. He'd have a few words with the lawman and check to see if there were any newly wanted men he could pick up while he trailed Wage.

The Dewton jail was a solid structure made

of new red brick. The marshal's big oak desk sat on a polished wood floor. This quiet town of farm families was growing faster than the spring weeds. It was almost a shame, since crime was sure to come with prosperity.

The marshal stood by the wall of wanted posters speaking with a bear of a man in a long dusty coat.

"Afternoon, Marshal," Zane said. "Willie Sue."

The big man turned with a fleshy grin that was missing more teeth than the last time Zane had run across him.

"Coldridge," Willie Sue answered with a nod. From six feet away Zane could smell the grease in his matted hair.

Willie Sue was a filthy man inside and out.

"Surprised to see you in Dewton," Willie mumbled around a wad of chewing tobacco.

"Just passing through, Willie." Zane scanned the wall behind the marshal, relieved to see that Missy's poster was not pinned up with the rest. "How about you? Not many criminals in this town."

"I'm after me a lamb this time." Willie Sue presented the poster gripped in his fist. "Don't suppose you've seen her?"

The marshal plucked the poster from the fat hand and tacked it back on the wall. Zane felt a little sick seeing the bounty hunter's sweat smeared across Missy's smiling face.

"Willie Sue, you just remember what it says about the lady being returned pure," the lawman admonished. "There won't be a penny in it for you if she isn't."

"Now, Marshal, there's just all kinds of rewards in this world and not all of them have to do with cash." Willie Sue glanced about for a spittoon and, not finding one, hacked the wad in his mouth onto the floor. "Now and then there's just the satisfaction of a job well done. Seeing this sweet thing home would be a reward all of its own. Know what I mean, Coldridge?"

He knew. The nasty laugh shaking the man's belly told it all.

"I recall the woman, now that I look at her likeness close up." Zane smiled, trying for a look of camaraderie, but he hated the meanness of some in his profession. "She was working in Luminary at Pete's before it was trashed."

Willie Sue squinted his eyes at the poster. "This one worked at Pete's?"

"I saw her myself, just last week. I heard, though, that when Pete's fell, she moved on, toward Kansas is the rumor. Chances are, a woman like that is headed for Dodge."

"I do thank you for that word, Coldridge." Willie Sue stumped toward the door then turned. "It's a rare day that one of our kind helps another."

As soon as the door closed the marshal went

to the window to stare after the figure crossing to the general store.

"I retire next month and I tell you I can't wait to be rid of men like that." The marshal turned away from the glass and cast Zane a sharp look. "Dodge, you say? The word is a man rode in here yesterday with a scarlet woman. My wife can't talk of anything else."

The marshal's wife would not be the only one talking about Missy. She was like a tropical bird dropped into a nest of sparrows.

"Marshal, can you point me to the new telegraph office? I've got a wire that won't wait."

Chapter Nine

Missy jingled the coins in the pocket of her gingham dress. In addition to sweeping she could now add bartering to her list of skills. In trade for her harlot's costume Mrs. Homer Crump had given a blue gingham frock plus enough money to purchase more writing supplies.

Respectable-looking once more, she stood outside the general store with Muff tucked under one arm, savoring the day. Last night's storm had been blown away by a day of sunshine and birdsong. Life sparkled.

She closed her eyes, feeling the warm rays touch her face. The red feather adorning her hat caught the fresh breeze and tickled her nose.

Mrs. Crump had begged to trade her matching gingham bonnet for the feathered hat, but Missy had refused. The satin and feathers were more than a head ornament, they were a keepsake, a memento of the days she had spent with Maybelle, Moe and the girls.

Still, Mrs. Crump had been correct when she'd warned that blue gingham and red satin did not complement each other. In Boston the fashion offense would be the fuel of gossip for a month.

In Dewton, a thoroughly Western town, her hat might draw a few stares, but was not likely to cause fainting spells. It was hard to know what would cause the biggest scandal back home, the homey gown or the crimson headpiece. A gently reared lady would never wear the softly worn cotton of a hired woman. That same lady would shave her head before she would cover it with a hat that hinted of sin.

Western women had the freedom of dressing with common sense. Suzie would be thrilled when she discovered that farmer's wives sometimes worked wearing their husbands' pants!

Day by day, the comforts of home seemed like restrictions. Memories of neck-scratching lace and corsets drawn too tight chafed at her skin as well as her soul. Had it only been a few days since she had given up proper tea in favor of rich brown coffee? Since the gentlemen of the east had faded to ghostly wisps compared to the dark mystery of Zane Coldridge?

She had pretended not to see him watching her earlier, while he loaded his saddlebags, but his gaze had followed her all along the boardwalk. She knew that he had stared at Mrs. Crump's front door long after it closed behind her.

Chances are he had been saying a silent good-bye. The truth hadn't yet hit him, as it had her.

It would never be good-bye between them.

She stepped out of the sunshine and into the dim interior of the general store.

A large man with a dirty coat and a face that looked as though it couldn't recall a washing was speaking with the clerk about coming into a fortune soon. Missy took a spot at the counter several yards down from him hoping his new wealth would enable him to afford a bath.

The clerk handed the man a stack of blankets to look at then gave his full attention to Missy. She'd like to tell him that the customer's sweaty palms were ruining his stock, but surely he would have noticed that on his own.

"How can I help you and your little dog, miss?" he asked with a pleasant smile.

"I'd like an ink pen, a journal and an extra bottle of ink, if you please."

"I keep those in the back. I'll be just a minute." The clerk disappeared behind a drape-covered doorway.

The big man turned. She felt his unnerving stare studying her from head to toe. Muff curled his lip, baring sharp puppy teeth.

"It's a fine afternoon," she said to redirect his rude perusal.

"So it is, ma'am." He presented a smile with more teeth missing than intact. "Getting finer by the minute, as a fact."

The clerk returned with Missy's supplies, and not a moment too soon. The man had moved closer by a yard.

She paid for her goods and had a coin left. "I'll take a ribbon, as well."

"Right up there by the window, miss."

Missy tried to forget the man in the dusty coat as she placed the coin on the counter then walked toward the front of the store, but she felt his stare prickling her back.

Pale afternoon sunshine streamed in through the window glass. A rainbow of bright ribbons lay across a wood dowel attached to the wall.

"Which one do you like, Muff?" she asked, setting him on the deep windowsill. She picked up a green ribbon then set it back on the dowel and selected a red one. "This is sweet, we'll match."

She lifted the fur hiding his face and tied it up with the ribbon.

"Aren't you a handsome boy?" she crooned and twisted the loops of the ribbon into a perfect bow.

"What's yer name, lady? Where'd you get that hat?"

Missy spun about. Muff barked with wild, ear-shattering yaps. The man took a step forward, backing her up until her spine pressed against the dowel of ribbons.

She couldn't speak without breathing and breathing meant smelling the rotten stench coming out of his mouth.

"See here, mister." The clerk hustled out from behind the counter. "You can't treat the lady that way."

"Not your business." The offensive customer shot the clerk a glare that seemed to pin the poor man's feet to the floor.

"Neither is my name your business." She lifted her chin and narrowed her eyes. His belly butted to within an inch of her ribs. It would be fitting to poke her finger into that roll of fat and drive it backward but she'd be washing for a week. "Kindly stop scaring my dog."

In truth, Muff was not scared but outraged at the intrusion of his territory, which he considered to be Missy.

"You'll fess up your name if you're smart." The threat hissed like a snake loose in the store. The clerk inched forward half a step, then scuttled back two.

A shadow blocked the light coming through the door but her assailant didn't appear to notice.

"Coldridge…" the shadow announced. "Mrs. Zane Coldridge."

The menace in Zane's voice spun the man about, unbalanced like an oversized top. Muff snapped at the filthy coat twirling past his muzzle. His sharp teeth ripped a jagged tear.

"Never heard you was married, Coldridge." The man backed away a step, looking from Missy to Zane. He touched the hole in his coat with an offended glance at Muff.

"You know it now." Zane reached out his hand. "Come on, darlin'."

With a single motion she grabbed Muff and her writing supplies. She scooted around the belly that nearly blocked her way then latched onto Zane's fingers.

Out on the boardwalk Zane rushed her toward his horse, tethered a few doors up. She ran to keep pace with his long strides. A duet of light and heavy footfalls echoed along the quiet street. A button popped off her boot.

Zane hoisted her onto the saddle and jumped up after her.

She nearly slipped over the other side trying to keep a grip on both Muff and her purchases but Zane's arm clamped quick and tight about her waist.

"Don't even think of climbing down." His breath whispered hot against her cheek.

Let him misunderstand her near tumble. If he believed she was struggling to be free he would hold her tighter against his flexing muscles.

"If you're going to be a bully about it," she mumbled. She oughtn't to feel a grin spreading from top to toe, not with Zane pushing Ace as though they were trying to outrun Lucifer himself.

But whoever that man was, the devil or just a creepy patron of the general store, by rights she should thank him.

Left on her own it might have taken some time to catch up with Zane.

She couldn't guess where he was taking her now and it didn't matter. This was adventure at its most romantic. In a dozen childhood daydreams shared with Suzie she could never have conjured one so fine.

Zane reined Ace to a halt and listened. The land seemed as peaceful as creation day. Birdsong and grass whispering in the breeze were the only sounds that came to him.

The horse dipped his head to munch on a weed. Ordinarily, Ace became agitated when they were being trailed. Four hours out of Dewton with no sign of pursuit indicated that Willie Sue had fallen for the wife story and was probably racing his unfortunate mount toward Dodge.

"Wake up, darlin'. It's time to give the horse a rest."

His sweat-dampened shirt felt cool when she lifted her head from the hollow of his shoulder. Sable-colored eyelashes winked open. She stretched both arms over her head and wiggled her fingers at the sky. The cramped fit of the saddle squeezed her plush hindquarters against him.

"Where are we?"

"About in the middle of nowhere."

"It's pretty here."

Seventy miles of open land between towns is all it was, along with dust, heat, wind and cold.

"You can see forever, just grass and flowers," she said.

Zane slid off Ace's back then lifted her down.

"Wouldn't it be something to be Muff and look at everything blossom-high?" she added.

At the sound of his name, the dog poked his head out from under the flap of the saddlebag.

"Come on, you little scamp." She lifted him from the pack and nuzzled her nose in his fur. "How long have we got?"

"An hour, maybe less."

Missy took her writing supplies out of the saddlebag while Zane led Ace to the creek for a drink. Coming back, he spotted Missy a dozen yards away sitting in a circle of flowers with her head bent over her journal.

Posies of every hue dotted the landscape as far as he could see. How had he failed to notice them until Missy pointed them out? Maybe he'd become hardened over the years, riding the rough land and no longer seeing the beauty before his eyes.

A yellow butterfly tested the feather on Missy's hat then spiraled up and away when Muff lunged for its colorful wings. The pint-sized dog bounded in and out of the grass, the red bow in his fur appearing and disappearing while he stalked a bug.

Zane sat down, lounging against a cottonwood growing beside the stream. Ace nibbled weeds several yards off. Ordinarily, an hour rest stop would be the time to get a little shut-eye, but he couldn't take his gaze off the scene spread in front of him.

Missy looked up, studying the clouds scurrying across the sky. She tipped her head this way and that then returned her attention to her journal. She dipped her pen in the ink bottle then wrote swiftly across the page. Once or twice she looked at him and smiled.

The woman had a way of seeing past ordinary and looking at beauty. That was fine, as long as a person didn't forget that snakes hid amid the grass and flowers.

Snakes also hid in a friendly smile. They slithered about in good-intentioned lies. His lie about Missy being his wife had been necessary to keep her out of harm's way but he didn't care for being dishonest. A man always paid the consequence for telling a lie.

This necessary lie would have Missy seeing romance and happy endings where there were none.

Missy set her writing tools aside then removed her hat. She plucked the pins from her hair and let the tresses fall to her waist in sunny waves. With a yip and a leap, the pup bounded out of the grass, bit a curl then yanked her down onto the turf. She rolled to her belly laughing and wrestling with the dog.

Even if romance lurked somewhere in his soul, it would be crushed in a heartbeat when Missy discovered his biggest deception. A happy ending would not be possible for this lonely bounty hunter.

At the time, his action had seemed reasonable. Any sane person would have done the same. This morning in the marshal's office, with Willie Sue sweating all over the poster of Missy, he had known there could be no other choice.

Damnation, but everything was a muddle now. He couldn't take back the wire that he had dispatched to Edwin Devlin, revealing that Missy would be at the Hotel in Dewton for the next week and telling her brother where he could deposit the reward when he recovered her.

If he was honest with Missy and told her about the wire to Edwin, she would run off. Then it would be only a matter of time before she fell into the hands of another man like Willie Sue.

So far, she hadn't asked a single question about what had happened with Willie Sue and that worried him. Missy normally had questions about everything.

Zane stood up, slowly flicking a blade of grass off his pants. It was time to face her with some sort of story. He'd bet the reward for Wage that she didn't notice that he was the snake in the grass.

Walking forward, he felt the serpent twisting in his belly. He crouched in front of her with it choking the life out of his conscience.

Missy sat up and scooted Muff toward a dragonfly buzzing about a blade of grass.

"You must have a million questions about what happened this morning."

"A million and one." The breeze picked up a strand of Missy's hair and blew it across her face. "Who was that man? Did you know him? Where are we going and are you leaving me there?"

She plucked a blue flower growing near her knee and twined the stem in the hair behind his ear. "Why did you call me your wife? Was that a proposal? If it was I would like to know about your ribbon."

"It damn sure wasn't a proposal." Something about her smile unsettled him. "Darlin', a bounty hunter's life isn't fit for a wife. The ribbon is no one's business but mine."

"Have you ever thought of becoming a lawman in some quiet little town?" She plucked another blue flower and tucked it behind her own ear, then stretched out with her belly on the grass and her chin in her palm. "They say that the marshal in Dewton is retiring."

That very thought had smacked him square in the brain as soon as the marshal had mentioned his intent, but he had swatted it out before it had a chance to settle.

Apparently this was a conversation that was going to last for some time so he flopped, stomach-first, on the ground, eye-to-eye with Missy.

"The man in the general store was a bounty hunter named Willie Sue." A little of the truth wouldn't give anything away. "I guess he was just looking for a good time in a way that low-life men do. When I spotted him through the window, looking like a randy old goat, telling him that you were my wife seemed the quickest way out of the situation."

"I could have been your sister."

Hell and damnation, that ought to have been the first lie to pop into his mind.

"Here's the thing, since I can't leave you anywhere without you getting into trouble, I'm going to have to keep you with me."

With a frown she snatched the flower from his hair. "How on earth have I gotten through my life without you to carry me away on your big bold horse?"

"That thought has crossed my mind a time or…four."

"Just because you seem to happen upon me at inconvenient moments doesn't mean that I can't handle difficult situations on my own."

"You talking about the cow, the flood, the brawl or Willie Sue?"

Missy flicked the blue posy at him but she was smiling again. "My sister and I have had more experience getting out of situations than you can imagine. Besides, don't tell me you've never needed help getting out of a fix?"

He laughed out loud and felt the joy of it to his toes. When was the last time he had done that? When he'd first encountered Missy, bold as brass in her underwear, he had laughed to his bones, but before that, he could hardly remember.

All of a sudden he realized that the carpet of flowers growing about them not only looked pretty but they smelled like an hour in heaven.

"I might agree to stay with you." She tilted her head with her lips pursed and her eyes picking the blue out of the sky. "So long as you understand that we will be partners and have equal say in how we catch Wage."

"You will do what I tell you to do, when I tell you to do it." Missy Devlin might be the death of him, imagining that she knew how to track and capture an outlaw. He had devoted his life to the calling and it was still a difficult job.

"Obedience is not my strongest trait, Edwin swears it."

He might like to meet Edwin Devlin and find out if the young man's hair had turned gray under the pressure of being the guardian to such a sister.

"Promise me you will work on it," he said with a sigh.

"Naturally, I will consider each and every thing you advise me to do, as long as it's reasonable. And as long as you promise me that you won't pull any sneaky tricks to leave me behind."

Snakes. The telegram he had posted earlier in the day slithered across his mind.

To Edwin Devlin, in response to the reward for Missy Lenore Devlin. I have secured your sister's safety in the town of Dewton, Nebraska, and paid for her…

"You're thinking up a way to get rid of me right now, aren't you?" Her eyes narrowed in accusation.

"It hasn't worked so far. I'm out of ideas by now."

Muff trotted between them with a butterfly proudly clamped in his mouth.

"If you do get an idea, do you vow to ignore it?"

A man with any sense would think of a thousand ideas and act on every one of them. Any woman who wore a harlot's hat with a buttoned-to-the-chin gingham dress was sure to draw attention. Sneaking up on Wesley Wage would be a problem.

"I promise that I won't do anything to try and get rid of you." A hummingbird flashed by overhead. The whir of its wings hissed in his ear.

"And we share Wage's reward, half for you and half for me."

A crazy man might agree to that. "A tenth for you and nine-tenths for me."

"I counter offer at forty-sixty."

"You counter offer?" His ears had to be playing tricks. He was going to extremes to protect the woman and she was bargaining over it?

"I'll be a bigger help than you might think."

At this point he was only hoping for not much trouble.

"Make it twenty-eighty and we have a bargain, darlin'."

"A bargain is not binding unless it's sealed with a kiss." She licked her lips then puckered them up.

"Or a handshake."

Missy shook his offered hand but then she kissed her fingertips and touched them to his lips.

What kind of a devil got into him to make him taste her ink-stained fingers?

* * *

Missy sat upon Ace's broad back on a knoll above the peaceful-looking town of Legacy Creek. She gazed down at Zane, crouched in the dirt with his elbows braced on his knees and his hat gripped tight in both fists. He stared at the town. Noon sunshine brushed a sparkle of blue in his hair.

That was the only thing sparkling about the man today.

All through the night he had seemed distant. Even though they had shared a blanket for warmth, Zane had withdrawn into himself. For all the heat he generated she might as well have been snuggled up to a wooden plank.

By dawn he had given up civil conversation for nods and grunts. He hadn't sat behind her on his horse today, but instead, walked beside with his hat yanked low over his forehead.

"Waiting here like a slug in the sunshine won't get the job done," he mumbled at last, then slapped his hat on his knee.

Missy didn't comment on the puzzling remark even though curiosity over his strange mood made her insides itch.

"The devil take it, then," he said out loud and straightened up. He shoved his hat on his head and mounted behind her in one leap.

"The devil take what?" She turned in the saddle and looked up at his face. The shadow of the hat brim couldn't hide the bleak expression in his eyes. "I hope you don't mean me, we made a bargain."

"It's not you, darlin'. Our bargain stands." Zane tipped her face up. His calloused finger felt rugged under her chin. The brim of his hat touched her forehead an instant before his mouth touched her lips. "There now, it's sealed with a kiss."

"What is it, then?" she asked, a little breathless. That quick show of tenderness nearly melted her off the horse. If Zane hadn't seemed troubled to his soul, she would have pressed for another kiss, one that would singe the ends of her hair.

"I've got business in Legacy Creek, and I wish I didn't." He lifted the reins from her fingers then urged Ace down the knoll. "I'm leaving you at the livery and I want you to stay put."

"Why the livery? Liberty Creek seems like a lovely little town."

"If we are going to be keeping company for a while, we'll need another horse."

"That is sensible." Sensible but disappointing.

She didn't even need to lean back to feel the shift of his thighs against her backside. The cramped quarters over the miles had made it a constant condition.

The livery turned out to be the first building, just outside of the town proper. A short distance beyond, Missy spotted a bakery and a general store.

"I'll get us something nice from the bakery while you take care of the horse." It seemed a more pleasant place to wait than a smelly stable.

Zane slipped backward off Ace and landed on the dirt with a solid thump. He reached for Missy and helped her down.

"Look, I'm collecting a bounty." He pressed her shoulders with a firm grip and gave her a stern look, a reminder that he was the one in charge. "I need to know exactly where you are and that you will be ready to ride in a hurry. Keep Muff close at hand."

"Suzie might hop right out of her chair if I wrote about an actual bounty collection. That's one adventure I would like to witness."

"You wouldn't like it." He shook his head and led Ace inside the dimly lighted livery. "I'll tell you all about it later if you really have to know, but please, Missy, don't set a foot outside of this door."

Fifteen minutes later, that "please" kept Missy inside the livery like a butterfly stuck in a spider web.

From the open door she watched Zane walk up the middle of the main street of Legacy Creek, his posture erect. He carried his hands loosely at his sides, within easy reach of his gun, Missy noted.

He seemed to know where he was going and, clearly, had no wish to go there.

Bounty-hunting, she believed, was not a job that Zane truly enjoyed.

She stared up the street for five long minutes after Zane walked out of sight. A dust devil whirled down the center of the road and nicked the side of the livery with pebbles. When it seemed that nothing thrilling was about to happen, she turned her attention to her new horse.

The pretty cinnamon-colored mare would be pleased to know that her rental days were over. Zane had purchased the horse not as a gift, he'd assured her, but an advance on her portion of the reward for Wesley Wage.

"Hello, pretty girl." She stroked the white flower pattern between the horse's eyes. "What should we call her, Muff?"

Muff growled at something rustling in a pile of hay.

"Mouse?" Missy touched the smooth leather of the used saddle that came with the horse. Her writing supplies were already tucked in a pack along with a towel stuffed into a pouch for Muff to ride in. "I prefer Daisy."

"Around here we call her Big Muddy," a voice coming from the far corner of the barn said. The owner of the stable hung a harness on a wall peg then turned to look at Missy. "She's one to loll about in the mud when she gets the chance."

"Well then, my horse and my dog are of like minds." She glanced at Muff, happily gathering bits of hay in his fur while pouncing after the rodent hiding inside the heap.

"That's the funniest-looking mongrel I've ever seen," the man said then turned his attention back to his work. At least he hadn't called Muff a rat.

A cloud must have passed over the sun for the light in the stable dimmed. Daisy's cinnamon coat smoothed to chocolate.

Compared to Ace, Daisy was short. Compared to Edwin's race horse, she was plump. It was easy to imagine the horse as a mud-roller.

Picturing Daisy in the same stable as her brother's pampered, high-strung animal brought Missy up short. She wouldn't fit in at all. Daisy was a creature of the West. Try as she might, Missy could not picture the sturdy little animal stabled beside the thoroughbred.

Hadn't Missy felt that very difference most of her life? She and Suzie had been a pair of wild flowers stuffed in a bouquet of stiff and proper roses. When the time came to return home, she wasn't sure that she could abide by the restrictions that proper society imposed. Everything would seem small. Life would be pale.

Worse than anything, Zane would be half a continent away.

"I have to go home sometime...there's Suzie. Mother and Edwin have their own full lives, but my sister is stuck in that chair." She pressed her forehead to Daisy's velvety muzzle. The horse's whicker blew warm, moist air on Missy's neck.

"Zane and I are meant to be," she whispered. "I feel it bone-deep. But Daisy, I can't picture him as a gentleman any more than I can see you in my brother's stable."

Muff yipped then vanished into the pile of hay. Outside a woman screamed.

Missy rushed to the open door with the stable owner fast behind her.

Several buildings up the street, a crowd had gathered with Zane at the center of it. He dragged a boy who didn't look more than seventeen toward the marshal's office. The group swelled to about fifteen and seemed increasingly unhappy.

A distraught-looking woman screamed obscenities at Zane. She picked up fresh horse dung from the road and flung it at his back.

"Rot in hell, bounty hunter!" a man's voice from the rear of the crowd called.

"You can't take a widow's only son!" a screeching voice shouted.

The widow clung to the back of Zane's coat while he pushed the young man up the stairs ahead of him.

Zane's face, viewed in profile, seemed to be made of stone. Missy had never seen a face so void of expression. If the hysterical woman clawing at his back gave him pause, it didn't show in the determined set of his jaw or his stiffened posture. He might have been outside of the drama for all that he gave away of his emotions.

"Damned bounty hunter." The livery keeper spat in Zane's direction. "Never would have sold him the Muddy had I known."

Missy glanced over her shoulder to see the man's face flushed with anger.

"I saw him save a baby's life, even though he might have lost his own," she said.

"Why can't he leave a poor widow in peace?" He spat again. Missy had to flick her skirt aside to prevent it from being hit by the yellow glob.

"He plucked me from the hands of a lecherous cad."

Zane shoved the boy inside the marshal's office and slammed the door behind him. The wailing quit abruptly when the widow fainted into the arms of two younger women. The pair of them immediately took up her lament.

"Come, Muff, come," Missy commanded. Now she understood why Zane had ordered her to stay put.

Muff erupted from the hay and dashed toward the back of the barn in pursuit of something brown and furry.

"Muff, leave it!" She scrambled after him and scooped him up just as a mouse squeezed through a dollar-sized hole in the livery wall.

She placed the pup in his pouch and plucked

several pieces of alfalfa from his fur. It would take more than a moment to clean him up so she straightened his red ribbon then closed the flap over his face.

With the excitement over, the crowd began to break up. Some wandered off with shaking heads, others with shaking fists. The weeping mother had been revived and was being escorted home by the younger women.

Heartache seemed to be a living presence following the bereft widow home. How could Missy ever have imagined there would be great adventure in the event? Suzie would never be thrilled to read of it.

Zane had warned her that this was something she would not want to see. What a fool she must have appeared. In the dime novels, no one ever wrote about grieving mothers.

Tears burned behind Missy's eyes while she gathered up Daisy and Ace's reins. Even though she had promised to remain inside, she didn't want Zane to encounter the liveryman.

"Come, Ace. Come, Daisy," she said. The horses followed her out the livery doors with amazing obedience.

"Damned filth," the livery owner grumbled as she passed him.

Red-hot anger throbbed in Missy's cheeks. If she were a man she would lay the fellow flat out cold with a blow to the chin.

"That boy was a criminal." She gave the hay-dusted liveryman a glare. "Don't pretend you won't be grateful that it won't be your place he robs next."

"A pair of turds boilin' in a pot is what you are," he mumbled then walked back into the shadowy barn. "Never should have sold you the Muddy."

So this was Zane's life. No wonder he saw the world as bitterly as he did.

The marshal's door opened and Zane stepped out on the boardwalk. He glanced about with harsh sunlight revealing deep creases at the corners of his eyes. Dark grooves cut the edges of his mouth.

When he noticed Missy coming forward, leading the horses, the bleakness in his gaze eased for an instant.

She dug deep for a smile, hoping on the butterfly moon that it would look heartening, that it would be what he needed.

Chapter Ten

⁂

"The stable owner did call her Big Muddy," Missy told him.

Zane watched her lips twitch as though she were trying desperately to hide her mirth while she stared at her horse rolling belly-up on the muddy bank of the creek.

The mare had turned out to be quicker than she looked. No sooner had he unsaddled the horses for the evening than Daisy trotted to the creek and began a high time in the muck. By damn, the animal looked as pleased as a fly in butter.

"No, Muff, no!" Missy cried out. The dog raced toward Daisy, yipping and yapping.

With her arms waving and her skirts flying, Missy chased him. Four short legs proved to be quicker than two taller ones. Missy trailed in the race by several yards.

"Come, Muff, come!" she yelled.

After this morning's business Zane had expected to be in a black mood for days, but only hours later he felt the shadow of his job lifting. Watching Missy, her dog and her horse brought him within an inch of a smile.

Muff reached the mud a leap and a skid ahead of Missy.

"Oh, you little imp!" She slammed her hands on her hips, glaring while the pup found a spot of green-brown ooze and mimicked the horse's roll.

Missy spun about, her lips thin with vexation and the laughter snuffed from her eyes. Evidently, what was laughable in a horse was not laughable in a white dog.

"I'll set up camp while you tend to your animals," he said in a voice a bit gruffer than he felt.

He'd sent a boy off to trial and likely prison this morning, he had no business feeling amused this soon, like a man with no remorse.

It wasn't that the kid didn't deserve what he got—he'd earned his due, but it was a sad thing to see a life go bad so young. The memory of the mother and sisters bearing the burden of sorrow would likely keep him sleepless tonight.

He'd experienced the ugly side of his job enough times to know that Missy would not find him fit company again this evening.

He started a fire, dug through his pack for

beans and jerky, and then set a pot of coffee on to boil.

This was the time he dreaded the most. Even Missy and her misbehaving animals would do little to lighten it.

He sat down with his back to the stream, staring at the fire until the land grew dark and the flames turned bright. He listened to the crickets take up their night song. Near the stream he heard splashing water and Missy's voice go from stern to a soft croon.

Apparently, Muff had been forgiven. What might life be like if a man could be so freely forgiven? The widow and her kin would be cursing him tonight, not forgiving…never forgiving.

Life would be easier if he took up another occupation. He could open a store, be a banker or farmer. Folks would thank him after a long day's work. Their thanks would be mean nothing, though, in the deep of the night when he felt his mother's dying breath under his cheek, when he heard the rasp of it choking her life away.

No, he could never take the comfortable way. His peace would always come at the cost of another's freedom. But, as tonight would prove, there really was no peace. His bank account might be comfortable, but not his soul.

Footsteps tapped the earth, coming away from the creek. Cotton rustled, which he guessed was Missy drying off her dog. Full dark pressed down on the prairie, except for a fat full moon on the rise and the small circle of light pushing out from the campfire.

"Take off your clothes, Zane." Missy's hand squeezed his shoulder. "Let's go swimming."

He could not have been more startled if Ace had suddenly asked to go for a run in the moonlight.

"It's crazy warm for this time of year," she said leaning close to his ear. A tendril of silky hair tickled his cheek. "Come on, it'll be fun."

Swimming with a beautiful woman and only starlight to guide one's conscience might be considered fun, or it might be considered wicked.

"That water is colder than you think." He jerked his shoulder to dislodge her tempting fingers. "I'll sit tight, here by the fire."

"Cold water warms right up once a person starts splashing."

Splashing, and touching, wet skin sliding over wet skin was probably not the kind of fun Missy had in mind, but it's the kind that had his hands itching and his mind simmering. He had enough sins to deal with tonight without adding the seduction of an innocent.

"You go on. The fire suits me fine."

"Sulking over things that can't be changed never did a body any good." Missy sighed, sounding defeated. Muff trotted toward the fire and curled into a sleepy puff. "But as long as you're at it, keep a eye on Muff, will you? He's had more fun today than I can abide."

Keeping watch over the dog might be the one thing that would get Zane into the water. Bearing responsibility for that ball of mischief would land any man on his feet. Luckily, for the moment, the pup looked like a pile of lamb's wool dozing soundly next to the fire.

Since the dog didn't stir when coyotes half a mile out began their mournful yipping, Zane didn't either.

One thing Missy had been right about, though, it had been hot for this early in the year. Even after sundown the earth held on to the heat. Tonight's campfire was strictly for protection and warming beans and coffee.

Zane unbuttoned his shirt, wishing for a breeze to cool his skin. He heard a big splash in the creek, as though Missy had jumped in all at once.

Of course, she would have. Missy Lenore Devlin was not one to do anything by cautious steps.

He heard laughter and more splashing. Here was a woman who dove into life head first and came up laughing. He tried not to wonder, but he did, what it would be like to make love to such a female. Would she sigh her passion and cry out with joy at every new and unfamiliar touch? Would she demand all of him? He knew she would, and would give back as much in return.

This was a trail his mind shouldn't be traveling, but he couldn't stop himself from wondering if she had taken off all her clothes before she jumped in the water.

He stripped off his shirt.

"You're missing some fun!" she called out.

Frogs at the creek bank croaked out mating calls to each other. Zane pulled off his boots, seeking some cooling relief, although the heat came from his brain as much as the waning day.

If the pictures playing in his mind were happening at the creek, he didn't dare turn to look, but he wanted to so badly that his eyeballs burned.

He would have left his pants on if she hadn't started to hum in a low, sweet voice that made the frogs stop to listen. But she did and he tossed them clear over the campfire, his denims and his red knitted drawers both at the same time.

The creek was just deep enough for Missy to float and the current slow enough that by fluttering her hands she remained in place.

She closed her eyes, feeling the ripple of the water pulse under her back. The threads of her chemise washed across her breasts, twisting across her nipples like tickling feathers.

With her eyes shut, the world seemed to become more vibrant. With sound as her predominant sense she listened to a chorus of frogs and decided that they croaked a melody as sweet as any parlor serenade. Crickets joined in the symphony, their chirrups quick with the warm weather.

A breeze must have come up. Grass whispered and sighed. She imagined it as the applause to the frog-and-cricket lullaby.

From way out, a cow mooed. This time she would be careful and not let the stealthy beast sneak up on her. At the first sign of invasion, she would rush for her dress.

Weightless in the water, Missy let her body and her mind drift. If she tried to capture the night tune on a piano keyboard, what notes would she use?

She began to hum, trying to figure it out. The water rippling past gathered her shift over her thighs and her belly. The wispy fabric caught beneath her breasts, leaving her lower half bare to the grin of the man in the moon.

She could wiggle out from the garment altogether and it wouldn't matter. Zane was stuck in his misery up at the campfire. Her privacy wouldn't be invaded.

All at once the frogs became quiet.

Drat! That cow couldn't have gotten here already. Missy pinched her eyes tight, clinging to the peaceful moment. If the bovine wandered into camp Muff would bark or Zane would rouse himself and chase it off.

A pair of splashes rippled the surface of the

water; no doubt frogs were fleeing a small night predator. She waved her arms in the water to maintain her float.

Something solid brushed against her hand. Something warm and muscular. She stroked the backs of her fingers against…a knee!

Her eyes popped open and she lost her float. Her rump hit the bottom of the creek with a soft thud.

It was Zane, all of him, with nothing between her stare and his privacy. She studied his bare knees for half an instant before letting her gaze travel upward.

She blinked hard to get the water out of her eyes. Thighs so hard and lean needed to be appreciated without creek water smudging the view.

He stood straight. The light of the rising moon reflected off the sheen of perspiration glistening on his skin. Something inside her belly began to curl. It wasn't only his posture that was straight. All of him looked straight and hard as could be. The curling sensation twisted clear to her nether parts.

With some effort she forced her gaze up, lingering only a moment on his flat, tanned belly. She stared at his well-muscled chest. It had to be an illusion that she could see his ribs thump with his heartbeat.

If she weren't convinced that this was her forever man, she would have modestly glanced away. But something in her soul recognized that those strapping arms would hold her for many years to come. For thousands of nights in her future she would snuggle into the sanctuary of his embrace.

He might not understand it yet, but his eyes gave him away. They stared down at her with the passion of a man for a woman, to be sure. But more than that, he looked at her with possession, like a man for his mate.

Since she couldn't think of a single thing to say to express those profound thoughts, she splashed and grinned.

She kicked her feet and flailed her arms, then stopped to admire the results of her watery attack.

Water dripped from his nose and his fingertips. It washed over his stomach without altering the stiffness of his posture or...anything else that was stiff.

Except his smile. He seemed to be trying to hold on to a scowl, but his lips quirked up at the corners and gave him away.

"Do you surrender already?" She threw out the challenge.

"Never." His answer rumbled deep in his chest.

He came down in the water inch by inch, like a predator toying with its prey.

Missy felt giddy with the game. "Oh, please,

Mr. Predator, have mercy on this defenseless little mouse."

"Defenseless little mouse, my Aunt Hattie!" All at once he lunged, taking them both under the water.

Missy came up coughing and laughing. She cupped her hands and poured water over his soaking black hair.

He laughed and did the same to her. She wasn't sure she had ever heard him sound like that. Like pure joy shook him to his soul.

In order to keep him doing it, she jumped astride his lap and ruffled his hair with both hands. She scooped up handful after handful of water and dribbled it over his face.

At some point she noticed that he had quit laughing. In the next instant she realized that her bare feminine folds sat smack on top of the part of him that hadn't grown soft in the water.

"I didn't mean to..." Her voice felt thick and slow.

She tried to move, to free him from the embarrassing position she had landed him in, but he grasped her waist, holding her still.

He moved his hips, sliding their bodies against each other. Missy's heart popped into her throat.

Calloused hands crept up her ribs and she could have easily moved off his lap, but she didn't. He gathered the fabric of her shift with the upward stroke of his fingers. He lifted it over her head and tossed it toward the bank.

He went still beneath her but his hands caressed her shoulders. His thumbs stroked her collarbone in little circles then traced a curly trail toward the top of her breasts. She wanted to close her eyes to better feel the touch of his rough thumbs against her flesh, but she couldn't.

She had become spellbound. Enchantment held her tongue against any maidenly protest. Sitting utterly still, she watched Zane's palms rub her nipples. Moonlight illuminated his fingers, dark against her pale flesh, petting and kneading. Nothing had ever felt so wonderful. Nothing, that is, until he pressed his hands to her back and pulled her to his mouth.

Her eyelids dipped and her breath came thick and heavy. Someone moaned, but she couldn't tell who.

One of Zane's hands stoked her ribs, her waist then her bare bottom. He moved beneath her, sliding against that part of her that had suddenly become the very compelling center of her attention.

She had become a wanton woman, too impatient to wait for her wedding night. Years ago, she'd overheard Edwin laughing with a friend about how first babies don't take as long. Now she understood why. It would be much more interesting to take the path that her body urged than to run for maidenly cover.

"What about you, Missy, do you surrender?"

"Yes…no, I want to." She felt confused, her body pulling one way and her intelligence another. "I will, but not now."

"Don't you want me, darlin'?" His breath blew hot in her ear.

"I want you." She slid off his lap, putting a foot of breathing room between them. "I just want more than you can give me right now."

Missy couldn't help leaning her head against his palm when he caressed the back of her neck.

"I can give you everything…right here and right now."

"Can you give me forever, Zane? Have you seen the butterfly moon?"

"You know there is no such thing," he said, leaning closer while she leaned back. "There's just you and me and this long, dark night."

"There's a marriage bed and a house full of babies."

Zane dropped his hand in the water with a splash and backed away. "Not for me, darlin'. I live a hard life."

"I saw that this morning." Missy brushed a hank of dripping hair away from his cheek. "I also saw that you hate it. You could make a living some other way."

Even in the dark she could see him considering his words. "I like the money bounty-hunting brings in… Missy, have you even considered how you'd feel always waiting on me, wondering if I'd even come home?"

Just as Suzie, mother and Edwin were likely doing at this very moment, waiting and worrying about her? She made a vow in her heart to send a quick wire when they got to the next town to assure them she was doing well.

"Having lots of money can be tiresome," she said. "It can bind a person just like being poor can."

Sitting still and naked in the water made the night seem suddenly cold. Chilly bumps prickled her skin. She tried to rub them away but they stood as stiff as toy soldiers.

"And you know plenty about being poor, I suppose," he said.

"I don't know a thing about it, I only know that money can't make you happy, not in some ways that truly count."

"That's pie in the sky, Missy. It hurts being a kid and not knowing where your next meal is coming from, if it even is."

She wouldn't know how that felt. She had never gone hungry for a single meal, neither had the children of the hired help.

"Were you wealthy before your uncle, when your parents were alive?"

"No," he said softly and his expression lost its hard, resentful lines.

"Were you happy?"

"I was." He gave up a reluctant smile.

"Tell me about your mother. She must have been a wonderful woman."

Zane's smile faded. He looked like a man caught between joy and sorrow. "I don't talk about the past."

"Maybe it's time you did."

A wolf howled far out and a calf bawled closer in. Zane sat stiff and silent.

"Does it hurt so much to remember those good times with her?"

"Like hell. I can't think of those times without thinking of the other."

"Tell me, Zane. What happened to your mother?"

"It's getting cold." Zane started to get up. Missy cursed herself for pushing him too far. Maybe she ought to learn to leave some things alone.

To her surprise, he moved behind her and sat with his naked thighs bracing her on both sides. He wrapped his arms across her chest and put his chin on her shoulder. His beard stubble felt nice and scratchy on her bare skin.

"She was shot to death in a bank robbery. It was a damned stray bullet. The thief's gun went off by mistake, he never even meant to hurt anyone. But Ma lay on the floor with a hole in her chest just the same."

"Oh, Zane, you saw it happen?"

"The sheriff pulled me off her body, all I took away was the ribbon from her hair."

So, that was the horrid story he had hung on to about the ribbon. She must have seemed a cold harpy to go on about it like it was some romantic thing to be written about and glorified.

"No wonder you treasure it so," she whispered past the guilty lump in her throat. "I'm sorry, Zane, I should have thought—"

"I should have told you." He kissed her shoulder in a seemingly unconscious gesture of affection. "Now you know my sorry past—no butterflies, no happy ends. Just an ugly career that lets me deal with my guilt."

"You shouldn't carry any guilt. You were only a child. The guilty one is the bank robber."

"Logically that's true. But the fact is, if my mother hadn't rushed forward to protect me she would have been well away from the bullet. I was playing in a spot where I was not supposed to play. She'd warned me not to stray from the edge of her skirt, but a customer had brought in a puppy and I ran over to see it."

"So now you have no peace unless you are capturing bank robbers." She reached up to stroke her fingers along his jaw.

"Now that you know way too much about me, I expect you will leave me at the next town."

"You wish it, Zane Coldridge." She turned in his arms and looked hard in his eyes. "One of these days you're going to see that butterfly moon and I want to be here for it."

"One of these days you're going to throw a dime novel in the trash. That's what I want to see."

"I'd never throw a book in the trash, even though dime novels might not be quite as gospel as I had once thought."

"Praise be, she's seen the light," he declared with a laugh.

"Just a glimmer of it, mind you." She snuggled into the warmth of his arms. "Speaking of seeing the light, you know you can still put bad guys behind bars in other ways than you do. Be a sheriff...or a lawyer."

"Couldn't stand wearing a suit and fancy shoes, practicing the law would make me a crazy man." He breathed out a long, hard sigh, rubbing the hair of his chest against her back. "A sheriff makes a tenth of what I do."

"Money can make life comfortable, Zane, but it can't warm your soul."

"I learned that a long time ago, darlin', but it can give you a warm place to sleep at night."

Missy wiggled out from his arms. She stood up and wrung the water from her hair.

"Warm and alone, Zane," she whispered then bent to pick up her shift. The short walk toward the fire seemed especially cold.

Missy sat beside the window of her second-floor hotel room staring out at the fog. The town of Foggy Johnson Creek certainly lived up to the foggy part of its name.

Whorls of white vapor pressed against the glass and made people on the sidewalk below look like ghosts wandering in and out of the lamplight.

She supposed there might be a Johnson or two in town, but what the folks of Foggy Johnson Creek called a creek was a broad body of water circling the town on three sides.

A soft knock on the door connecting her room to the one beside it made Muff jump off her lap and hit the floor with a puff of dust. Clearly, the animal was not meant to be a Western dog. Back home, in the manicured confines of the garden, he'd never gathered so much as a burr.

Before she could rise, the door swung open and Zane filled the door frame. He looked nervous, as though a single step into her room would land him on a bed of coals.

"We need to discuss business," he stated.

These were the first words he had spoken in nearly twenty-four hours, ever since she had left him to shiver alone in the creek last night.

She pointed to the rocking chair beside hers but he glanced at it as though it were a trap.

"Mercy be, Zane. I don't have an eternity rope to bind you to that chair. You are free to go back to your own room at any time."

"An eternity—?" He shook his head. Clean

dark hair skimmed his shoulders, his black eye-brows dipped in a frown. Crossing the room, he sat in the dainty seat that appeared two sizes too small for him. "Darlin', last night I—"

"What kind of business?"

She wasn't ready to discuss last night, but still, the relief that crossed his face was disappointing.

"Hunting down Wage. It's time you earned your twenty percent."

"Are we hot on his trail?" All of a sudden her mood lightened. With the excitement of chasing the criminal, she would be able to set aside her emotional turmoil. It was purely distressing to find the man of her heart only to discover that he did not have one.

Well, he had one, of course, just not one he was willing to share with her.

"I've decided that we aren't going to chase him."

That, Missy knew, was no way to catch a crim-inal. Clearly, she ought to be the one in charge.

"It seems to me that he will get a good distance away if we don't," she said, allowing a note of disapproval to shadow her voice. "I won't earn a single penny sitting idly beside this window."

"That's why I'm the one in charge and you are going to do as I say."

She hesitated only an instant before replying, "Yes, of course." As long as it was logical and she had a worthy part in the plan. "What are we going to do?"

"We've already done it. We've gotten ahead of him."

"Cat and mouse and we are the cats!" The idea sounded adventurous, at least. "What if he doesn't come here? We could be waiting until I'm in my dotage and your mustache turns gray."

"Darlin', if you live to be a hundred you won't be in your dotage. But he *is* coming here, and soon. I've heard rumors, none of them indicate that he will be here."

"That makes no sense. I think you've been addled by spring fever." She leaned forward and pressed her fingers to his forehead, certain he had become delirious.

"It does if he planted those rumors himself, or paid someone else to do it. No doubt, he expects me to be looking for him in Omaha or Lincoln." Zane looked away from her and out the window. He peered through the fog where the Farmers' and Merchants' Bank of Foggy Johnson Creek was barely visible through the mist. "This is a thriving little community and that bank has got to be as ripe as a peach ready for plucking."

He stared silently at the building across the street. "He'll be here, and soon. Mark my words."

Chapter Eleven

By noon the following day, fog continued to lick at Missy's window. She tapped her fingernail against the glass.

Zane had assured her that watching the bank was crucial since Wage was certain to scout the area before committing his crime.

Crucial but tedious. She had worn her vision out staring at the foggy street while Zane lurked behind buildings and haunted dark corners of saloons.

Surely she could be of more benefit lying in wait near the bank doors than she could be in this room, watching like a sleepy-eyed owl unable to resist a fit of yawning. All she needed was a suit of feathers to make the look complete.

Besides, she had things to do. Muff needed a trim. Who was to say that she wouldn't meet the wily bank robber in the mercantile while she purchased a pair of scissors?

She had promised herself to send a wire to her family. Even bank robbers visited Western Union.

One never knew! It was certain that the criminal would not come knocking at her hotel door.

Zane would not be pleased if she went out. He had given a stiff-as-starch order. She was to sit at the window and watch.

He must realize by now that she was not good at sitting and even worse at obeying orders. Chances are he never really expected her to stay in the room, anyway.

Missy bounded from the wing chair. She plucked her feathered hat from its peg by the door and secured it with a long pearl-tipped pin.

If she didn't locate Wage, she would simply come back to the room, take up her boring position beside the window and Zane would never know the difference.

If she found the thief, he would be so pleased that he wouldn't care.

"Be a good boy, Muff, and I'll bring you a rawhide strip to chew on," Missy said, closing the door behind her.

Filled with a fine sense of adventure, she fairly flew over the hall carpet and floated down the staircase. Owls, after all, had wings as well as eyes!

Out on the boardwalk, Missy curled her chilly fingers deep into the pockets of her blue gingham skirt. Clearly, this town was cursed with perpetual fog. During the time that she had been here, not even a tickle of sunshine had pierced the gloom. It was no wonder that the folks she had encountered this last hour had greeted her with frowns.

Earlier, looking out of her bedroom window, she hadn't guessed how cold it would be without a coat. Fog gathered in doorways and whirled in milky swirls about lampposts left burning, even during the day. It penetrated her dress and made her feel as damp as a workday sponge. The jaunty feather on her bonnet sagged with pearls of moisture clinging to its tip.

The misery would have been worthwhile, worthy even of a full chapter in her journal, if she had caught a glimpse of Wesley Wage. But the only thing that hiding in an alcove for forty minutes and staring at the bank door had earned was a chill that made her bones clatter.

Nearby, through the window of Hanraty's General Store, she had spotted a welcoming fire. A shivering spy would be useless, so she had gathered up her sodden skirt and crossed the road. She spent a penny on a treat for Muff then joined a pair of shoppers at the stove with their backsides toward the heat.

It had been fascinating to learn from her fellow heat-gatherers that the town had, indeed, been cursed with perpetual fog. Zane would claim that the fog was a natural occurrence, due to the river, but it appeared that the good folks of Foggy Johnson Creek would never believe that their founder hadn't cursed them.

This would make fascinating reading.

Now, out once more in the elements, she hurried two blocks toward the telegraph office where she would spend the rest of her money on a message to her family.

She wouldn't reveal where she was, of course. An exotic torture could not make her hint at her latest adventure or that her partner was a darkly handsome bounty hunter. She wouldn't give away that he had captured her heart and her body as easily as if it had been the subject of a broadsheet.

That information would send her entire social circle into a dead faint and keep their tongues busy for months to come. All that Mother and Edwin would need to know was that she and Muff were safe and that life went on with boring predictability. Suzie, naturally, would know better.

Across the street and two doors down, Missy spotted smoke curling out of the chimney of the telegraph office. She dashed across the dirt road and up the steps.

Warm air washed out to greet her when she opened the door.

At the counter, a tall, broad-backed figure waited for the clerk's attention. She choked down a gasp and closed the door in the second that the man turned.

Zane! Of all the places in town, and all the minutes of the day, he had to be here, now!

Missy lifted the mucky hem of her skirt and dashed down a small alley between the telegraph office and a bakery.

He couldn't have seen her; she'd closed the door before he'd fully turned. Still, it wouldn't do for him to find her away from her assigned post at the upstairs window.

Rounding the corner, she ran behind the row of buildings. Soft earth muffled her footsteps and fog concealed her. Even so, she glanced behind, dreading pursuit.

Out of breath, she came to a familiar building, the Foggy Johnson Livery. She recalled a dry gully near the back stable door with brush growing alongside. It would make a perfect hiding place. If Zane caught her she could simply say that she was checking on the horses.

She crouched low in the shrubbery, thinking of a way to explain how she could be checking on the horses while hiding in the bushes. It didn't help that the newly sprouted leaves did not fully hide her blue gingham dress.

It was quiet behind the barn. Ace and Daisy had been the only guests when Zane had checked them in the day before. Her heart beat too loudly against her ribs, her breathing sounded like a windstorm and the snort was likely to bring the stable keeper running.

The snort! She hadn't snorted.

Warm breath puffed against her neck. A soft muzzle nipped at her hat. She whirled and fell hard on her behind.

Looking up, she stared into the face of a plain brown horse. It had average brown eyes, an everyday brown coat, a black mane and tail that one saw dozens of times a day, and a brand that marked it as belonging to the Green Island Livery.

"Number Nine!" Missy stroked the long jaw. She stood up and inspected the animal for injury or mistreatment. "You look half well kept, at least."

Number Nine swished his tail and whickered.

"I know," she whispered, plucking a burr from his mane. "It's a horrible thing to be kidnapped, especially by such a loathsome criminal, but really, you were better off. The other horses at the livery probably drowned."

Number Nine was saddled and in hiding. Clearly Wesley Wage was about to commit a crime.

"Is my journal still in your saddle pack, or did that wretch toss it out?"

Missy opened the flap and felt inside. The journal was there! She longed to take it out and make sure it was intact, but she needed to get the horse out of the shrubbery. If Wage couldn't find his mount, it would certainly complicate his crime.

The back door to the livery was only a few yards beyond the shelter of the brush. She would put Number Nine inside with Ace and Daisy, then hurry back to the telegraph office and alert Zane to what she had discovered.

Life, as she had long believed, was a wonderful adventure.

"The wretch, my dear Miss Devlin, got a respectable laugh out of your drivel," a voice stated, too close to her ear. "It made for an amusing evening in my bleak little hotel room."

Not again! Missy turned with the speed of a cornered slug, buying time and trying to devise a plan to, this time, keep her rented horse.

Clearly, physical confrontation was not an option. The man, although slim, was bigger than she was. And mean, Zane had said so.

She faced him with the smile she had learned as a toddler on her mother's knee, the social smile that hid a woman's feelings when confronted with someone who was, most honestly, creepy.

How did a man keep his skin so pasty white while traveling the prairie? Vampires who scoured the forests of Transylvania and lurked in the pages of the many books she had read would not look more undead than he did.

Lacking, though, was the strange allure of the undead. This man's hairline grew well back on

his head. Black pinwheel curls made his flesh
seem paler than could be healthy. His cheeks
had no muscle tone; they sagged into jowls that
tugged his mouth down in a pout and made his
lower lip protrude. His narrow nose, pinched tight
at the nostrils, made his breath hiss in and out
of his face.

Only years of practice kept her smile in place
before his pompous smirk.

"Oh, mercy, you gave me a start!" She couldn't
pretend that she didn't recognize him. He had
called her by name. But he didn't need to know
that she and Zane were a team, soon to put him
behind bars and happily claim his bounty.

Missy fluttered her fingers at her throat. She
wrinkled her brow and sighed, presenting the
image of a wounded bird or a crushed flower.

"Truly, sir, you thought my work was drivel?"
she asked.

"Drivel in the truest sense. Really, Miss Devlin, your prose shows that you are quite naive."

He took two steps forward, close enough so
that she smelled the odor of his breath; mint, covering alcohol. A true illustration of his charac-
ter, she determined. As sometimes happened, the
guise of a gentleman covered an unprincipled
individual.

"Drivel in what way?" She casually picked up
Number Nine's reins while her brain whirled. She
needed to stall until she thought of a brilliant es-

cape plan. "Can't you be more specific? Surely you found something of value in it?"

"It was good for a laugh." He stared down his razor nose at her.

"Well, a writer takes her critiques where she can find them." She sighed, lifting her bosom. Men were usually distracted by that. "Thank you for yours, Mr.— I'm sorry, I didn't get your name when we last met, things being as they were."

"Where are you going, Miss Devlin?" He grasped her elbow, halting her first step toward the livery. Leaning close, he whispered in her ear, "You very well know my name. You and your paramour have been a thorn in my side for some time now, but I believe I've just gained the upper hand."

"I can't imagine what you are talking about." She turned and snatched her manuscript out of the saddle pack then thrust it at Wesley Wage. "Is this drivel or is it funny? Since you seem to be a literary expert as well as a horse thief, you owe it to me to point out where I went wrong."

Good, his hands were now occupied with holding her manuscript. She turned. She would mount Number Nine while his attention was riveted on her book.

"You really are rather fetching, Miss Devlin." He dropped her journal. It fell open in the dirt, creasing the pages. "But I have pressing business to attend to and I'm sure you know what it is."

His hand shot out, reaching for Number Nine's reins. Missy whipped them behind her back and tangled them in her fists.

"Not with my horse, you don't!"

He only laughed and circled his arms around her. Tugging her tight to his tailored vest, he attempted to uncurl the leather straps from her clenched fingers.

"What a pet you are," he mumbled. Heat and mint brushed her ear. "I can't imagine what to do with you while I make good on my business."

Missy lifted her knee and drove it into his soft crotch. His breath whooshed out of his lungs and he groaned, but his fingers dug into her wrists with a strength she would never have guessed at.

Zane stood before the counter of the telegraph office, waiting for the clerk's attention and wondering what had become of his good plain sense. Day by day, he seemed to see the world through more fanciful eyes, almost as though he were looking at it as Missy would. Damned if colors didn't appear brighter. The air even smelled sweeter.

Exactly one hour earlier, he had been lurking in a doorway near the bank. He should have been keeping a hawk eye out for Wage, but his attention drifted too often to the pretty face peering out of the hotel window from across the street.

Missy Devlin looked like an angel and no mistake about it. He had been ten times a fool to stare at her the way he had, with his heart as well as his eyes.

He couldn't recall ever meeting a woman like her. Peering out the window sleepy-eyed, with her sunshine curls caught up in a blue ribbon, she was a picture of delicate womanhood. Any man seeing Missy at that moment would have given his right arm to protect her.

Any man wouldn't know that the sweet sparkle in her eyes was really a flash of intelligence and a call to adventure that went bone deep.

Sometimes, the most delicate-looking creatures were the hardiest. For instance, butterflies. If a man didn't watch his step, he might just get caught up in a butterfly moon.

Maybe that's why, after only half an hour of watching for Wage, he had abandoned his hiding place next to the bank.

After that, he'd searched for the criminal from one end of town to the other, giving the task only half of his attention. It was unlike him to be so careless.

In the end, he stood outside the telegraph office, perplexed by what he was about to do. Clearly, he had been bewitched by some sort of a spell.

With a shiver, he reminded himself that he did not believe in spells.

But when had he come to want Missy's bright

company more than the outrageous bounty that her brother offered?

He had been standing at the telegraph counter, mentally composing the wire to Edwin Devlin that would cancel his interest in the reward, when the door opened with a rush of cold air.

He heard a gasp and turned around.

Missy! Her face had been turned, hidden by the closing door, but he'd bet a year's pay that she was the only woman in Foggy Johnson Creek to sport a flopping red feather on her harlot's bonnet.

"Sorry for the wait, mister, what can I do for you?" the clerk asked.

Zane stared at him for a moment then he studied the closed door.

"You a married man?" Zane asked. "Maybe you have a regular woman in your life?"

"No, sirree! Never put my neck in that noose." The clerk's sizeable Adam's apple slid up and down with his declaration. He swiped his brow. "Not this fellow."

"Sensible… I suppose. I'll catch you later about the wire." Zane tugged at the brim of his hat, giving the man a nod in parting.

He left behind the warmth of the telegraph office and stepped into the fog. Missy had disappeared. Wherever the woman had gone he would bet his mother's ribbon that she was hell-bound for some misadventure or another.

Zane took fast strides up the street and when he didn't find her, turned and paced the other direction. Ten minutes later he abandoned the relative security of the boardwalk to search the alley where any lowlife might take refuge. Without a doubt, Missy would be drawn there like a bee to spring clover.

The thought set him running. In his mind he saw her confronting every one of the scoundrels at once, helpless and at their mercy.

Someone yowled in pain. After a heartbeat a curse sliced through the fog. It sounded only a block or two up, probably behind the livery. It was a man's voice, but that didn't mean that the madcap Miss Devlin was not involved.

He reached for his gun on the run.

Damn! Children's voices, and too nearby to risk drawing his weapon. In this fog they could be anywhere.

From fifty feet away he spotted a pair of figures. Through the wispy vapor they appeared to be dancing.

"Let go!" Missy hissed.

"I vow, I'll mail the cursed thing back here when I get a hundred miles away without being followed. Ooof!" The taller figure grunted when Missy bit his hand. "You little bitch!"

Still forty feet away, Zane stretched his stride, watching the tug of war going on between Missy and Wage.

Wage held the reins of a horse in one fist and a journal in the other.

Missy also gripped one corner of the journal. She appeared less than willing to let go of it. With both of her dainty hands she tugged on the leather-bound volume. The book shifted back and forth between them like a two-manned saw.

Missy raised her knee. Wage pressed his thighs together.

In the same instant he must have heard the pump of Zane's boots on the dirt for he let go of the reins and the journal. He clamped one arm about Missy's chest and turned her, facing Zane.

Missy looked hot and furious. If sheer anger could win a battle, the bank robber would be done for. Her feet kicked and flailed, but Wage, in his dandy's suit, held her fast.

From the front of the livery, Zane heard a woman's voice calling to the children. Missy's breath wheezed in her lungs.

"Back off!" Wage demanded. His nostrils pinched to slits with the exertion of holding Missy still. "Hand over that ribbon in your hair, Coldridge… No funny business or I'll make her pay for it, I swear I will!"

Missy's mouth moved but her voice remained trapped under her assailant's arm.

Zane ripped the ribbon from his hair and flipped it to Wage. Second by second, Missy's face purpled with the need for air.

"Please do quit squirming, Miss Devlin. I won't keep you with me an instant longer than necessary. Just long enough to know that Mr. Hero, here, hasn't followed."

"Ma, come quick!" a boy's voice screeched. "There's a man's got a lady behind the barn!"

Footsteps, light and feminine, tapped the dirt in the alley beside the livery.

Zane's gun felt like a hundred pounds of dead weight for all the good it did.

"Hold out your hands like a good girl. We wouldn't want the kid to see anything unpleasant."

Missy nodded her head vigorously and touched her wrists together.

"Lovely, we have a nearly pleasant end to this little problem, then." He frowned at the blood dripping down his palm.

Wage let go of Missy for an instant, needing both of his hands to tie up hers. What he didn't see was her sideways glance...her grin.

Zane cursed, but quicker than the wink she shot him, Missy shoved the journal at Wage. For some reason, he fumbled with it rather than keeping his full attention on his captive.

Distracted, he failed to notice Missy touch her headwear and pluck a pin from her hat.

His yowl echoed in the fog.

"Oh, my!" gasped the woman standing at the corner of the livery.

"Gads!" the boy declared. "She pinned him in the rump!"

Up to the hilt! With one smooth move she had buried the pearly pin in her target and snatched Zane's mother's ribbon from Wage's fist.

Gads indeed! She was something! But Wage's face had gone red with pain and anger. In half a second he would retaliate against her. Already, his fist had curled into a tight, bony ball. He drew it back, clearly intending to flatten Missy's face.

The woman beside the livery screamed, the boy hollered.

Zane roared and lunged.

Chapter Twelve

Wage pinioned her journal under his arm. The cad! In the instant, though, Missy could not keep hold of Zane's ribbon and retrieve her manuscript without taking the blow bearing down upon her face.

She ducked beneath the sweep of the bank robber's fist, keeping the precious bit of fabric secured in her fingers.

Her ears quaked at Zane's sudden roar. If her hat pin didn't deter Wage, the unholy fury coming from Zane would.

Wage had no choice, really, but to run. His fists punched the small of her back, shoving her into the path of Zane's charge.

Her skirt hem tangled on the tip of her boot. Her arms waved madly, reaching in vain for something to break her fall. The ribbon fluttered and snapped. She slammed into Zane's chest and they went down. She saw the ground coming at her nose but in the instant before impact Zane's arms squeezed about her. He twisted.

She slammed down on top of his chest. His breath whooshed out of his lungs with a grunt. Instead of colliding with hard-packed earth, she scraped her nose on the button of his shirt.

"My hero," she panted, and pushed off his chest. Surely she had broken at least one of his ribs.

Rolling sideways she lay beside him with a pebble digging into her back.

Hoofbeats pummeled the earth, growing fainter by the second. Zane's breath wheezed in and out of his lungs.

"He's getting—" she gasped "—away!"

Zane lifted his head and peered after Wage. "He's not sitting down, though."

Missy lifted her head to peer after the fleeing figure.

"Drat, he's got my journal."

She turned her face to peek at Zane. "He does look absurd, doesn't he, with his hind end in the air and my manuscript pages flapping?"

"Oh, my gracious!" A rustle of petticoats rushed forward. "Are you hurt?"

Zane eased up on his elbow, ignoring the woman standing over them and wringing her hands.

"You could have saved it," he said. Inch by slow inch he tugged the ribbon from her fingers. "You could have kept the thing you hold most dear."

"Not most dear."

He looked into Missy's eyes, as though searching for something that went deeper than the things that eyes could see. She would bet her next breath that he saw their future together. He might not like it, but surely he could no longer deny it.

"You've scratched yourself." He dabbed the lace on the tip of her nose.

Brown eyes, shimmering like the sunshine far beyond Foggy Johnson Creek, searched her soul. Surely he would see the rightness of the love she had for him. Fluttering lace felt like butterflies against her face.

And then he kissed her.

"Oh, my!" The forgotten woman hovering over them gasped. Her skirt fluttered in retreat. "Come along, Gregory, Amy, everything here seems to be in order."

After that...Zane laughed.

Something was wrong.

From his seat at the restaurant table everything seemed normal. His steak was cooked rare, Missy smiled and chattered about the day's adventures while Muff slept under the table on a pillow in a basket.

Still, something was wrong.

Everything seemed humorous.

Logically, he ought to be angry. He ought to be cursing his partner for abandoning her post and, therefore, setting up a situation where Wage once again escaped and where she had put herself at great risk.

If his mind were clear, he would be riding hell-bent away from Foggy Johnson Creek, hot on the criminal's trail with Missy left behind forever.

Instead, he was having dinner, compliments of Murphy's Steak House, and smiling at the glow of the new ruby-tipped hat pin securing Missy's hat to her hair. The pin had been a gift from the proprietor of the general store.

If he could erase from his mind the sight of Wage's rear end bobbing over his saddle like a ball afraid to touch the ground, he might be able to regain some sensibility. But, with his eyes open or closed, the scene played over and over, and everything was funny.

Missy, it seemed, had become quite a heroine in town, having saved the bank from being robbed. Even their hotel rooms for tonight had been paid for by the local citizenry.

The prospect of another evening in Foggy Johnson Creek made him feel uneasy, though. It wasn't because of the constantly dreary fog, or the fact that Wage got farther away by the hour. How far could he get in one day with a pin buried in his rear? The pursuit could begin after a lazy morning in town and they would still capture him.

His anxiety was due to the fact that every eye was on his partner. When she laughed, ears would twitch her way, when she picked up her fork, nearby diners would turn to look. She had become a Foggy Johnson Creek celebrity and the besotted folks of the town doted on her every breath.

It couldn't be long before one of them matched her face to the poster that, until this morning, had been pinned to the wall behind the marshal's desk. Even though the handbill was now hidden in his gear along with half a dozen others he had collected, someone might make the connection.

The sooner they lit out, the better he would feel. Unfortunately, feeling better about keeping Missy by his side was something that did not make him feel in the least better.

To make matters worse, his conflicting emotions ought to tie him up in a sour mood, but he still felt like laughing. What had become of his sober-minded self? Where was the heart of brick that had seen him through the difficult years?

This laughter, so ready to spout from his mouth, was new and almost frightening. It felt good, so good that it must be a weakness. But then, Missy didn't suffer from weakness and she laughed often.

Soon, very soon, he would have to do something to set his emotions right, but not tonight. This evening he would enjoy being the man he might have been if his early life hadn't taken a bitter turn.

This evening life sparkled, Missy sparkled and he was happy.

The walk from the restaurant to the hotel wasn't precisely a romantic stroll under the stars but fog swirled about Missy and Zane and wrapped them in a milky cocoon that Missy imagined shut out the rest of the world.

Their muted footsteps whispered on the damp wood of the boardwalk. Lamps glowing from windows along Main Street cast yellow shadows into the night. Passing them by, one by one, Missy watched Zane's face. The smile on his lips held from one light to another.

What would happen next, would he burst out in song?

Something had come over him. It was wonderful, to be sure, but she wondered how long his easy humor would last. Seeing the world as rosy was not something that came naturally to the bounty hunter.

Too soon, they came to the open door of the hotel and, most likely, a return to the usual tug of war between them. She stepped through the doorway but Zane stopped her with a hand on her shoulder. It felt firm. The warmth of his palm went through her cotton dress and heated her to the bone.

"It's chilly, but would you care to walk for a while?" he asked.

Would she! For the first time ever, Zane Coldridge had asked her to share his time and space. They had spent plenty of time together, this was nothing new. But before tonight, she had been forced upon him by circumstance. This was a new Zane, one who smiled and laughed and requested the pleasure of her company.

What on earth had happened to make him so congenial? After letting Wesley Wage escape, she had expected at best a grumble, and more likely a good scolding. It would not have been a surprise to find herself locked in her hotel room, doomed to stare out the window until it pleased her eighty-percent partner to let her out.

"The air does have a nip," she answered. Not much of one but she shivered on purpose.

His grin, a compelling blend of high spirits and mischief, made her feel clammy and hot all at once. He laid his arm across her back, caught her shoulder in his palm and drew her close to his vest.

"Even so," she said, "a walk would be just the thing."

And then she couldn't think of another thing to say. How uncommon.

Silence stretched up and down the street. No one was about on this foggy evening to make comment upon. Nothing new with the weather, either. Simply fog and more fog.

How was she to form a compelling conversation when the man consumed her senses? So close, the smell of clean clothes and soap didn't quite mask the wild prairie scent of his skin. She heard the gentle rush of his breath and the whisper of his denims as he walked.

Glancing up and sideways, she appreciated the fact that he had shaved for dinner. The hint of a cleft in his chin made him so handsome that she was feeling a bit queer, weak in the knees and short of breath, even though they strolled at a snail's own pace.

If a conversation didn't distract her in the next instant or two, she was going to melt into a puddle right here on the Foggy Johnson Creek boardwalk. That would give the townsfolk a thing or two to talk about.

"Why is it, Zane, that you haven't locked me away in the hotel room?" His smile held. Not even the shadow of a frown wrinkled his brow. "Truly, I thought you would be furious with me for letting Wage get away."

"Darlin'," he said then looked her in the eyes with a brown-sugar gaze that made want to her sigh.

Oh! Had she actually done it? Out loud? She

must have for he chuckled and hugged her to his chest.

"I am…or I ought to be." His breath, laced with his dinner of steak, potatoes and beer, whispered against her ear. "But I think I've been bewitched."

Missy pulled back and studied his eyes so that she could judge the sincerity of that statement.

"As if by magic?" Surely he must be teasing, which in itself was as strange as him believing in magic.

"As if by you." He turned a corner and led her onto a path that ended at the creek. "Magic is for foo—…for other folks."

At the end of the path was a bench. Without taking his hand from her shoulder he sat down, drawing her along with him.

"Someday, Zane Coldridge," she whispered. "Just you wait."

He didn't answer, but she felt the negative shake of his head when his hair, worn loose and midnight-shiny, brushed her cheek.

Water in the creek rushed past with a playful gush and bubble. A frog croaked, then a night bird answered.

This was magic, whether the strangely content man gazing at her lips as though he were still hungry, recognized it or not.

"You must be, at least, a little upset that I let Wage go," she said, needing to clear the air on the subject. "If you are, I understand and I take the blame."

"He won't get far, not with a needle stuck up his backside." Then Zane laughed all over again.

When he quit, his eyes glittered as though they reflected starlight, even though there was none.

He lifted his arm from her shoulder and withdrew the pin from her hat. The red feather bounced and danced when he lifted the hat from her head.

Without a word he tugged a strand of hair out of its neat coil of curls. He sifted it through his fingers, and then loosened another.

In silence, he freed her whole coiffure from its bindings. The heavy mass lay across her breast, the ends curling up at her waist.

He picked up a tress where it sloped over her bosom and rubbed it between his thumb and finger. His big tan knuckle brushed her breast. Under her shift, her nipple twisted up as tight as a puckered kiss. A sensation that she could only liken to yearning reached to her belly and lower. She had the indecent impulse to sit on his lap and spread her knees wide.

How odd…and pleasant.

"My mother…" His voice seemed to catch in his throat. "My mother used to wish she had a daughter with hair this color. She never did, but she always told me if she did she'd tie it up in pretty, lacy ribbons. Ma put great store in ribbons."

She knew she ought to say something, but couldn't imagine what.

"My mother does, too," she said at last, then felt like a fool. It sounded as though she had boasted that she had a mother, a very alive mother with ribbons, while he did not. "I'm sorry, Zane. That wasn't the right thing to say at all. What I meant was—"

"Shush." He pressed his wide, calloused thumb to her lips. "I know what you meant, and thank you. If it hadn't been for you, I would have nothing left of my mother. You are the single person in this world who knows what that ribbon means to me."

She sighed against his thumb then turned her head to free her mouth. "But if I'd stayed in the room like you wanted me to, the ribbon would not have been in danger."

"True." He laughed softly then touched his forehead to hers. "But if you had stayed in the room you wouldn't be the adventurous woman I have come to—"

"Evening, folks." The marshal's voice filtered through the fog before his portly figure appeared in the mist. "Just making my nightly rounds."

"Everything here is as peaceful as can be, Marshal Brody. Only the frogs are jumping," Zane said.

"And all due to your lady." The marshal nodded at Missy. "This would be one hell of a miserable night if the bank had gotten robbed."

"I like to help when I can," Missy declared.

"This is one adventure you can count on being immortalized in a dime novel," Zane said.

His reply didn't sound like sarcasm and he was still smiling. She didn't dare hope that he now approved of her calling, but it was a night of wonders.

"Is that so?" the lawman asked. "Are you a writer, Miss Devlin?"

The night, it seemed, could not get any finer. To be able to answer him, "Yes, I am," was pure bliss.

He looked at her for a long, silent moment, seeming to scrutinize her face.

"You look familiar to me, Miss Devlin, I can't quite place..." He bit his upper lip in concentration. "Have you visited Foggy Johnson Creek before?"

Beside her, Zane grew suddenly stiff, his fingers clenched in her hair, tight enough that she nearly yelped. His smile vanished like a campfire being doused by a water bucket.

"I'm new to the West, Marshal." She turned her face to frown at Zane, who was beginning to grind his teeth together. "But if you've been to Bos—"

All at once Zane yanked her to her feet, his

fist clamped around her elbow. "It's late," He announced. "We've got an early start in the morning."

With only a mumbled farewell to Marshal Brody, he spun her about and hurried her away from the creek.

She tried to turn to say goodbye but Zane kept her in front of him so that she could not even look backward. All she could do was wave her hat to the side in an improper farewell.

"I'll be up all night trying to think of where I've seen you," the Marshal called, but Zane had already whisked her around the corner with a grimace that would stretch to the moon and back.

Chapter Thirteen

◦◦◦◦◦◦◦◦

Well before daylight Zane tapped on Missy's door. A thud bumped the other side…Muff on the defense. His yapping screeched up and down the hallways, sounding like a pack of miniature wolves bent on predawn mayhem.

Two rooms down, a man opened his door. He peered through gray eyebrows, stabbing Zane with a bushy glare.

"What's the fuss?" he grumbled. "There's folks who like to sleep at night."

Apparently, unlike Zane, Missy had been one of the blissful dozers. When she opened the door a full minute later, her eyes were still washed with dreams and her hair tangled over her shoulders in a sleepy golden mess.

"What are you doing just opening the door like that?" He tried not to glance down but she had been sleeping in her shift and it didn't cover much.

"If you didn't want me to answer, why did you knock?" She rubbed her eyes and covered a yawn. "Quiet, Muff."

Missy scooped the dog up and pinched his muzzle shut with two fingers.

"Here, let me take the scamp." He reached out. Muff was growing fast. When he'd first seen him, the pup could fit in a coat pocket. Now he might have some trouble napping inside Missy's saddle pack.

Missy handed over the dog but arched her eyebrows in surprise. Maybe he'd never asked to hold the mutt before.

"Get dressed. We're leaving," he grumbled, but it took some effort. A grumble used to feel the most natural thing in the world.

"Now?" Missy looked toward the window. Fog pressed against the glass so thickly that there was no clue as to the hour. "What time is it?"

It was nearly four-thirty, and Zane hadn't slept a wink.

Last night, the marshal had been a thought away from recognizing Missy from the wanted poster. First thought on waking, he might. Waiting for daylight to get out of town might be too late. Even though the lawman might not want the reward, he had knowledge that Missy didn't need to know just yet. Not until Zane admitted that he had wired her brother.

"It's time to go, is what time it is."

"All right." Missy shrugged…she stretched.

Even in the dark he saw more of her than was decent. "I'll wait for you in the hall."

He stepped out and closed the door. Leaning against it, he took a deep breath. Behaving in a "decent" manner toward his partner was becoming more difficult by the hour.

"What's come over me, dog?" He stroked the small white head and received a lick on his thumb for the effort. "What was that for?" Had the mutt somehow picked up on his change of heart?

Something had shifted inside him. He wasn't laughing out loud any longer—the marshal had blown out that candle when he'd nearly recognized Missy—but still, the cloud that had shadowed him since childhood had lifted, and the dog had noticed.

What that meant to his future, he couldn't say. If Missy had a part in it, he didn't know that either.

What he did know was that he needed to get her away from Foggy Johnson Creek. Far too much attention was focused on Missy. A week or two ago, he would have been ready to hand her off to the first decent person who was ready to take her home. Now, something had changed and he didn't know what it was or how to deal with it. The only thing he did know was that he was taking Missy away from here.

He didn't know why, he didn't know where. He only knew that hours of lost sleep had convinced him that he had to do it.

A half mile outside of Foggy Johnson Creek, the fog dissolved. Missy sat in Daisy's saddle watching the stars blink across the sky. Apparently, daybreak was still some time away.

She yawned then turned in her saddle to look back at the town. Foggy Johnson Creek, her hotel room and her cozy bed had vanished. In their place was a giant pillow of fog.

"The Curse of Foggy Johnson Creek," she murmured. Soon, she would write a fascinating chapter about it.

Zane rode ahead of her, his posture easy on his big black horse. An entire book would be required to portray him.

The cheerful Zane that she had glimpsed so briefly was gone and a version of the sober Zane had returned. Something had changed, though. While she had been with this Zane for less than an hour, she noted that he was as likely to smile as to frown.

At the start of their acquaintance, his big, bold self had captivated her. Last night, his cheerful change of mood had delighted her. This morning a new man had emerged, one who was, most likely, the true Zane Coldridge. From the beginning she had loved him, but this new man was one she could make a future with, if he could only see it.

Without a doubt, she was tied up in a love knot that would never be undone. It bound her to him. Unless her man came to understand this, the knot would tangle her up…strangle her even.

"Did you see that?" Zane asked in a near-reverent tone.

"See what?" She had been too absorbed in watching Zane's back roll with the gait of his horse to notice anything else. Whatever Zane had seen in the predawn could not have been half as interesting.

"A star shot across the sky." He pointed his finger straight up then traced a line down toward the horizon. "I can't recall ever seeing one so big."

"You never can predict what magic you might see when you open up to the possibilities."

He shook his head and glanced back. Where a week ago she would have seen a scowl on his face, she now saw interest in his eyes, sprinkled with a dose of reluctance to be sure.

"It's all natural phenomena, darlin'." He shot her a grin. "Nothing more."

She snorted and earned a mental picture of her mother's frown of disapproval. A lady never snorted. A lady always deferred to a gentleman's opinion.

Missy snorted again. She was not cut out to be a lady, in spite of her mother's best efforts to make her one.

"You swallowing dust?" Zane's question was punctuated with a rumble of laughter.

"Ace's hooves are stirring up enough to choke me, if you must know."

She urged Daisy forward so that she walked nose-to-nose with Ace. Within a minute Daisy had fallen back, walking placidly behind what she clearly believed to be the dominant male.

"Smart animal you purchased," Zane commented. "She knows her proper place."

"Her proper place is back in the stable, having dreams of her morning oats." Missy yawned hugely, with as much drama as she could muster so early. "Why did you drag me out of bed before the birds? The world wouldn't have ended if we had eaten breakfast before we left."

This time it was Zane who snorted. Then he cursed under his breath.

"What was that?" Missy asked.

He turned in the saddle, fixing her with a glare. "My eighty percent of this outfit says we needed to be on the trail early."

"My twenty percent wanted to stay in bed, if that means anything at all."

"It doesn't." All at once his scowl slipped to a grin. "Not when it comes up against my eighty."

With his point made, he turned around with

his face set toward the horizon, which still did not look as though dawn was about to spring over it.

She closed her eyes, trying to take an upright doze. Daisy would follow along after Ace like a proper female so there was no need to chart her course. Mother would be pleased with Missy's new horse.

And so the morning passed and then the afternoon, with Missy following behind Zane and conversation limited. She had lost interest in the bold shape of his broad back some hours past and now entertained herself with identifying mythological gods and goddesses in the shifting shapes of clouds that built a black mass toward the evening horizon.

"Oh, my word, I just spotted Neptune!" She pointed to a morphing figure in the clouds. "Maybe we'll get some rain."

Zane slowed Ace and let her catch up. "It looks like rain for sure, but what has a planet got to do with it?"

"Not the planet, the Greek god of the sea. Same as Poseidon."

"Looks like my uncle neglected that part of my education," he said then shot her a wicked smile. "And the ladies had other things to teach."

"Were you a good student, then?" Curse the blush that heated her face. "Paying attention to your instructors and…and completing assignments?" Drat, it was difficult to seem worldly with cheeks as red as sin.

"I was a wicked student."

Zane reined in Ace and let the distance close between the horses. He touched her cheek, brushing aside a hank of hair that blew across her face.

The sun slipped below the bank of clouds, leaving behind its crown of golden rays. He lifted her chin with his thumb and kissed her. Butter and sugar simmered in a pot would not have been half as delectable. His mouth lingered long and tender. Morning bristle where he hadn't taken the time to shave prickled her lip. When he ended the kiss, lips parted from lips in a slow pull. Maybe he couldn't stand the separation any better than she could for he swooped in for one last peck.

"I drove the ladies mad with my stubbornness. If any of them had known Greek gods, they wouldn't have had the patience to teach me. They just about had to nail my pants to a chair to get me to learn reading, writing and sums."

"They never made you go to school?"

"Even if there was a school, and I don't recall there being one, it wouldn't have welcomed Maybelle's boy."

"Suzie and I had a governess and a private tutor. Between them, they made us learn every boring thing they had probably been forced to learn."

"We couldn't be from two more different

worlds." Zane stared at the gold-and-red streaks of clouds melting into sunset. "It's like you're fire and I'm ice. I wonder if it could ever work for us, darlin'?"

"It doesn't take higher education to know what happens when fire and ice get together, Zane Coldridge." While she watched, a star glowed into view. "The ice takes the fire's heat and they bubble and boil into one."

"So they do." He looked at her with an expression she could not read, for all her studies. "We'd better find a place to set up camp."

The lightning storm was too far west for Zane to hear the thunder, but that small relief did not keep him from worrying. Violent weather had a way of covering a lot of ground in a hurry.

Missy sat close to the campfire, writing in her journal. Twisting flames cast red-and-gold highlights in her hair where it fell across her back, loose and wavy. He was glad that she didn't braid it the way many women did before retiring.

She glanced up, silently watching the show on the horizon.

"I've never seen a storm like this," she said. "In Boston they aren't nearly as grand." With a small hitch of her shoulders, she bent her head over her journal and continued to scribble across the page.

They wouldn't be. This disturbance was extreme even for the wilds of Nebraska, and he'd seen many of them over the years.

Typically, lightning would flash and thunder would boom, big and loud, but pretty normal for springtime. This storm sat on the horizon like a huge flickering lamp, with the sky never going fully dark between thunderbolts. Closer to it, the rumbling would probably sound like a battle of cannons.

If the weather shifted this way, things could get dangerous in a hurry.

"You ever seen a twister, darlin'?" he asked, forcing the strain from his voice. That was what he feared most about the events to the west. Right now the air was still and the thunder too far off to be heard, but he'd seen things change from one breath to the next.

She glanced up with a smile. "Not yet."

The blamed woman looked as though she were hoping for one, another adventure to write down in her copybook.

"Same for a prairie fire, I expect," he said.

This time she looked at him with a frown. He hoped she had more respect for raging flames than for killer winds. The hullabaloo in the distance could easily cause either one.

"Not that either." She dipped the tip of her pen in the ink bottle. "I did watch Mr. McNulty's carriage house burn down right outside our parlor window. Suzie and I nearly made it out our front door to get a better look before Edwin caught us and locked us in our bedroom. It was quite a thrill to see since no one was injured. Not even the mouse that ran out the barn door only a step ahead of the McNultys' cat."

No need to get her opinion on the flood that might swamp them in a few hours. She had lived through one of those and claimed the outcome to be magical.

It was true that folks should have perished in the Flood of Green Island and no one had, but even with his new outlook on life, the concept of magic lay beyond his mental grasp.

"You worried, Zane?" Missy asked. At last he detected concern in her expression.

"Hell, no." He sat down beside her and gathered Muff onto his lap. The pup began to gnaw on his thumb, but in a friendly way. "I've been through a dozen storms like this and worse."

It was a lie, but it sounded reassuring, even to him.

"I'm, maybe, a little nervous," she admitted, then scooted closer to him and snuggled next to his chest. He wrapped his arm about her shoulder and pulled her tight.

"Nothing to be worried about." He tried not to stiffen at the sudden gust of wind that howled along the ground and stirred up a wave of prairie dust.

"Tell me a story about you and Suzie, something that no one else knows. What horrible thing did you sweet pair of hellions get away with?" He wanted to know, to picture her, a child, at her mischievous best. If her voice drowned out the sound of the wind rustling across the earth, so much the better. "Don't spare a sordid detail."

She was silent for a moment, tapping the tip of her pen on her journal page. A smile played at the corners of her mouth. She sighed and shrugged her shoulders.

"Surely, you can think of something," he urged.

"Mostly, we got caught... Let me think."

She gave him a smile so sweet that, for half a second, he believed he had misjudged her, that she had grown up an angel, a picture of proper decorum and her mother's shining star.

"The best thing we ever did without getting caught had to be the mouth-inking."

"Mouth-inking! Spill the details, darlin'. I won't sleep a wink if you don't." A flash of distant lightning brightened the mischief in her smile. Edwin Devlin must have led a hell of a life.

"First of all, it was in a worthy cause. Almost everyone who ended up with a black mouth deserved it for what they were about to do to poor little Desmond Thornton."

"Almost everyone?"

"There were a few innocent victims, but that couldn't be helped." She sighed, grazing the curve of her breast against his shirt. "You need to understand that our social group was petty and mean. Desmond had a stutter. On the Halloween that we were ten years old there was a party at the McNultys', whose carriage house burned down.

"Before you even think it, Suzie and I had nothing to do with that." She shot him a brief but severe frown. "Our snide group of peers had planned to humiliate poor Desmond by giving him a firefly in a jar and claiming it was a fairy with a magic pill that would cure him of his stuttering.

"The magic pill was nothing more than a glob of shoe black and sugar. The plan was to feed him that rot at the party and then laugh themselves silly at his appearance.

"It was a simple thing, really, for Suzie to dump a bottle of ink into the punch bowl. The punch was a dark color to begin with so that it resembled witches' brew. I organized a blindfold game where everyone had to drink the brew as a part of it. When the blinds came off those black mouths weren't laughing at Desmond, I can tell you. If only you could have been there, Zane, it was something to see."

"How is it you didn't get caught, with you and Suzie having the only clean faces?"

"Naturally, we had to drink the brew along with the others, and we howled up a storm with the best of them."

"What happened to Desmond?"

"He had to get a black mouth, too, so he wouldn't be singled out, but he never found out about the fairy and the bootblack. A couple of years later he quit stuttering. Later on, every girl and her mama was after him, he turned out to be handsome, and of course, rich as anything."

"Did that include you and your mama?" Even though they were having a light conversation, all in fun, something stirred inside him. The only time he had ever been jealous was watching other kids and their mothers through windows in the dark of night. This stirring felt something like that.

"Suzie and Mama." She grinned at him and winked. "I was in love with a fantasy man. In my dreams he was always big and bold with rough hands that were gentle enough to untangle my hair without so much as a pinch."

"You are…" Where was his breath all of a sudden? "You are about to steal the heart right out of my chest. Did you know that, Missy?"

Her eyes opened wide.

"That's been my intention all along, in case you haven't noticed," she whispered.

He'd known, all right, but had been too much of a fool to explore what was in front of him.

"Now you know one of my dark secrets, what about yours?" Her eyes called a challenge. "Don't tell me you walked the line growing up."

"I was a beast." He matched her grin and set Muff down. The dog pattered over to the far side of the fire and curled back to sleep next to the saddle on the ground. "I can beat your mouth-inking."

"You really know how to win a woman over, Zane Coldridge. Don't leave out a single, hideous word." She leaned into him with a shiver. Knowing Missy, it would be a shiver of delight rather than a reaction to the quickly cooling temperature.

"One afternoon I was hiding from the ladies. They were determined to teach me world history, as far as they knew it, anyways, and I was set on not learning it. So I ran off and sulked in the bushes that grew beside the pond on Old Man Jensen's farm. He was a mean cuss, the ladies never spoke highly of him.

"So, here I am hiding, and along comes the farmer with a bag tied up with twine. He ties the strings of the bag to a reed then tosses the bag in the pond. Now, just before the bag sinks into the water, I hear a noise coming from it. The old buzzard doesn't wait around, he takes off real quick, so I jump into the pond and pull out the bag to see what's making all the racket.

"It turns out to be a litter of pups, not even old enough to be weaned away from their mother."

"That was heroic, Zane." She cocked her head,

distant lightning reflected in her eyes. "But I want to hear about some mischief."

"Get ready for a razor-strap's worth, then." He looped his arms around his knees, settling into his story. If he'd ever passed a more pleasant evening he could not recall it, threatening weather not withstanding. "So, I put the pups in my pockets. Five of them, and all cold and whining, did I say that it was November? I was darned cold myself, with my clothes soaking from the dip in the pond. Anyway, I figure the farmer needs a lesson, just like your ink-mouthed friends did.

"Next, I tie up the sack, with the knot identical to the one the farmer tied. I snag it on the same reed that he had left it on. Then I take the pups home to Maybelle's and get them good and warmed up. After dark, I sneak into Jensen's barn where I figure the mama dog is. There she is way back in a corner looking pretty miserable without her babies. I set them at her teats and then I hide in a pile of straw, waiting for morning.

"A while before daylight Old Man Jensen and his wife come out to milk the cows. He hears the pups whining and lets out a yelp. His wife asks what's the matter, hasn't he ever heard a pup before? He tells her how he tossed them in the pond last night. She says how it would serve him right if they came back to haunt him.

"I had to bless Mrs. Jensen for the suggestion since that was what I had planned for him to believe. I didn't even have to let out my ghostly howl, which might have given me away. He called her superstitious and said that somehow the pups had worked their way out of the bag and made their way home. Mrs. Jensen called him a fool, the pups hadn't yet learned to walk. He dropped his milk pail and stomped out of the barn. After Mrs. Jensen left the barn, I followed Mr. Jensen to the pond. He was kneeling beside the water holding the dripping bag, tied with the very knot he thought he had tied, still intact. He's the one who looked like a ghost, all white and shaking like a leaf.

"Those pups lived to ripe old ages and all their pups did the same. It seems that Farmer Jensen never had the courage to toss another animal into the pond."

Missy's mouth rounded in a circle of delight; her eyes blinked wide. "Leave it to you to be a hero and commit mischief all in one adventure. I bow to your superior deviltry, Mr. Coldridge."

Somehow, this was the highest praise that he had ever received. Not that he had received much. Occasionally, a casual bed partner would comment, once in a while a grateful lawman, but usually his actions drew vicious words and angry gestures.

Superior deviltry. The honor was enough to make him grin without restraint. He felt like crowing. He felt young and happy in a way he hadn't since the loss of his mother.

Without hesitation, without sadness or regret, he slipped the lace ribbon from his hair. He moved sideways a foot, just far enough so that he could gather Missy's loose hair together and tie it up in a bow.

"It looks prettier on you," he murmured, amazed that it didn't hurt to give the ribbon up.

Missy touched her hair, her fingers hovering over the worn scrap as if it was made of dreams.

Maybe it was. Dreams, memories and something he had never considered—hope for the future.

Tears glistened in Missy's eyes. Her smile trembled. Clearly, she understood that by handing over his ribbon, he had handed over his life. In this woman, dreams that he had never believed could come true, had. He'd bet the sun, the moon and the stars that she understood this without a word being spoken.

He needed a moment to think, to comprehend the turn his life had just taken. If he didn't back off for a moment to get things sorted out inside, he'd be weeping like a newborn.

"What are you writing?" He asked, grasping for a piece of solid ground.

* * *

What was she writing? Of all the times for the man to take a sudden interest in her career, why did it have to be now?

Something unspoken had passed between them, a shifting that would leave their lives forever changed. It was the thing she had been waiting for.

But Zane seemed afraid of it. Like a night-loving creature that had accidentally poked its head into bright daylight, he had withdrawn.

What she had just written would not give him the shadows he sought.

"Just descriptions, is all." She flipped the journal closed and hoped the ink didn't smear. "Is there any coffee left?"

"Not a drop." Zane reached across her lap, picked up the journal and opened it.

"Here, let me find something for you to read." She grabbed for the book but he held it out of her reach, grinning like a fool.

"I'd like to look at what you just wrote. It must be something if that blush is anything to go by."

"That's not a blush. It's the heat from the campfire," she insisted. "You look as flushed as I do."

That was a fib. Although he didn't look flushed now, in a moment he would.

She snatched at the journal but he laughed and held it away from her flexing fingers.

Watching him devour her most private thoughts was too much to bear. How could she judge how he would take the inner workings of her heart? Especially when they pertained to him. Any second now he might run for his horse and race for the safety of bachelorhood.

She stood up, shook the dust from her blue gingham skirt, and walked to the far side of the flames. The storm was still a good distance away, but it looked menacing. A sudden gust of wind tugged at the ribbon in her hair with greedy fingers. She hugged her arms about her middle against a sudden shiver.

Just now, Zane would be reading about his eyes. That was tame enough, but in a moment he would be reading about the shift of his muscles beneath his shirt. She turned at the waist to glance at him. No doubt he had read down the page and was shocked by her fantasy of that shirt gone missing.

Perhaps her mother had been correct in her view that a woman with a pen could only lead to social disorder. Missy should have remained on her piano bench as her brother had ordered. She liked the piano bench.

Missy turned back toward the storm on the horizon, but closed her eyes. Yes, the man did have a shape to make a woman weep and an inner virility that made her knees—and other places—quake.

And now he knew it. Along with knowing that his hands were made to touch her most intimate… Oh, mercy! Why couldn't he be reading about clouds or flowers or Muff's latest nibble?

At least he wasn't laughing. What was he doing, anyway? She spun back to look at him again. Lord have mercy if he hadn't flipped back to the beginning of the passage and started to read it again!

Maybe she ought to just walk away, stroll off across the prairie, never to be seen again. It would be easier than having to face him after what he had just discovered about her interest in the part of him hidden by his drawers.

"'With half a glance of his warm, whiskey eyes,'" the perverse man read out loud, "'I become a puddle of sticky syrup at his feet.'"

"It's not proper to read an author's work before its been edited," she explained, but doubted that the edited version would be less adoring.

Zane snapped the journal closed and set it on the blanket beside his hip. Missy returned her gaze to the show in the west. She heard footsteps crunching on the dirt, coming toward her.

A gust of wind howled along the ground, it swirled about her boots and up her legs. From a stand of trees several yards from the campfire Ace snorted. Daisy whickered.

"'The stroke of his hands against my flesh

makes it rise in a chill, even though I am steaming inside.'"

Evidently, the wash of his breath over her ear did the same thing.

"You are no gentleman, Zane Coldridge, reading a lady's private thoughts."

"I'm not reading." He nipped her earlobe. "I have it memorized."

"You cad."

"You temptress." He turned her about with his big hands, gentle yet firm on her shoulders. He pinned her with his whisky-colored eyes.

For pity sakes! She really was syrup at his feet.

"You bewitching little seductress," he murmured with his lips a hot breath over hers. "You've taken my miserable, independent life and made it yours."

"Have I?" She stood on a pinhead balanced between life as she had known it and a brand-new future. She couldn't breathe.

"You have." His mouth moved over hers, touching her lips with words. "Now, what do you intend to do with it?"

"Love you forever," she mumbled against his mouth but what she had to say was too important to be misunderstood so she pulled back half an inch. "I intend to love you forever."

"I'll take your forever, darlin', and give you mine." With his arm about her back pulling her close to his heart and the wide palm of his hand cradling the ribbon in her hair, he kissed her. "Wesley Wage be damned, we're changing course and heading for the nearest preacher."

Chapter Fourteen

Zane tried to stop kissing his brand-new intended—the preacher was only a day or so away—but Missy melted into him like…well, like sticky syrup.

It would be easier to find a thread of self-control if he kept his hands away from the front of her dress, but that skein had unraveled some time ago. To his chagrin, his fingers trembled over the buttons of her shirtwaist as though he had never touched a woman in his life.

His brain struggled weakly to understand the turn his life had taken. How had he gone from free as a dried-out tumbleweed to snared and willing in the course of a few days?

Oh, hell, maybe he had been snared from the very beginning. Maybe he ought to quit thinking, there was no way he was about to figure anything out. Not with his body in control of his reason. He ought to be alarmed. As a lover he had always been polite, always tenderly in control.

Somehow, Missy had turned him on his head, spun him about and left him with as much restraint as a bumbling adolescent.

It seemed a clumsy eternity, but he managed to free the pesky wood buttons. He slid the dress backward, over her shoulders. He pressed it down to her elbows, smoothing the goose bumps on her skin with his thumbs. All that stood between him and the heart of his captor was that flimsy shift dotted with fancy blue bows.

The preacher would have to wait, because he couldn't. He yanked on a bow. The lace that hid her from his gaze slid downward. Flashes of distant lightning flickered over fair skin.

He touched her with both hands. The backs of his fingers grazed her flesh. With his thumbs, he outlined the outer curves of breasts that would fill his palms. His knuckles circled pink buds that had grown tight and pebbled. Uncovered, she smelled of nectar, fresh, sweet and ripe.

"Do you want to wait for the minister?" His voice felt dry, like leather left out in the sun all summer. That was it for being polite and in self-control. He couldn't judge what he might do if she said yes.

"I wonder if it's after midnight. Really, there's no way of telling." She sighed, deep and full, pressing the plush weight of her breasts into his hands. "If it is, and we find a preacher in the morning, then this could be our wedding day."

"I don't suppose the preacher would begrudge us a couple of hours." The man would have to be made of rusty nails if he did, Zane thought.

Thunder rumbled in the distance, but the sound was faint. He could barely hear it over the thrumming of the blood through his veins. There was time and more to find shelter.

He swept Missy up and carried her toward the campfire and the blanket beside it. His steps were quick, scattering rocks and crunching twigs. Her bare bosoms jiggled against his flannel shirt. With every bodily sense aware, he heard the friction of flesh against worn cloth.

At the blanket's edge, he knelt with Missy cradled in his arms. The breeze caught her skirt and billowed it over her knees. Plain cotton stockings hugged her legs and borrowed an orange blush from the campfire.

The air began to smell damp but he refused to acknowledge any scent but the carnal flesh an inch from his nose.

He might have tasted the storm coming, but instead, he tasted Missy. The tip of her breast filled his mouth, plump and white-hot. He suckled and felt her pulse beating against the rasp of his tongue.

"I wish I'd figured out some things a long time

ago," he gasped, working to free her from the rest of her dress.

"Ordinarily, I'd hang on every word you had to say, Zane." She lifted her hips and in one movement he swept her free of every stitch. "Just now though, you might put your mouth to better use."

"Yes ma'am," he whispered against the curve of her waist and up her ribs. "I intend to do just that."

When Zane's mouth tugged at her breast she longed for him to kiss her mouth; when he kissed her mouth she ached for him to nuzzle her neck. She was greedy, her appetite for the man knew no limits. She wanted him to touch her everywhere at once.

She closed her eyes while his seduction washed over her in waves, tossing her up and up toward something that she needed as much as her next breath. She didn't know what that something was but it was so close that she felt she might pull apart.

Scratchy wool bit her bare behind. Flannel and denim skimmed her front when Zane's weight settled on top of her. His belt buckle pressed a cold rectangle on her belly, but upon contact with her searing skin it soon simmered.

Her body and her heart lay open to him. Her legs, pinned to the blanket beneath him, wanted to do the same.

She longed to open wide. Both her body and her soul had been like a flower bud all her life. Now, at the urging of the man pressing his hips in a slow grind on top of her, she needed to bloom.

The longing that made her body squirm settled in her womb. Her brain whispered some nonsense about modesty but the craving that had lodged in her nether regions knew better. It directed her, dizzied her and murmured that this was the way that bonded the souls of a man and a woman. "The two shall become one flesh," she remembered.

Sometime during the battle between modesty and desire, soft flannel turned to smooth, hot skin. Crisp denim became muscled legs rubbing along her inner thighs, gently pressing them open. The belt buckle on her belly had been replaced by something long, hard and hot.

This is where the souls would join. The heart of a man and love of a woman would interweave.

She opened her eyes. Zane was staring at her, his eyelids glistening.

Fireglow touched his arms, painting his biceps with bronze shadows. Amber and gold fingered his chest in a sensual dance of light. A lick of pulsing red seared her nipple where it tangled in the dark, coarse hair of Zane's chest.

"This is different, isn't it?" she whispered. He'd been with other women, probably many times, but this was different.

He nodded, the weight of his male part heavy against her belly. "So different, darlin'. My body's been through this dance before, but I swear, it's my first time."

A kiss came next. It started tenderly, a peck and a gentle embrace of lips while his hand stroked toward the center of her craving.

His big rough fingers parted her curls and hovered over her swollen flesh. As soon as his finger slid inside her folds and began to stroke, the kiss exploded into an inferno, hot and greedy. Her hips lifted, as though he were a composer drawing sensual notes from her body. She was an instrument, responding to his touch. The symphony he conducted within her reached toward the sky, climbing to somewhere she had never imagined.

When she thought she had surely reached the stars, she felt the pressure of his manhood replace his fingers. It pushed at her and she opened her legs.

He entered slowly and she closed around him, welcomed him with a thrust of her hips. He pushed back and they rocked together, hurtling toward the place that made them one flesh.

Zane sat beside the campfire with his open palms stretched toward the warmth of the flames. He gazed at Missy's form buried beneath the blanket with a foot of blond curls peeping out the top.

Under the bend of Zane's knees, Muff sat tall, keeping a close watch on the sky to the west. Once in a while he growled with his furry ears erect and twitching. With Zane's mother's ribbon tied in a bow about his neck, the little dog made a funny sight.

"It hasn't made a turn toward us yet, little man, but it could."

Muff leaped to his paws and barked at the dark where shadows moved in the wind beyond the campfire's glow.

"You need to quit your trembling. It won't make that storm go one way or another." He scooped Muff up and tucked him under the blanket with Missy.

The lace of Missy's shift and the curve of her breast brushed his hand when he snuggled the dog close to her.

"Sure love to crawl inside with you both, but I've got some walking and considering to do," he whispered.

What had happened had happened and he wouldn't change that for the world. This was his wedding day and he'd never felt better in his life. But there were some troubles that came with it and he needed a good airing to settle things into place.

He walked down a slope toward the stream, and then paced up and over a small knoll. He didn't go far but he needed a little distance to think over the great change his life had taken. If there were any disturbance at camp he would easily hear it.

First he would deal with his troubles, put them in their proper perspective, then move on to rejoice over the path he had taken, or more correctly, the path his bride-to-be had set him squarely upon.

Number one, the problem that niggled at his heart most insistently, was the telegram that he had sent to Edwin Devlin. If Missy ever found out about it, and he didn't see how she would not, she'd be hurt. She might be angry enough to turn her back on him for good. Who could blame her, really? To anyone looking from the outside, it would appear that he had drawn her in with sweet nothings only to keep her close at hand until he could collect the money from her brother.

Zane squatted beside the stream and listened to the water run over rocks and around reeds. The babbling rush ought to soothe his nerves but the number-two problem was nearly as big as number one.

Missy was from a world he didn't know and was sure he wouldn't fit in with. His own life of living from town to town, earning the anger of most people he met, was no life for a wife. And babies, how would he tote a family around after men like Wesley Wage?

Zane picked up a stone and skimmed it across the surface of the stream. Splash, splash, sink.

Like one problem, two problems, sunk in the water. And that's all there were, two, but they were big ones.

He stood up and began to pace. Sometimes ideas came with movement. Action, the regular setting of one foot after another, put his mind in an orderly place.

A shaft of moonglow sliced over his boot toe. He glanced heavenward to see the moon shining down through a break in the clouds.

The sight of the brave little moon breaking through the chaos of the storm made him stop and stare. In the past he hadn't been much for signs, but he studied it, wondering if maybe…

First thing, he would wake Missy and tell her about the wire to her brother. He'd tell her the truth and silence her anger with a declaration of his undying love. If she tried to leave him he would kiss her and kiss her again until she listened to reason.

To describe Missy as remarkable was to do her an injustice. She was everything good, pure and fun. It might take an hour or two, but she would forgive him.

Problem number two was easier. The answer reached right out to embrace him. The town of Dewton needed a sheriff. He could honor his mother's memory by protecting the growing population and keep his family safe at home in the process.

Zane leaped in the air with a shout. His problems had answers that would work! If they wouldn't, why would the moon be beaming out of the storm like it was?

He'd received, of all the unexpected things he had never expected, a magical sign. Missy would be pleased.

Suddenly the air rushed out of his lungs, his heart slammed against his rib cage and knocked him back half a dozen steps.

As he stared at the little moon pushing back the storm, a yellow-winged butterfly flitted up from the grass, followed by another and another until, across his line of vision, the sky appeared to be covered with them.

Impossible, but there it was, a horde of blue, yellow, red and gold wings glittering in the moonlight.

"I'll be damned," he whispered to the night. "I'll be hog-tied damned."

A rolling cloud smothered the moon, but he had seen what he had seen. There was more to life than his dried-out heart had ever dreamed of.

He let out another shout, but it was muted by the sound he had dreaded most this stressful, wonderful night.

The rumble of a freight train's engine shook the air, coming fast and straight. The ground shuddered even though the nearest train track was more than thirty miles away.

Zane ran toward camp but the distance back was longer than he had remembered. His boots seemed made of lead. Rain lashed his face with big stinging drops that blurred the land before him. The distant rumble grew so loud that he could not hear his boots pounding on the earth.

He cursed himself for giving in to the whim to walk off his problems. It had been pure folly to let Missy out of his sight on a night like this.

Wind pressed Zane backward. Leaning into it, he fought for every step toward the dimming campfire. Wet hair whipped across his face, stinging his eyes.

Violent gusts buffeted him from side to side, back and forth. Sand and bits of flying grass pelted his hands and head. He raised his arm to shield his vision.

Where was Missy? He'd expected her to be standing, fearfully clutching Muff to her middle, looking for the man who should have been there to shield her.

The blanket she had been sleeping under had blown and snagged on the pair of saddles lying a few feet from the dying fire.

A woman in a white shift shouldn't be hard to spot in the dark, but all that met his gaze was hurtling debris. Perilously close, the tornado swept over the earth, roaring and sucking up everything in its path. Through the glare of fractured lightning he watched its long funnel eat up the land.

"Missy!" he shouted, but couldn't hear his voice. "Miii-sss-y!"

Prairie sod, no longer firm under his boots, looked as though it had taken on unnatural life, as though it had become ocean waves, but made of sand and torn-up sections of sod.

The horses were missing as well as Missy. Swaying on his feet, trying to hold on against the wind, he prayed that Missy had taken the animals and now rode toward safety.

Surely that is what she had done. Right now she was probably looking for him, riding into peril because he had felt the need to go walking about.

God forgive him.

"Ace!" he yelled, knowing that it was beyond hope that the good animal would hear him. He let out a shrill whistle, even knowing the horse was gone.

A flash revealed the shimmer of something stuck in the blanket that flailed over Ace's saddle.

Mercifully, the wind shifted. The freight-train noise grew more distant. The ground settled under his feet and he was able to dash toward the saddle.

He yanked the pearl-tipped thing from the blanket, pricking his palm.

It was a hat pin.

Missy's hat pin. The very one he had last seen buried in the fleeing behind of Wesley Wage.

Chapter Fifteen

Missy tugged against the twine binding her wrists. The narrow brown cord was wrapped so tight that it felt like barbed wire cutting into her flesh. A pair of red welts was all she had gained for her struggles.

Good and truly trapped on Number Nine, with Wesley Wage's rigid arms about her, she tried to think of a way out of this mess.

Today was her wedding day and she would not spend it as a captive to a bank robber…or, as seemed increasingly likely, swallowed alive by a tornado.

Before this day was done, she would stand before the preacher and become Mrs. Zane Cold-ridge, legally wedded and bedded.

"You are no gentleman, Mr. Wage." The fitful wind caught her words and blew them back at his face.

Behind her, she heard the wanted man chuckle. She leaned forward so that she wouldn't feel the ripple of it against her back.

"That is a fact, Miss Devlin," he yelled over the war cry of the storm. "Though I was raised to the highest of social standards."

"Let me down, you fool!" she yelled back. She jabbed backward with her elbow but only brushed the cloth of his dandified coat. This earned another humorless chuckle.

With two riders on her back, Number Nine struggled. The horse tried her best to outdistance the sweeping funnel cloud that seemed closer by the minute, but the poor animal was a stable rental, surely frightened and longing for the comfort of her stall.

"What was that, Miss Devlin? I can't seem to hear you over the wind."

Aunt Hattie's left foot! What was she to do now? If it were simply a matter of her own survival, she could ride along with the villain until a moment of escape presented itself. But with Ace and Daisy tied to Number Nine's stirrups, Zane was stuck. Without a horse, he might not survive.

Missy shivered, but not from the damp weight of the air. She thought that she could free the horses, but there would be a loss involved. The cost of freeing them would likely break her heart.

She stiffened her back, set her mind, turning it away from the hurtful truth that saving Zane would likely cost her Muff.

The pup was tied up in Number Nine's saddle pack and once she got the horses free, there wouldn't be time to free him.

The brave little dog didn't deserve to be left behind. He had acted like the biggest and bravest of canines while Wage was abducting her.

The villain had come upon her during a sweet dream of flowers and wedding vows. She had assumed that the man holding her hands together was Zane until Muff started to bark as fierce as though he was a full-grown wolf and she opened her eyes.

Before her mind understood that she should fight, the twine had been secured about her wrist, her mouth clamped over by Wage's soft, stringy hand.

While she had been biting and kicking her assailant, Muff had chomped onto the man's ankle and pant leg. A wild beast could not have been half as brave.

In the end, Wage had produced her pearl-tipped hat pin, pointed it at Muff's throat and ordered her up on the horse. Her plea to leave Muff behind had been turned down. It seemed that Muff was the price of her cooperation.

Now, she was faced with the unthinkable.

She would be forced to leave her little protector behind.

One thing mattered…freeing Ace. If she didn't, Zane might be killed. Even as bold and brave as her intended was, he couldn't outrun a tornado.

She turned around, looking up the long pinched nose of her kidnapper. Her hair flew about his half-bald head like slapping fingers. "Let Zane's horse go, I'll do anything you ask."

"I truly would be a fool to do that, now, wouldn't I? I aim to collect that price on your head."

"Clearly, this storm has addled your brain. You are the criminal with the price on his head."

"Play the innocent, then, maybe you are. It makes no difference either way."

So be it, he'd slammed the easy door in her face. She would pick her moment then leave her best little friend in the care of an unprincipled criminal, and a brain-addled one to boot.

"You are a fool to the bone," She shouted in his face. "But are you a killer, too?"

"You offend me, Miss Devlin. In my line of work there is the occasional and unavoidable act of violence, but so far, no killing," he called. "I assure you, I'm the highest-minded of criminals."

"Kidnapping women and puppies while they sleep is less than admirable!"

He cocked his head and arched a razor-thin eyebrow. A pea-sized ball of hail smacked him between the eyes. "You'll barely be bruised by the adventure…and according to your journal, you are quite fond of adventure."

"There's adventure and there's madness, you fool." This was not adventure. This was life and death.

"And Zane?" She longed to scratch Wage's face, to rip at him with her teeth, but her bound hands prevented her. "You'd let him die?"

"He's a resourceful man. In my experience, he keeps turning up like a bad penny." A sudden gust buffeted them so that Wage had to grab tight to Missy to keep his balance in the saddle. "You'll make me comfortable, Miss Devlin. Financially speaking, that is. I don't intend to lose you. With his horse restored, Coldridge would be on us like a shot."

Suddenly, the wind felt like a living creature… a demon let out of the underworld. It plucked at the roots of her hair; it stole her breath and roared in her ears.

The funnel that had been dogging them was so close now that Missy sensed a change in air pressure. It was likely that she and Wage would die in the next moment or two, but not before she gave Zane his chance.

The wind pushed. Hail beat down, stinging like an attack of bees. Wage fought to stay in the saddle while urging the terrified horses away from the sucking center of the storm.

Escape was simple. Missy leaned sideways,

with the draw of the wind. Wage toppled and Missy landed hard on his groin. He squealed, piggy-like.

She scrambled to her feet. Half-blinded by sand and debris, she felt her way along Number Nine's neck and shoulder until she came to the place where Ace's reins were secured.

With her hands tied and numbed by ice pellets, she couldn't manage the knot. The leather was stiff; her petticoat blew about, snapping at her fingers and obscuring her view of the tangled leather.

Too soon, Wesley Wage struggled to his feet, buffeted to and fro while grabbing his crotch. He hobbled toward Missy, shoved her hands away from the knot then untied it.

He slapped Ace's rump. The horse trotted several yards away and pranced in a nervous circle.

"There!" Wage shouted and grabbed her hands. "The damned animal's free, now get back on the horse."

"I won't!" She raised her knee, threatening his injured area. He let go of her bound wrists.

"If you don't come with me you're going to get sucked up in that thing!"

She reached for the saddlebag, but that knot fought her as well. Muff whimpered inside. Wage spun her around.

"Look, Miss Devlin, come or don't, I'm out

of here." He pulled into the saddle, fighting the gusts that tried to blow him down.

He stared down at her, his eyes grown round and lidless with fright. He reached for her with flexing fingers.

She stumbled backward, shaking her head, her hair wild and hissing like Medusa's serpents. Suddenly the hail quit.

"Two thousand dollars isn't worth my life!" he yelled, then kicked Number Nine hard in the side. He rode away with Daisy bouncing behind.

Missy ran and stumbled. Up again, she covered her face with her arms to protect it from gusts that came from every way at once. She plodded in a direction that she hoped was away from the twister's path. With the noise, with the prairie being heaved and spewed about, she couldn't tell.

Beside her she recognized the solid thump of Ace's hooves.

"Run!" She shooed her arms at him. "Go find Zane!"

Instead of running, the big horse leaned against her. She grabbed onto his mane and twisted her trussed-up hands in it.

She let the horse drag her, while she held on for dear life, praying all the while that Zane was in a safer place.

Daybreak shone bright without a cloud in sight. Neither was Missy in sight.

Tracking was impossible with the ground torn up as it was. The path that three horses would have taken had become unreadable.

With his hat blown probably back to Luminary, the sun shone bright in his face. Heat waves blurred the horizon. He shaded his eyes with his hand but the land gave nothing away.

An hour of walking toward the east revealed nothing. For no reason other than to ease the strain on his eyes, he turned north. One direction was as good as another since he had no idea where Wage had taken Missy.

Two hours north proved futile so he turned west. His shadow, this early in the morning, stretched long and for three more hours was his only company.

Before he met Missy, his shadow had been the only company that he required most of the time. Now, without her, every second stretched out long and full of emptiness.

"Where are you, darlin'?" he whispered. All at once he shouted, "Missy!"

With any luck, Wage had gotten them away from the tornado. So far he hadn't found what he feared the most. In all his hours of searching he hadn't seen any sign of death for woman or beast.

If Wage hadn't gotten them safe away, Zane would have found the evidence closer to camp. This reasoning gave him hope since he had searched the area thoroughly last night. But in the dark he might have missed something. He turned to walk southeast, toward last night's campfire. He couldn't leave the area until he knew for sure Missy wasn't out here, wounded and needing him.

Only after he searched every square inch of the area would he give up and go after Wage. If he had to follow to hell or beyond, he would find the man and, he prayed, his own wife-to-be.

He was within five miles of camp when he spotted the buzzards. A dozen or more circled in the crystal sky, not even a mile to the west.

It wasn't Missy they were waiting on…it was a wolf, or a deer. Maybe even Wage. But not his Missy.

He began to run. It was wildlife that the vultures waited for. Wildlife…wildlife…wildlife…

Then he spotted Ace, still a quarter of a mile in the distance, standing over a heap of white lace lying still as death. He didn't need to see blue bows before he roared a curse and raced forward on legs burning with a last surge of energy.

He collapsed to his knees, his lungs aching with the run and the grief. He pushed Missy's hair away where it covered her face. Even under a crusting of grime, her skin looked too pale.

"Missy?" He touched her cheek, then her throat, feeling for a pulse. She wouldn't be dead yet, otherwise the carrion birds wouldn't still be circling. He rejected the thought that it was Ace's presence keeping them aloft.

Ace whinnied and nudged his shoulder.

"There it is, fella. Just a flutter but it's there." He patted Ace's nose. A lifetime of luxurious care could not repay the horse for standing beside Missy through a tornado.

Zane ran his hands over her body, checking for broken bones. Everything seemed intact. Nothing broken, no obvious bleeding, what, then?

He lifted her shoulders and eased behind her. Pray God that he wasn't making an injury on the inside worse.

He touched her head, feeling her scalp through her hair. There had to be some kind of injury keeping her unconscious.

He found swelling at the back of her skull and a small cut.

"Missy, darlin', wake up."

Silence, deep and complete, answered him.

Had Missy not been unconscious she would have exclaimed over the charming house they were approaching. Since she seemed closer to dead than alive, cradled against him in the saddle, he did the exclaiming for her.

"Just look at that!" Who knew what a person in her state might hear and rouse to. "Right out here in the middle of nowhere there's a pretty yellow house with flowers blooming in window boxes…and lace curtains, too. Blamed if I don't see a pie cooling on the windowsill."

He glanced down to see if his words had any effect. If she were herself, Missy would be dragging out her copybook and writing everything down.

"You know, darlin'," he said against her cheek, "your writing tools didn't get blown away. You recall how I tucked them into my saddle pack for safekeeping? I told you how precious those words were to me? Well, after I found you we went back by way of camp and picked up Ace's saddle. Everything was inside the way I left it."

No response, not even a twitch of an eyebrow.

"That's all right. We'll send for a doctor. You'll be yourself in no time."

But Zane was not himself and never would be again. That other man, the one he had been before Missy, he never wanted to be again. Even though pain wrenched his insides, he welcomed it. He welcomed life.

Before he had loved Missy, his emotions lay close to the surface. They never went deep, for joy or for sorrow. Over the years his line of work had turned him that way.

His former line of work, that is. Now that his soul had woken up he could no longer face the grievous side of the profession.

On Missy's behalf, he admired the pretty quaintness of the house. She would be surprised when she woke up and discovered that she was not so far from the place where her adventures had begun. Luminary was an easy ride away.

A day's ride south was Dewton. That's where he would build Missy a home, like this one, and take up the career of lawman.

He took note of the details of the house, setting them in his mind for the near future. Shade trees anchored it at both ends and flowers in full bloom edged the walk to the front door.

A pair of rocking chairs on the front porch and more pots of posies in bloom declared that friendly folks lived inside. A painted sign hung on the white picket fence: The Reverend Raymond Gilroy, it read.

He would need the services of Reverend Gilroy the moment that Missy woke up. For now, he needed a place for her to recover. Surely they would not be turned away from the home of a man of God.

If it had been the man of God stepping out on the front porch he would not have told what some might consider a bold-faced lie. To Zane it was only a minor stretch of the truth.

But the woman greeting him with her hands folded at her waist looked less welcoming than a snapping turtle.

She resembled the creature, too, with a sharp beak of a nose and a shallow chin. Her high-necked collar looked like a shell that was too tight to pull her head into. He felt a jab of pity for her until she opened her mouth.

"Another whore from Luminary for Reverend Gilroy to redeem?" She frowned, gazing through slits in eyes so piercing that they could likely spot every indiscretion between here and town. "And this one not even decently clothed. Is she drunk as well?"

"Mrs. Gilroy—"

"That's Miss Gilroy, and kindly keep riding. This is no place for her kind."

Miss Gilroy sniffed, turned on her heel and ran smack into a man coming out the door.

"Please excuse my sister," the man said, looking at Zane with apology. He blocked his sister's retreat into the house. "Hortense, as we have discussed in the past, this is exactly the place for her kind."

"Her kind," Zane said through gritted teeth, "is my wife. She was injured in the tornado last night. We need shelter and a doctor."

"By all means." The reverend, a tall, muscular man with apparent strength to spare, rushed down the flowered path and reached for Missy. "Please, make your horse comfortable in the barn, it appears the animal has been through an ordeal as well."

The preacher, clearly much younger than his sister, bounded up the steps with Missy cradled in his arms.

"Hortense," the preacher directed, "prepare the guest room."

"She is hardly dressed, Raymond. You will bring shame on us both."

"Don't be a prude. This woman is a lamb of God, the same as you, clothing not withstanding."

Zane watched Hortense Gilroy's stiff gait as she followed her brother into the house.

One of the Gilroys might be a lamb, for all his size, but the other was a snapping turtle with a wicked bite.

"I remember your lady." Dr. James Griffen inspected the back of Missy's head, probing gently with long slender fingers.

"My wife," Zane corrected because Miss Gilroy stood in the doorway, listening.

"Your wife?" The doctor touched Missy's wrist, checking her pulse, then he listened to her heart through his stethoscope. "She did what she could for that poor girl, Harriet. Not many folks would have. No sirree, Luminary hasn't been the same since she wrecked Pete's saloon."

A loud sniff brought Zane's and Dr. Griffen's attention to the doorway, but all that remained of Hortense Gilroy was a flash of her starched skirt.

"Did Pete rebuild?" Zane asked, uncomfortable with Missy being only miles from that greedy man.

"No, he's moved on. Some say to one wild

place, some say to another. With Pete gone, there's talk of the town going respectable. There are rumors of a school and a church, even a music hall. People still talk about your wife and her skill at the piano. There's a fresh wind blowing through Luminary and it doesn't leave room for a place like Pete's. Even Maybelle is considering taking on a partner and turning her place into a hotel."

The doctor rolled up his stethoscope and put it in his bag.

"Will my wife be all right?"

"She took a blow of some kind to the back of her head. I'm afraid there isn't much I can do to help. Modern medicine can't cure everything. When it comes to the brain it's hard to predict."

Zane felt as though the floor had opened under his chair. "What can I do?"

"Read to her. Talk to her. There's so much we don't know about head injuries, but it makes sense that keeping her mind stimulated might bring her around." He touched Missy's forehead with his palm. "If there's something that you know she hankers for, offer it to her. And pray."

"I'll admit that my knees have become a bit rusty of late."

"A common ailment, son, but easily cured." Dr. Griffen picked up his bag and walked toward the hallway door. He turned before closing it and smiled. "I'll be in Luminary for a day or two if you need me. There's a new baby coming. It's quite the occasion for the town since its ma and pa are legally wed."

"Thanks, Doc."

Things were changing in the Wild West. Civilization was coming as fast as the trains could carry it.

He was changing, too. Now, as his knees hit the floor, he was aware of the lie standing between him and his prayer.

He wouldn't mind discussing this with the good reverend; his job was all about dealing with sinners. It was the sister that would keep him quiet, though. A private word in this house would be impossible with her ears hearing every secret confessed behind a closed door.

Zane hadn't expected to find a collection of dime novels at the parsonage, but it seemed that the Reverend Gilroy had developed a fondness for them when a "wounded dove" had left them behind on her way to respectability.

"Johnny Swiftdraw Encounters the Indian Chief Great Thunder Sky," Zane read the title out loud. "Darlin', you sure you like this stuff?"

As he had expected, she gave no response, not even a twitch of an eyebrow to show that she had heard him. Still, he thumbed the worn pages until he had read the story to her, cover to cover.

"Here's one about a bounty hunter." It must

have been someone's favorite for the pages nearly
fell apart in his hand. After an hour, he closed the
book. "Sorry to say so, but there wasn't an ounce
of truth in this one, either."

"It's all trash." The spinster Gilroy stood in the
doorway with a tray in her hands. "See if you can
get some of this broth down her. It will do her
more good than those nasty words."

Zane stood up, crossed the floor and took the
tray from her.

"Some folks live and breathe the adventure
between these pages. Look, they're nearly worn
through."

Zane set the tray on a table beside the bed.
Steam rose from the bowl in a swirl of life-giving
nutrients that he doubted Missy would be able
to swallow.

Hour by hour his worry had grown. How long
could a body last without food or drink?

Hortense Gilroy snorted through her beaked
nose. "Empty minds filled with foolish thoughts,
if you ask me."

There had been a time when he'd thought the
same. But Missy didn't have an empty mind.
What he used to consider foolish thoughts had
turned out to be wisdom, a fresh and joyful look
at a weary world.

Zane knew he shouldn't do it, but the smug set
of Hortense's mouth as she gazed down at Missy

pushed him toward an act that he would regret in the morning, maybe.

"You are a wise woman, Miss Gilroy, this is trash." Apparently her vanity had been appeased. She gave him a stiff, superior-looking smile and a nod. "Here is something that my wife wrote that I think you might find...well, educational."

"Anything of an educational nature in this house would be uplifting. Please, Mr. Coldridge, do read it."

He shouldn't do it really, but he reached for Missy's journal where he had placed it in her motionless hand, hoping that she might sense it and come around.

The pages fell open to one of his favorite passages, one that he had read over and over, to himself and to his bride-to-be.

He cleared his throat and swallowed a gulp of self-reproach. Still, it would do Miss Hortense Gilroy good to learn an ounce of humility.

"'My breasts swell with yearning,'" he read aloud and with confidence. "'The very nipples twisting with the need to be touched. Not only by his strong brown fingers...'"

Miss Gilroy turned pale. One hand clenched nervously at her tightly buttoned bodice. The skinny fingers of her other hand looked like bleached sticks splayed across her belly. She didn't appear to be breathing.

He was wicked and couldn't stop even though

the spinster's face had blossomed with crimson splotches. "'…but…his…suckling…lips.'" This last he drew out for emphasis and, mercy forgive him, he smacked his mouth.

"You—" she gasped in a lungful of air "—are vile!"

"And you are not the first to have noticed."

She backed out of the room with both hands pressed to her flaming cheeks. "Vulgarity…and in this house of all places. My brother will hear of this."

"What happens between a man and his wife is holy, Hortense, not vulgar."

To say that he and Missy were man and wife stretched the truth a bit, but what was between them did feel holy. If she hadn't been hit in the head, this would be their wedding day.

A few moments later, he guessed that Reverend Gilroy was hearing about the vulgarity under his very roof. The intensity of his laughter booming down the hall must have brought the man to his knees.

The front door slammed. Miss Gilroy showed off a temper that probably left the hinges bent. With all that he would be happy never to cross paths with Hortense again, Raymond Gilroy was a man he might like to call friend.

Hortense, pleading a sick headache, took dinner in her room.

Raymond turned out to be pleasant company, a

compassionate man with a robust sense of humor. If Missy hadn't been sick to death in the other room Zane would have liked to pass an hour or two at the table with him. As it was, though, every minute spent away from her stretched like an hour.

"There must be something we've not thought of to bring your wife around," the reverend said, twirling a dollop of cream into his cup of after-dinner coffee.

Zane's brew sat in front of him, untouched. He watched the steam curl across the dining table as though an idea might come swirling out of the vapor.

"Has she any family?"

Zane nodded. He'd made every effort to keep a step ahead of her folks, but now he would have to let them know what had happened to their girl.

"In Boston. A mother, brother and twin sister." He tapped his dinner fork on his plate. "I'll send them a wire first thing tomorrow."

"Boston, that's a long way off." Raymond swallowed a deep swig of his coffee then added more cream. "They will be some time in getting here."

But come they would, and without Zane having admitted to Missy his sorry role in the whole bounty mess.

In the beginning, contacting Edwin had been simple business and the best way to keep Missy safe. Falling in love was something he had never anticipated. If she discovered what he had done before he had a chance to explain, she might see his actions as the worst sort of betrayal.

None of that could be helped now, her life was at stake and she needed her family. If she didn't come around before they arrived and he didn't get a chance to explain…well, he'd dwell on that problem later. For now he waited, living for every twitch in her sleep to be her awakening, praying to see her beautiful blue eyes blink open.

"What does your wife favor, other than—" Raymond grinned in the direction of his sister's open bedroom door then whispered "—literature?"

In spite of his heavy heart, Zane grinned back. "Well now, there's…" He stood so abruptly that his chair fell backward, clattering on the floor. "Her dog, Muff!"

The reverend looked puzzled. "I don't recall seeing a dog."

"I assumed he had been lost in the storm, but maybe not." There was a chance that he was with Wage.

"A good-sized dog might have made it to safety."

"The mutt does have a good-sized spirit." Zane set the chair to rights. "I'll go looking for him… now…tonight, if you can do me the favor of caring for my wife."

"I'll tend to her as if she were my own sister." He rolled his eyes and shrugged. "Make that my own dear cousin."

"I can pay you for your trouble," Zane said, backing toward Missy's room and anxious to be on his way. He should have thought of Muff hours ago.

The Reverend Raymond Gilroy raised his hands, palms out. "No need. I'm pleased to be of help."

"There you go again, brother," came the whiney voice of his bitter sister, from somewhere down the hall. "We could use that money and you well know it."

"She wasn't always so…" Raymond shrugged his shoulders again. "I pray for her hourly. And don't worry about that wire, I'll ride to Luminary and send it first thing in the morning."

"Much obliged." A short thanks, Zane knew, but every second mattered when finding a small white dog on a vast and dangerous prairie.

Inside Missy's room, he rummaged through his saddlebag, making sure he had what he needed for a fast trip.

After the quick check, he knelt beside the bed. Lord, if Missy didn't seem smaller and paler every time he looked at her.

"I've got to go, darlin', but just for a little while. I'm going to find Muff." Did her eyes twitch just now? He'd bet his life they did. "Hold on, Missy, don't you go anywhere. We'll have our wedding day. Soon as I come back that's just what we'll do."

This time, her eyes rolled as though she was struggling toward the surface. The sooner he found that scrap of dog, the sooner he would have his intended back.

He kissed her lips then dashed out of the room.

In his rush to be on his way, Zane nearly plowed down Hortense, who was passing in front of Missy's doorway. Her sour frown would be enough to curdle the dinner he had left on his plate.

As he rushed through the dining room, toward the front door, he snatched a biscuit that he hadn't had the appetite for earlier.

Action was what he needed. Somehow he would find that pup and bring him back to Missy's arms. She would wake and they would begin a new life together.

Light penetrated Missy's closed eyes. The storm must be right on top of her for the lightning to appear so bright. She tried to open her lids but they felt like raw steaks dredged in sand.

Instead of thunder she heard the rustle of fabric, like a starched skirt, maybe a stiff petticoat... and a snort.

With the greatest effort she cracked her eyes open for half a second and saw a woman standing in the corner of a room holding a piece of paper in her hands. Oddly, it looked like a wanted poster.

What on earth? Where was she and how had she gotten here? The last Missy remembered was digging her fingers into Ace's mane and holding on for dear life, desperate to find...

"Zane?" Her voice clogged in her throat with all the clarity of mud. The effort of whispering his name made her feel as if she had competed in an uphill race and come in last.

Footsteps clicked across a wood floor. She forced her eyes open, calling on the pitiful bit of strength that she had.

The woman stood at the foot of the bed, frowning...no, wait, smirking?

Well, she was in a bed, that much she knew. If she had gotten to a place of shelter, maybe Zane was the one who'd brought her here.

"Zane?" she managed again.

The woman at the foot of the bed was very definitely smirking and...staring at Missy's chest?

"Gone," she stated, and Missy didn't know another thing until she woke again in the dark and found a man sitting beside her bed reading a dime novel by candlelight.

He laughed at something and shook his head. Fair brown hair that seemed to carry a dose of sunshine in it flopped over his brow. He skimmed it back, revealing cheerful brown eyes.

He squinted, reading by candlelight.

"I think you might like this one." With his eyes tracking the words, he tapped one finger on the page. "It's all about a bounty hunter who comes face-to-face with—"

"His mother's image on a wanted poster," she mumbled.

"Well, now!" The smiling man set aside the book and leaned forward with his elbows on his knees. "Welcome back, Mrs. Coldridge, you gave us quite a scare."

Mrs. Coldridge? My word, she must have missed some important events since the storm, like her own wedding.

"My...husband?"

"He brought you here, yesterday noonish."

Praise be, they were safe, both of them alive. She closed her eyes while relief washed over her. Once again she heard the scratching of a stiff skirt.

She opened her eyes to see the starch-like woman standing in the doorway.

"I'm the Reverend Raymond Gilroy and this is my sister, Hortense Gilroy. We are pleased to have you staying with us."

Clearly, the reverend was pleased. Welcome shone in his smile and genuine hospitality warmed his eyes. His sister looked as though a rodent had just scurried across the room.

"I don't know how I can thank you, Reverend. I don't remember anything since the storm."

"You wouldn't, you've been out since your husband found you unconscious and brought you here."

Not married, then. Zane would have said they were for appearances' sake.

"Is he hurt?" She turned her head to look for him—surely he would be at her side if he weren't—but the simple motion made it feel as though rocks were rolling around in her brain.

"Lie back, now." The reverend touched her shoulder. "You've been through an ordeal and need your rest. Hortense, bring Mrs. Coldridge some of that broth, if you will?"

Hortense answered with a frown, but she turned with a snap of petticoats and marched from the room.

"Don't worry about Zane, he's not hurt, but plenty worried. We all were."

"Where is he?"

"On a fool's errand, if you ask me," Hortense mumbled, coming back with the cup of broth. "Of course, no one would…ask me, that is."

"Thank you, Hortense, I'll help Mrs. Coldridge." He looked at his sister, his eyes alight with brotherly mischief. "I'm sure you've got a kitten to torture or a puppy to drown."

Raymond Gilroy lifted Missy's head and put the cup to her lips.

"Please forgive Hortense," he said. "Our puppies and kittens are perfectly safe. Sometimes I like to see if I can surprise a smile out of her."

After she finished the broth he lowered her head to the pillow.

"We were all worried about you. The doctor told Zane to think of things that were important to you. He read you books, but in the end he went after your little dog. He didn't want to leave but nothing was bringing you around."

"Muff!" How he must be suffering. Wesley Wage would be more likely to abandon him than care for him.

"There now, don't cry." He took her hands and wrapped his big ones around them. "Let's say a prayer together for their safe return."

While the reverend talked with God about keeping Muff safe on the open land, she prayed with him that He would return both future husband and pup to her unharmed.

In Missy's estimation, the reason for Hortense Gilmore's foul disposition was clear. Each morning the woman put on clothes that were scratchy, stiff and utterly suffocating.

With spring in full bloom, who wouldn't be driven to distraction by the high-necked garments of drab wool? Mercy, but it seemed that everything the unfortunate Hortense owned displayed various shades of gray.

Sitting on the front-porch rocker with a bowl

of snap peas in her lap, Missy decided she could easily smother in the charcoal-colored threads of the borrowed gown she wore.

Snap a pea at one end, peel off the string, snap the other end. Watch, snap and watch again for Zane's return. That had been her occupation for the last couple of days. Raymond must have plucked every pea from his lovely garden just to give her something to do.

Hortense turned the corner of the house, carrying a pail full of water. She passed in front of one of the prettiest flower borders Missy had ever seen. Red hollyhock and blue delphinium made the dress she wore look even more depressing. How could the wearer of such a frock help but be anything but downcast?

But wait! If she wasn't mistaken, Hortense smiled as she dribbled water onto the flowers.

"Your flowers are beautiful, Miss Gilroy," she called out. "You must have a knack for growing them."

Hortense jumped, most certainly startled. She dumped out the rest of the water, drowning one small purple posy just poking its head above the soil. She glanced toward the porch with her customary frown. Missy was sure she saw a kitten dash for cover.

"What I have is a chore. It's my dear little brother who sets out all these…weeds then expects me to care for them."

"Just the same, they are lovely."

"Humph!" Hortense dropped the bucket. She mounted the stairs with her back stiff. "Water and weed, and all for what? The whores and sinners to enjoy?"

"Your brother seems like a wonderful man." Missy tasted a pea. The flavor was as sweet as Hortense was sour.

"I suppose he—" She shook her head, folded her hands primly at her waist. "Wonderful doesn't stick his sister out in the middle of nowhere with only jackrabbits for company."

Clearly, Hortense needed companionship. A trip to town would be just the thing. New clothes might cheer her, something cooler with a dash of froth and color.

"Hortense, we should make a trip to Dewton, the two of us. We could shop for summer gowns."

"And give up your perch here on the porch?" She sniffed and looked down her nose.

"After Zane returns, naturally." Missy wasn't about to budge from her perch until her man and her dog rode into the yard.

"It's been two days or more. Really, how long do you think it takes to find a dog, or its corpse? That man is gone. He's stolen what he wants from you and now…well, now he…" She reached in the pocket of her dress and pulled out a folded sheet of paper. "He isn't coming back. They never do."

With a flick of her wrist she unfolded the paper

and dropped it. The broadsheet drifted onto the bowl of snap peas. Missy gasped at her likeness staring up at her.

"This fell out of his belongings. I guess he was in such a hurry to get away and collect that reward he didn't notice."

"If he was in a hurry, it was to find Muff." What the bitter Hortense didn't know is that Muff wasn't lost on the prairie. It would take Zane a good long while to rescue him from Wage.

"Tell yourself that, then, Miss Devlin. But in the long run it will hurt all the more."

"Not all men are like the one who hurt you, Hortense."

Missy scanned the wanted poster, reading and rereading what her brother had posted. She ought to be angry for his interference in her life, but instead, her heart swelled with affection. In spite of what he had to believe was another one of her follies, he had posted a huge amount of money to see her safely home.

"Men are what they are." Hortense stared down at her, surely not aware that the lines tugging the corners of her mouth spoke of secret pain. "Name one who isn't a liar to his core."

"Zane Coldridge for one, my brother and yours."

"I don't know your brother, but I do know mine." Even though Hortense looked at her with venom, Missy wasn't sure that her intention was to cause pain so much as to express her own.

"Your…whatever that man is to you…lied when he claimed you were his wife and lied again when he lit out of here. It's been time and enough to find that dog."

Hortense Gilroy crossed her arms over her cinched-flat bosom and stared out past the flower garden.

"One would think he would give it up and come racing back to your side, with you all but on your deathbed," she said. "You can bet your tainted soul that he lied about rescuing little Fluff…or whatever."

A soul was not a thing to be bargained, but Zane was coming back. She'd bet her next breath on it.

Chapter Sixteen

"That woman will bring shame on this house, mark my words." Hortense's voice carried through the open window. Eavesdropping hadn't been Missy's intention, but bent over the flowerbed just below the window, she clearly heard the conversation.

Along with Hortense's bitter words came the scent of freshly baked peach pie. Pie-baking, it seemed, was Hortense's redeeming grace.

Late last night when Missy had been unable to sleep, the reverend had sat up with her. He apologized six times over for his sister. Her story was a sad one, made heart-wrenching by the fact that she had become so bitter.

According to the reverend, there had been a time when Hortense had been as fun-loving as the next girl, sweet and trusting even. But then

she met a man who loved her pies overmuch and
claimed to love Hortense, too. The fellow was
a cad, and her brother had tried to warn her so,
but Hortense had set her cap and wouldn't listen
to good sense. She planned to elope. Hortense
waited on the front porch from dusk until dawn
with her satchel on her lap, but her beau had run
off that same night with a whore from Luminary. Hortense decided the tragedy was due to
Raymond's negative attitude. All that remained
of the sister he had known was her skill with a
rolling pin.

"It's only a hat." Raymond's voice carried out
the window. "And who is going to see it but the
two of us?"

"It's red…with indecent feathers sticking out
of it, for mercy sake."

Missy bent over, plucked a flower and stuck
it in Emily's hat. She patted the purple blossom,
remembering the painted face of her generous,
if fallen, friend.

"She can't stay here, Raymond. That man is
never coming back. All he wanted was money."

"If that's the case, Hortense, Miss Devlin will
need our friendship. Can't you even offer that?"

"And when she turns up in a family way, what
then?"

"Try and remember what your knees are for,
Hortense. I don't even know who you are any-
more."

A door slammed inside. Seconds later footsteps pounded across the dining-room floor and stopped at the open window above the spot where Missy knelt with a handful of crushed peonies.

Raymond glanced down, saw her and closed his eyes, his breath hissing through his teeth.

"I'm sorry you heard that. Truly, I don't know what to say."

"This hat was a gift from a woman in Luminary." Thank goodness the personal treasure had been stored in Zane's saddle pack during the storm. "One of Maybelle's girls, but a dear friend all the same."

Raymond rested his hands on the windowsill and leaned out. "Maybe I know her, then, in a professional sense. My profession, that is, not hers."

"Emily."

"Emily Perkins? Emily and I have had some wonderful conversations." Raymond reached out the window. "Here, let me take those and plunk them in some water and see if they revive."

"Reverend, what your sister said is true." Missy looked up through the sunlight. "Zane and I are not married yet. And…well, I could be in a family way." She handed up the flowers. "I guess you should know that."

His smile down at her was warm and without hesitation. "In my experience, weddings and christenings don't always follow that order."

Hers was one wedding that would happen first. Zane was coming back, no matter what Hortense thought. Any day now he would come riding in with Muff.

A black voice in the back of her brain reminded her of the West that Zane knew. In that brutal place anything could happen. Through no choice of his own, Zane might not be able to come back.

"I need to go to Luminary, Reverend. It's long past time I wired my family and let them know where I am."

The next morning Missy sat on the buckboard, wedged between the Gilroys.

"If you'd rather eat nails than go to Luminary, Hortense, you should have stayed home," the reverend said.

Hortense sniffed the air. Craning her neck, she peered at clouds hanging like a dirty sheet over the sky.

"That, brother dear, was a cruel thing to say."

"Hortense is sensitive to severe weather," he said. "She hides in a closet and—"

Hortense turned her face toward her brother, her mouth snapping open and closed, apparently seeking words to express her outrage.

"That's where I'd be," Missy vowed quickly. "I've been through two storms out here and let me tell you, they are not like the ones back home."

Hortense arched an eyebrow at her but held the words about to spit from her tongue.

"Next time you head for the closet—" a shiver raced across Missy's shoulders when she glanced at the sky "—make sure there's room for me."

"Make room for a—" Hortense stared at her, straight in the eye. For half an instant her features softened. So quickly did the expression pass that it might have been a trick of wind and clouds playing over her face. "Clearly, I have no control of where you hide."

"There's Luminary ahead," Raymond announced. "Looks like we'll make it without getting wet."

Blessed be for meteorological good luck. The dull wool gown that Missy had borrowed scratched her skin without mercy. Any little bit of moisture would make her itchy and miserable.

Luminary didn't look any different from the last time she had been here, in spite of the rumors that the town was changing.

By the time Raymond pulled the team to a halt in front of Maybelle's, Hortense looked pale. Her hair frazzled out of its pinched bun.

"You can't make me go in there." Hortense's fingers dug into the seat of the buckboard. "We only came to send a wire. We were to do that and go home straight away... Raymond, please."

Raymond, please? Missy snapped her head around, away from the sign over Maybelle's door that advertised dancing ladies, to stare at Hortense.

Of all things, she dashed away a tear with thin, trembling fingers.

"It's a horrible, sinful place with women doing wicked things."

"Oh, for pity sake, sis." Raymond turned her chin, looking hard into her eyes. "The storm is going to hit and hit hard. Do you want to get caught out in it?"

"You know I don't, but really, I can't go in there."

"It won't be so bad." Missy patted Hortense's hand. "There won't be customers this time of day and there's a nice room at the top of the house to hide in. It locks from the inside and the out."

"Take me home," Hortense whispered, or more precisely, croaked.

At that instant lightning hit the ground less than a block away.

With a screech, Hortense dove from the wagon and shot up the front steps. She was inside Maybelle's before the shock of light faded and the ground quit shaking.

"Would you mind looking after my sister? The horses are spooked. I need to get them settled in the stable around back."

"I'll do what I can." Missy shimmied off the wagon without taking the time for a hand down.

Rushing through Maybelle's open front door

felt something like coming home. Candles and lamps gave the crimson room a rich glow. It was a warm cocoon in contrast to the threatening weather.

This time of day, the main room was deserted. Hortense gasped at the painting above the bar.

The youthful Maybelle, smiling down with an indecent proposal, must have robbed the small bit of breath cinched tight in Hortense's corset.

She swayed with one hand splayed over her breast.

Missy rushed forward and caught her under the arms. Hortense's weight and extra height sagged against her. She grunted with the effort to keep her burden upright. In the end her knees buckled and she wound up pinned between Hortense and a purple rug.

"Hortense! Wake up, I can't breathe."

Missy wiggled and grunted and finally managed to sit up with Hortense's head propped against her shoulder.

"What's going on in—" Maybelle, scurrying into the room, stopped in her tracks. She plucked her glasses from the top of her head and slid them onto her nose. She peered hard at the pair of women on her floor. "Well, dearie me, how on earth did you get there?"

She rushed forward and knelt down, taking a bit of Hortense's weight from Missy.

"We came in the front door. This is Raymond Gilroy's sister, Hortense."

"Yes, so I see. The poor dear."

"I don't know about the 'dear' part but, still, I couldn't have let her hit the floor smack-on."

"Clearly, but how did you...and where's your—" Maybelle glanced about the room then back at Missy. Her eyes widened. "Oh, dear me!"

A man's heavy footsteps sounded in the hall, coming quick.

He turned the corner and peered into the room with concern on his face, dashed with a hint of "not again."

"Oh, for pity's sake! How did you get there?"

"Edwin?" Missy gasped.

Wheels rolled across the carpet and came to a stop beside Edwin.

"She came through the front door," Suzie explained.

From down the hallway came another gasp, and then a decided thump.

"Mother?" Missy asked.

All heads, with the exception of Hortense's, turned toward the empty doorway.

"She's likely missed the new fainting couch by a good ten feet," Maybelle noted.

Mother had, in fact, missed the fainting couch by only a few steps. Missy sat on the floor and pillowed her mother's head in her lap.

"It's me, Mother, Missy." She stroked one pale cheek and touched hair that had, over the years, managed a pretty blush of silver in with the brown. "Wake up."

Edwin stepped over Missy and their unconscious mother in one long stride, carrying Hortense in his arms. He laid her on the fainting couch and patted her hand.

"Ummm..." Hortense murmured.

"I think she's coming around," Edwin said. "Who is she?"

"Hortense Gilroy... Oh, Mother! Are you all right? Anything broken or bruised?" Looking up at Edwin she added, "Hortense is the reverend's sister. I've been staying with them."

"Oh, praise be!" Mother expelled a deep breath and sat up. "The things we've been imagining... and hearing! And no, I'm not hurt, I've missed that couch so many times this last week the floor feels as familiar as my own bed."

Suddenly Missy found herself wrapped in a hug, enclosed by the comfort that only Mama's arms could give. Just as suddenly, her mother held her at arm's length, studying her from head to toe. "What on earth are you wearing? For pity sakes, it looks like dirt and feels like...sand! And please, dear, take off the hat before someone comes in and sees it."

"Mama," Missy whispered and felt her throat

tighten with unshed tears. "I'm sorry that you worried."

"This young lady needs some air." Edwin reached for the plain wood button defending the neckline of Hortense's dress.

Hortense's eyes blinked open in confusion at the very instant that Missy exclaimed, "Edwin, no!"

For a full three seconds Hortense's bleary eyes considered the face of the man bent over her. For one second a smile transformed her. From shrew to princess in a heartbeat.

In the next second, Raymond blew in the front door on a wave of wind and rain. Four doves, Emily among them, descended the stairs, all in time to witness Hortense slap Edwin's hand away and bolt upright with a screech.

What a string of events. Missy's fingers pulsed, itching to write everything down. Zane would want to know each delectable detail when he returned.

A muffled giggle filled the silence that followed the slap and screech.

"Susan Lenore Devlin! Where are your manners?" Edwin admonished. No doubt he was recalling his long-held belief that their parents had made a grave mistake in naming both twins after their mischievous Auntie Lenore.

Raymond rushed to his sister's side, trying to

look full of serious concern, but really, even he couldn't quite cover his amusement.

"But she…and then…and Missy's hat and…" Suzie covered her mouth but her giggles only came harder, infecting Missy like a virus.

"And this dress! And Mother and Miss Gilroy both on the floor, then that…screech…and Edwin's face." Missy gulped and struggled for control. "It's just too—"

"Horrible!" Hortense cried and scooted away from Edwin to cower on the far end of the couch.

"It's all right, sis, he's not a customer." Raymond sat on the couch and put his arm around his sister's shoulder in time to keep her from bolting when thunder pounded across the roof. "This gentleman has got to be Edwin Devlin, from Boston."

Missy stood up, fluffed a skirt that defied fluffing and walked over to Suzie. She settled on the arm of the wheelchair, hugging her sister tight and whispering that there were about a million and a half things they needed to get caught up on.

Once again, the room became silent with the pummel of rain on windows the only noise to fill it.

"Reverend Gilroy," Missy said, with her composure mostly restored. "This is my family—Edwin, Mother and Suzie. And you already know the ladies."

The ladies twittered and winked. Mother, being helped up off the floor by Edwin, gasped. Edwin spun about.

Raymond, with a grin that looked like mischief incarnate, hesitated five full seconds before informing Edwin that he knew the ladies in a purely pastoral way.

With the excitement settled and the introductions met, Edwin pivoted toward Missy, his expression set, severe.

"You, my dear little sister, have some explaining to do."

And so she did.

"Well, you wouldn't let me come west on my own. And it was my dream, after all. I meant to send you a wire all along, for gracious sakes. Then so much happened. When you hear it, well, you'll agree that it was all for the best."

"I'll agree to no such thing." As far as disapproving frowns went, Edwin presented his best. "You can't imagine the worry you caused Mother, not to mention the things we made up to tell the neighb—"

"Where's Muff?" Suzie asked, craning her neck this way and that, searching every dim corner of the parlor.

"I'm certain that he's fine," Missy said with a nod.

Hortense, who hadn't shifted her gaze from Edwin, said, "I doubt that. Your sister has encountered some trouble that you'll likely have to deal with."

Edwin pivoted back to stare down at Hortense. "I've all too much experience in that area. Maybe you would care to fill me in on the problem?"

"I've fallen in love!" Missy declared before Hortense had a chance to make things ugly. "Mother, do you need room on the couch?"

"No, just this once, I seem to have my legs under me."

A tug on her hair brought Missy's ear close to Suzie's mouth. "Tell them what they need to hear and later I'll have every delicious detail."

Edwin plunked down on the couch with his head bent, staring at the floor, his fingers tangled together in a vicious knot.

Her brother took five—she counted—deep breaths before looking up. When he did, he appeared weary, a few years older than when she had run away from home. Poor Edwin didn't deserve the worry she caused him. She would try to be gentle in the delivery of her news.

"Is there anything your mother and I need to worry about? And where is the dog?"

Hortense arched her eyebrows but, mercifully, kept her mouth pinched tight.

"The instant that Zane gets back with Muff we are going to get married and be deliriously happy." There, it was said, everyone could relax.

Somehow, though, Edwin didn't seem reassured. For some reason he had begun to look a little green around the mouth where his lips clamped together. Mother very subtly shook her head at him. How odd.

"Who—" Edwin asked and, really, he didn't appear well "—is this Zane?"

"Our Zane?" Maybelle exclaimed. With a hop and a clap, she rushed for the bar. "Come on, ladies, help me pour champagne for a toast."

"There couldn't be a better man," Emily tossed back as she trailed after Maybelle. "Truly!"

"High praise if I ever heard it." Edwin scrubbed his face with his hands.

"You don't know the half," muttered Hortense.

"Tell us all about your young man, dear." Mother stood behind Suzie's chair placing one hand on each of her daughter's heads. "What does he do for a living?"

Certainly Mother and Edwin were eagerly hoping to hear banker, lawyer or, at least, honest, hard-working farmer.

"I saw him rescue a baby from a raging river. He saved me from a flood and the clutches of—" Oh, better leave that story for Suzie alone. Already, her sister's mouth had opened in a perfect circle of anticipation.

"Pete!" Three doves exclaimed at the same time.

"Yes, there was Pete, but I meant—"

"Little sister," Edwin said on a defeated sigh.

"What does the man do for a living? How does he intend to support you?"

"Not to worry. He is an exceptional man," Maybelle squeaked. "I nearly raised him myself."

"He's quite a delight," a dove with ink-black hair and a sultry voice added, but Edwin didn't look reassured.

Rain flew against the windows. Vicious in its intensity, it ate up a long moment of silence.

Missy felt the pressure of her mother's hand move to her shoulder and squeeze, giving encouragement.

Some news had to be delivered standing, so she stood and folded her hands across her waist.

"Zane Coldridge is—" All at once Edwin pressed into the back of the couch and covered his face with both hands. Missy carried on, knowing that what she had to say would not put an end to his misery.

"A bounty hunter?" he groaned. "Well, hell, Missy, just kill me now."

"How did you guess that?"

Edwin stared blankly, silently, at the rain streaking down the window.

"But only until he finds a job as marshal." She hoped that bit of news would help her brother breathe again.

Mother touched her wrist to her forehead and took three steps toward the couch before she noticed that it was full. She took a deep, steadying breath, pinched her cheeks and turned to Missy with a great, suspiciously false smile.

"Our Missy is in love with Zane Coldridge." She shot a strange look at Edwin, then Suzie. "Isn't it wonderful?"

"I am in love, Mother!" Maternal arms embraced her. "I so want what you and father had."

"Oh, my baby." Her mother whispered. "I will pray for that very thing."

After a long moment, her mother released her.

"With all the excitement," Missy said, "I just now wondered. What are you doing here?"

She glanced from Suzie's grinning face to her mother's tearful one to Edwin's unreadable one.

Her gaze slid to Hortense. The silent message was clear. Zane had responded to the broadsheet and claimed his reward. That is how they knew to come. Zane was not coming back, Muff was not coming back.

"Mother? Edwin? How did you know where to find me?"

Edwin stood. He wrapped her in a hug. "Are you well and truly happy? You do look it."

She nodded against his shirt.

"We posted a reward for your safe return and—" He held her at arm's length, looking deeply into her eyes. "We got an answer…from Emily, here. We took the first train west."

Maybelle and the girls pressed flutes of champagne into everyone's hands.

"A toast to Zane's return and the coming wedding." Maybelle lifted her glass. Bubbles fizzed, catching the lamp glow.

Suzie lifted her glass. Mother sipped and dabbed at a tear. Edwin swallowed his libation in one gulp. Even Hortense took a taste and shrugged her shoulders.

Chapter Seventeen

"Something is going on." Missy settled into a stuffed chair and peered out the window. She watched a lantern swinging in the wind across the street. "Something very odd."

"We're so full of pie, I think we were hallucinating." Suzie leaned back in her chair and groaned, rubbing her belly.

"Pie is a clue, make no mistake." Missy leaned forward, catching her sister's full attention. "You saw them kiss as well as I did."

"It could be a passing fancy." Suzie tapped her finger on her chin. "Or not. Our brother has never been the passing-fancy type."

"So true, and Hortense laughed." Missy burrowed into the soft back of the chair, studying a drop of rain racing down the window. "Raymond says she used to, but I've never even heard a pleasant word come out of her mouth. And if she bakes one more pie…"

The dress she had borrowed from Suzie was lacy and soft, a garment that was nearly her own. Another bite of pastry might split it open.

"I'll bet Edwin hopes this rain goes on all week so that Hortense won't go home, is what I think," Suzie said.

"Edwin might go broke by then." Missy sighed. "It can't be cheap renting the whole brothel and paying the girls as much as they would have made with the gentlemen."

"It's been nearly two weeks. He can't keep it up much longer."

"You all should go home." They knew, now, that she was safe, that she wasn't going anywhere without Zane. "Desmond has got to be heartsick without you. You know that mother is convinced that the moment you turn your back some eyelash-fluttering fortune seeker will grab him up."

"Luckily for me, Desmond can spot a fortune seeker from across a room."

"He's always been insane over you."

"He hasn't changed a whit for me since I landed in this chair," Suzie said.

"He wouldn't, though. He saw the butterfly moon when you were all of, what? Thirteen?"

"When did Zane see it?" Suzie asked.

How did she admit that he hadn't? The family, even Suzie, would never believe that he was coming back if she did.

Rain and only rain is what kept him from coming to her.

She would dump her pens and copybook into a horse trough before she would believe anything different.

"Don't cry, sis." Suzie's hand touched her chin, turning her gaze away from the swaying blur of lamp below. "Zane will come walking through the front door anytime now. I feel it in my bones."

A tall man, dark-haired and handsome, did step through Maybelle's front door the very next day. With his tailored coat and stylish derby thoroughly drenched, Desmond Thornton swept Suzie out of her chair and danced her about the crimson parlor.

Clearly, nothing could prevent a man who had seen the butterfly moon from being with the woman he loved.

Missy loved Desmond, too. He had been like family forever and soon might truly be, but his presence pricked her, a tiny reminder that another day had passed and Zane seemed to have vanished into the great unknown.

Love, it seemed, flourished within the walls of the whorehouse on furlough.

Each coo and cuddle between Suzie and Desmond seemed like an accusation against the missing Zane. Every not-so-secret glance between Edwin and Hortense reminded Missy that she was alone.

Earlier in the day she had tried to find solace by writing in her journal but the pen felt as though it was dragging across her heart rather than the paper.

All that was left to her was music. With a sigh, she rose from where she sat beside Mother on the couch, watching Cupid do his best in the parlor.

She crossed the purple rug to the piano and plunked down on the bench. She needed to play something rousing, maybe even scandalous.

She had tapped out the first four notes of the devilish "Can-Can" when someone settled beside her on the bench.

Hortense, wearing her customary wool but with the top button loose, looked at her without a smile but also without bitterness.

"I think that I would enjoy that shopping trip to Dewton," she announced.

Missy's fingers skittered across the keys, because really, from Hortense, this equaled being on her knees begging forgiveness.

"I can't think of anything I'd enjoy more, Hortense." Suzie and Mother could come and they'd make a grand time of it. She could use a grand time.

Hortense smiled. She ducked her head, gazing

at her hands folded tightly in her lap. "With any luck, we'll both need wedding gowns."

Now, that cramped Missy's throat with tears. She leaned sideways and gave Hortense a hug. To her surprise, Hortense melted into it as if they had been longtime friends.

"You and Edwin! We knew it!"

"It's fast, I know, but Edwin says when you see the butterflies, well, that's just it."

"Who saw them?"

"Your brother saw them, but I feel them, right here." Hortense splayed her fingers over her belly. "And just so you know, I saw the way Mr. Cold-ridge looked at you when you were sick. I was so jealous of that. I was a shrew. That man would give up the world for you."

For the next three hours, Missy sat by the window, gazing up and down Ballico Street, watching for the man who would give up the world for her.

"The only one ever to have seen this much rain had to be Noah," Suzie remarked, rolling to a stop beside Missy's chair. "Edwin wants to see us in the kitchen."

"He probably wants to take us all home."

"He didn't say."

"I'm not going, Suz."

"After what you let me read about your Zane, I don't blame you." Suzie clearly tried to smile but couldn't. "Don't worry. That man is coming even if he has to follow you all the way to Boston."

She wouldn't be in Boston, though, she would be right here. Nothing Edwin could say would change that. Even without Zane, she could never return to the stifling life of a pampered lady.

Everyone was gathered about the kitchen table. Raymond sat beside his sister.

Maybelle, dressed as sweetly as a doting grandmother, set a plate of cookies on the table.

"Sit down, Missy. We have some matters to discuss," Edwin said. He looked nervous, which could not be good. Her brother never looked nervous.

"I won't discuss going home." Missy sat down with her back as straight as she could make it. "Nothing you can say will change my mind."

"Later, then." Edwin looked at everyone in the kitchen with utter joy shining out of his eyes. Well, he had seen the butterflies, after all.

He slipped out of his chair, bending on one knee before Hortense. "Marry me, Hortense, I love you. I'll cherish you always. I've spoken to your brother and how does tomorrow sound?"

Hortense covered her mouth with both hands. She looked...pretty, with curls springing about her nodding head and tears leaking from her eyes.

"The day after tomorrow, if you please. I'll need a gown, and a few flowers from home if they're not all drowned," she said.

Mother clapped her hands. "Oh, my! Welcome to the family, Hortense, dear. At last, a daughter with both feet firmly on the ground. Not that Missy and Suzie aren't my heart and soul, you understand."

Love and joy overflowed the kitchen. It sang off the walls and danced a happy jig. Missy glanced out the window to see nothing but rain and a long, empty street.

"What do you say, Suz?" Desmond slipped down on one knee before Suzie in her chair. "Let's give the gossips a heyday back home. Marry me now, right alongside your brother and Hortense!"

"You know how to sweep a girl right out of her chair, Desmond Thornton." Suzie kissed his lips thoroughly then laughed. "Oh, the lovely stir that would cause! But mother is set on a big social bash of a wedding, I'm sure."

"Mother," Mother announced, rushing over and kneeling to hug both Suzie and Desmond, "is set on no such thing, although I have been set on you, young man, for the longest time."

"Ladies will be fainting in the street when the folks back home get word that our Suzie has snatched Desmond right off the market…so to speak, and without a social hoopla," Missy declared.

"Those ladies faint when a black cat crosses in front of them." Mother stood, she straightened her spine and took a fortifying breath. "They could all use a trip to the Wild West to give them some starch in their backbones."

Both of her siblings, married! Missy wanted to cry a bucketful of self-pity. Her smile actually hurt.

Hours later Missy stepped outside of Maybelle's front door and stood under the porch roof. She watched the persistent rain patter the boardwalk two feet beyond the ruffle of her hem. The smile that she had secured in place for so long slipped.

Inside, wedding plans had everyone in high spirits. The ceremony was to take place in the parlor. Mother, Maybelle and the ladies bustled about, making things sparkle, adding a bit of lace to this and an extra candle to that.

The spirit of the butterfly moon bound everyone in dreams of a joyful future, but Zane had not at anytime seen, or expected to see, the butterfly moon. She tried to fight the image, but it became too easy to visualize her bright future fading.

Missy covered her face with her hands, ready to weep her despair, but the door opened behind her and she snatched back her hands and her tears. She turned with a forced smile and met Edwin's frown.

"You know we've got to talk," he said.

"Edwin, you think you know what's best for me. I get that, but I can't go home, I won't."

"There is something that you don't know."

Edwin leaned against the wall and folded his arms across his chest. He stared at the tips of his boots for the longest time before looking at her.

"I told you that we came because Emily sent a wire, and that was true. I've already paid her the reward. But, sis, she wasn't the only one to have claimed the money."

He reached in his pocket and pulled out two sheets of paper that were clearly telegrams. He gave one to her.

Blustery wind tugged at her skirt and raced up her legs. She curled the telegram in her fist, crushing it without looking at it.

"You can't crush the truth. He told us where to find you in Dewton."

She loosened her fist and felt the paper nibble her palm. Still, she would not look at it. "Maybe he did do that, but that was before. I'm sure he regretted it later."

"Look, sis, I don't doubt that the man cares for you, only a fool wouldn't, but where is he? There's been time and more for him to get back, whether he found Muff or not."

"The rivers are swollen. He probably can't get across."

"He could have sent word."

"What's to say the telegraph wires haven't washed away?"

"There's this." Edwin held out the other sheet of paper. "Reverend Gilroy received this one."

She folded her arms across her chest and shook her head.

"You're stronger than that. Read it," Edwin said.

"How long have you had this?"

"Too long." Edwin stared out at the rain and uttered a curse. Her brother never cursed within her hearing.

"I waited…I hoped I wouldn't have to…well, it's past time to go home."

"Not for me it isn't." She snatched the paper from his fist and crushed it. "I'm going to wait right here until Zane comes to get me."

"Just like Hortense, sis? Sitting on that porch and becoming bitter?"

"Go inside, Edwin."

He kissed her cheek. The wood door banged closed behind him. Wind blew the water falling from the overhang sideways at her. She opened the telegram sent to the reverend, blinking moisture off her lashes.

The words had blurred with water and repeated folding. Most of them of them were illegible.

She read a faint *forgive me,* a bolder *leaving a burden,* a smudged and dirty *sin.* The message was short but the word *mistake* might have been printed only a moment ago.

Forgive, burden, sin and *mistake* did not sound like the words of a man pledging his undying love. Not a single mention of the blow to her head, he never asked if she had even survived. His missive was one of remorse, his words a lifetime away from her dream of happily ever after.

She tossed the telegrams into the mud beyond the porch.

Chapter Eighteen

Ballico Street was little more than a mud puddle, but with sunshine glittering off the standing water, it seemed to Zane like nothing less than the gold-paved streets of Heaven.

He was home. A journey that should have taken a couple of days had turned into an odyssey of mud and frustration. At times it seemed that he had fallen into a nightmare where, try as he might, he could not return to the woman who depended upon him, maybe for her very life.

Had she recovered? Riding the prairie in ankle-deep muck had given him too much time to reflect and worry.

Nothing but death would keep her away from him again. He prayed hourly that they were not already separated.

The bundle under his jacket stretched, squirmed then resettled, warm and dry under his coat.

He patted the bulge. "Don't you worry, little one, only another block to go."

At last, only one block more to Maybelle's where he could stash his traveling companions for a while. He glanced back at Daisy and Number Nine. All of them, he and Ace included, wore mud up to their knees.

The front door of Maybelle's opened and Maybelle stepped out. She walked beyond the overhang, spreading her arms and stretching like a lazy cat in the sunshine. Other than Missy, there was not a soul on earth he was happier to see.

"You look like home and heaven all in one," he said to her.

He had expected to be greeted with a hug, or at least a smile. The scowl made him more than uneasy.

"You took your sweet time getting here, young man, I ought to—"

Whatever scolding he was about to get was cut short by Muff peeking his head out of the saddle pack. He whined and wiggled, trying to get out.

"I've brought you something," he said.

"Well now, you did bring back little Muff. I did say you would all along." Now she smiled. "No wonder it took you forever to get here, with the menagerie you've brought along."

She reached for Muff. "You better get inside and set some things straight."

Some things would have to wait. "Not now, I've got to get to Reverend Gilroy's place. Can you take care of this for me until I get back?"

"No need to go all the way out... Oh, my word... Where on earth!" she exclaimed when he opened his coat and handed her the sleeping toddler.

"This is Little Blue."

Maybelle hugged Little Blue to her bosom and twined a loop of his fine blond hair about her finger, all the while muttering, "Oh, my word."

"When he wakes up you'll see the bluest eyes in God's creation."

"Where on earth did you get him?"

"I won him."

"You what!" Maybelle hugged the two-year-old closer.

"I'll explain it all later. Muff and I have got to get to the reverend's. With any luck, this is my wedding day."

"Oh, dear, you might well need some luck with that."

Her words hit him like a physical blow. It felt as if a fist had grabbed his throat, choking his voice.

"Missy isn't at the reverend's, she's here," Maybelle said, not taking her gaze off Little Blue.

Missy wasn't dead. His heart kicked to life again.

"In Luminary?" Alive, and only moments from him!

"For the moment, dear, she's just inside but—"

He leaped from Ace's back and swept Muff from the saddle pack in one move. Maybelle's voice followed him, no more than a buzz in his head. He ran into the parlor, not caring that Maybelle would scold him for not cleaning boots that bore more mud than leather.

And there she was, the answer to his prayers, the substance of his dreams, healthy and whole. Sitting on the couch on the lap of a stranger.

Kissing him, laughing, her face declared her joy.

Black clouds gathering in his mind suffocated reason. Anger and grief nearly took out his knees. The brim of his Stetson seemed to press tighter about his head.

"Darlin', get off that man's lap," he gritted between clenched teeth.

She noticed him for the first time. Her big blue eyes grew round in an expression he knew too well. She all but shimmered in delight.

Who was this woman? Apparently, one with no shame. Only days ago she'd vowed her love and he'd vowed his. He set Muff on the floor.

"Zane Coldridge! I thought you wouldn't get here in time."

"Looks like I didn't."

Since she made no move to get up, he scooped her out of the stranger's arms. What kind of man grinned at having his woman plucked away? He must be a fool.

Zane kissed her hard. He kissed her long. He would wipe the taste of the grinning greenhorn off her lips or die trying.

Something was wrong with the kiss. He was looking for the missing spark when he felt a finger tapping his shoulder.

"Mr. Coldridge, I'll take my wife back, if you don't mind."

What the hell! He minded, all right. He curled his fist, ready to let it fly when Maybelle bustled up with Little Blue, awake and reaching for him.

"Zane, this is Mrs. Desmond Thornton…Suzie Thornton."

"It's a pleasure to meet you, Zane. Truly… a pleasure!" Suzie Thornton shot him a wicked grin and reached for her husband.

Zane couldn't hand her back quickly enough.

"Suzie…Devlin…Thornton?" He looked between Suzie and her husband. "If you want to call me out I won't even draw my weapon."

"No offense taken, by me at least… Humph… Clearly not by my bride, either. You've got to know, this kind of thing happens all the time with the Devlin sisters. Well, not precisely this, but a man gets used to the pair of them after a while."

"Papa," the little boy whined and reached for Zane.

"Papa?" Suzie's mouth fell open. Her brave husband pushed it closed with one finger. "I've read so much about you, but not..." She reached over and cupped Little Blue's cheek.

"He's recently come by," Maybelle said. "Won in a poker game, I expect, but Zane will tell us all about it later."

"Missy's out back by the stable," Desmond said. "But you'd better be quick if you have something to set straight."

For the first time, Zane noticed the bags and valises in the parlor. More than one person was taking a trip today.

Missy dangled her journal over the horse trough near Maybelle's stable. It trembled in her fingers. She had vowed that nothing could make her go home. Even without Zane, she had been certain that nothing could make her give up the adventure, the personal freedom, of living in the Wild West.

But she had been wrong. Something could make her go home. Her courses were late. Only a day, but a very big day.

Glory, but how would she support a child by pushing a broom or playing piano in some tawdry saloon? It's not as though she could deposit an infant in a basket like she had Muff.

In the space of a heartbeat, a new path had been set before her. All she had to do now was dump her old, impossible dreams into the horse trough. Just a slight opening of her fingers would see it done.

"Darlin', I hope that's not me you're giving to the livestock."

Her fingers did open, but in surprise. Zane caught the journal before it hit the water. She spun about, angry with herself for wanting to launch into his arms in a clinging, pathetic hug.

"Where's my dog?" she demanded instead.

Before Zane could answer, a ragged ball raced across the yard. His barking scattered a family of sparrows from a bush but he didn't pause to consider them in his race toward her skirt.

She scooped him up, knowing that Suzie wouldn't care a whit about the dirty paw prints marking her lacy pink gown.

Zane moved forward, his arms coming at her with an apparent embrace in mind.

"Hold it right there, Mr. Coldridge." She braced her open palm on his chest. "You're too late."

"You're alive, I'm here and Raymond Gilroy is a short ride away. Timing's just right, darlin'."

Drat! Why did he have to call her *darlin'?* As if his smoky brown eyes weren't enough to weaken her will all by themselves.

"It's too late to collect your reward. Edwin's already paid the whole thing to Emily."

He shot back three steps, as though her hand on his chest had been a pistol instead of fingers that longed for nothing more than to linger over the rapid thud of his heart.

"It's a disappointment, I'm sure," she announced.

He turned away from her then paced heavy-footed from the trough to an arbor that divided the yard from the stable. His coat flared open with his bold strides. He took off his hat and threw it on the grass. Hair that glinted true black in the sunshine whispered against his shirt. He kicked a rock. She forced an extra shiver of ice to her voice.

If it hadn't been for the second telegram, the one Zane sent to Raymond Gilroy, she might have relented at the devastated look he shot her.

But really, who wouldn't be dashed over losing that big fat reward?

A horse whinnied. Because she couldn't stand to see the regret in Zane's expression, she turned to look at the animal being led into the stable by Moe.

"Number Nine!" She set Muff on the grass. He trotted to a bush and lifted his leg. Heavens if her pup hadn't become a dog during the very long time it had taken Zane to bring him back.

"There's another one, too, Miss Missy," Moe called, leading Daisy into view.

Now, that shook her. Hopefully, Zane didn't see the moisture gathering in her eyes. He must have looked a regular Noah, leading his little zoo across the flooded plains.

Truly, it might have taken a lesser man a month or more to get here. She could almost believe his distress was because of her. Almost, but his own cursed words *forgive me, burden, sin* and *mistake*, kept her from running to him.

"Well, then." She prayed that her voice did not give away the quiver tightening her throat. "Since you've returned everything that Wesley Wage took from me, you must have captured him. I'll take my percentage of the reward…partner."

Zane reached her in three long strides; he gripped her upper arms. Drawing her to within a foot of him, he gazed down. She couldn't look away from the anguish on his face. It was dashed impossible to appear aloof with a tear rolling down her cheek.

"I didn't capture Wage. I could have, maybe I should have, but there were complications that delayed me as it was. Lord, Missy, I was wild to get back to you. The extra time it would have taken to turn him in wasn't worth it."

"Complications? What could be more simple, or important, than coming back?" Her composure broke. Another tear rolled off her nose. Oh, curse it, still another pooled in the corner of her mouth. By some mercy she didn't sob out loud. "You didn't know if I was dead or alive, I didn't know if you were!"

"There were things that couldn't be helped. I wired Reverend Gilroy about it."

"Yes, so you did." That very telegram kept her from blubbering out her love for him right now.

She shook herself free of his grip, but didn't back away.

"Maybe you'd care to explain those complications."

"Maybe I would!" The visage of grief, so plain on his face a moment ago, vanished. His eyes narrowed and his lips set in a determined line.

He caught her hand and hustled her toward the house. Before they stepped through the back door, he paused.

"Just to make it clear, I love you. That wire about the reward, I sent it before I knew that." He swooped in, quick as a flash and kissed her. "I tried to tell you but I was scared."

She shook off his kiss and snatched her hand free. "Scared of an honest explanation? Really, Zane, was I that intimidating to a rough-and-tumble bounty hunter?"

"My future was in your response, darlin'. Still is."

Swiping the tears from her face, she straightened her spine and presented him with her back.

She strode down the long hall toward the parlor. Muff scrambled past, bursting into the room with a happy yip.

Her family, growing as fast as Cupid could aim his arrow, gathered about Maybelle. Each and every one of them cooed and gurgled over something that she held in her arms. The tight knot of admirers prevented Missy from seeing what it was.

"That was the complication," Zane whispered in her ear, coming up from behind and standing way too close.

Heads turned, everyone was smiling, for mercy sake. Her life was crumbling about her and her family looked like a group of grinning buffoons.

As one, they stepped back to reveal a little boy, still round with baby fat.

"That's my son. Yours, too, if you'll have him."

The man was insane. He'd betrayed her, broken her heart and now wanted her to raise his... son? She ought to be ranting, she ought to be raving. Endless days spent together, talking of this, discussing that, nearly married for mercy sakes, and he'd never mentioned a child.

She ought to be behaving like a braying lunatic, but instead, she approached the boy. She yearned to hold him, as though he had been the answer to her lifelong prayers.

His cherub face looked irresistible, his fair hair

would feel like an angel's kiss. But it was his eyes, so sunny and sweet, that compelled her to reach out and touch his cheek.

"You never mentioned a son, all this time and you never said a word. Were you afraid of me then, too?"

The boy squirmed in Maybelle's arms, said, "Down, play Muff!" Maybelle set him on the floor and he scrambled after the dog. Emily followed them down the hall.

The back screen screeched open and slammed closed.

"Oh, no, dear." Maybelle took Missy's hands in hers and looked earnestly into her face. "He is come by recently. Zane's about to tell us all how he won the boy."

The big, bold bounty hunter, living only for his next capture, had won a child. That was a story needing to be written down, if ever there was one. She nearly ran back out in the yard to fetch her journal, which was at this moment lying on the grass near Zane's hat and likely being eaten by Muff.

But no, that was something the old Missy would do, Missy the dreamer.

"We're all ears, Mr. Coldridge," Missy said, flanked on both sides by her family, those lifelong and those recently come by. Even Raymond Gilroy stood among them, having just arrived to bid his sister farewell. "Please do tell us your tale, but in a hurry. Our train won't wait. Isn't that right, Edwin?"

Her brother frowned at her, sighed then shrugged his shoulders. "We'll need to be in Dewton by three."

"Not if I can help it." Zane's voice sounded more a growl than good American English.

"There's nothing you can say to change what has happened." Without thinking, Missy placed one hand over her belly, feeling protective of the secret that might be growing inside.

Oh, drat! Maybe not so secret. Mother had noticed the ageless gesture. She looked suddenly pale and more than a little unsteady. To her credit, she did not rush for the couch. Instead, she braced her hands on the back of Suzie's chair. Missy hoped that she was the only one to notice that her mother's knuckles had turned white to the bone.

Zane Coldridge looked as afflicted as Mother did. He might think that whatever he had to say would change her mind about him, but it would not. She knew what she knew, no matter how she wished she did not.

"Mr. Coldridge," Hortense said, her cheeks flushed and her hands wrung together in front of her. "I'd like to say something before you begin, if I may."

"Hortense?" Zane seemed surprised, as though he had not noticed her before. Truth be told, she did not resemble the woman Zane would have last seen, with her happy disposition and a newlywed blush to her cheeks.

For a long moment Hortense stood before him with her head bowed. At last she looked up, meeting his puzzled gaze.

"This is something for everyone to hear." She glanced at Missy then back at Zane. "I said some hateful things to you and about you. For the extent that I'm responsible for your current situation, I do apologize."

From close at hand, Missy heard a whispered "Thank you." She glanced sideways to see Raymond looking heavenward and smiling.

Apparently struck speechless, Zane merely stared at Hortense. He cleared his throat. "None of this is because of you, Hortense. And I apologize to you as well, for… You'll know what for."

Hortense's cheeks flamed. "Don't think another thing about that… Truly, I tried my best to convince Missy that you were a cad and never coming back. At the time, I believed that is what men did, until I met Edwin. You wouldn't know this yet, but we were married day before yesterday."

Zane bent and kissed her cheek. "Congratulations, Hortense. Don't think you are to blame for anything, things that had nothing to do with you kept me from getting back."

"I'm sure we're all desperate to hear what they are," Missy said. Actually, she *was* desperate to hear them, even though she forced her voice to sound mocking.

Hortense returned to the line of family facing Zane and slipped under Edwin's arm. He hugged her close with a besotted grin on his face.

Missy would wait awhile to tell her brother her news, let him enjoy a few weeks of wedded bliss before he had to deal with another of his sister's mishaps.

"I was desperate," Zane began, looking only at Missy. "You looked like you would slip away at any moment, even the doctor didn't know what to do. The only thing to do was wait…wait and pray. I did that, then I thought Muff might be the one to bring you around, so I lit out. I was going to bring him back or die trying."

Beside her, Raymond nodded. He must think this was the truth so far, the truth as he understood it anyway.

"It didn't take long to catch up with Wage. He was camped a day from Foggy Johnson Creek. Probably headed there to finish the job that you interrupted with the hat pin to his backside."

Missy noticed every eye widen, heads turn her way, but she kept her gaze on Zane, determined not to be swayed by adventuresome memories of the past.

"I was desperate to get back to you, so I took the horses and Muff. I left Wage stranded by his campfire. I wanted to hand him over to the law, or at least take the time to give him what he deserved for what he did to you." Again, heads turned her way. A look of pure horror crossed Mother's face. "But, darlin', I couldn't spare the time.

"Under normal conditions I would have been back in a couple of days, but the rain was a beast and the rivers hard to cross. The horses could barely keep the pace I asked of them.

"A day later I came upon a campfire a few miles outside of Brittlewood. There was a tent set up and a poker game going on inside, just a few men from town wanting a good time. Well, the horses were spent and it was getting late so I asked to join them. Near the far edge of the tent was Little Blue, asleep on a damp blanket and shivering even in his sleep. As time went on the man who admitted to being the boy's father got drunker and meaner. When he was out of money, he offered up his son. Now, the other men seemed pretty uncomfortable with that and got up to go home."

The family was so silent that a pin dropping in the building next door would have seemed an explosion. Surely, everyone must hear Missy's heart throbbing against her ribs. She'd give anything to believe his story. If only she hadn't re-read that blasted telegram so many times that it had become burned into her memory.

"I wanted to get up and go with them, every

minute off the trail home was agony. I started to go but then Little Blue coughed. His own father was too drunk to notice that the boy looked flushed with fever.

"Forgive me, Missy, I knew you needed me, but how could I leave the child with that man? So I said I'd play for the boy, but only if he signed away his rights. By damn, he did it. Wasn't much to beat the drunken cuss and gather up Little Blue. His pa never even said good-bye.

"I didn't know what to do, darlin'. What was I to do? I supposed he might have a mother in Brittlewood, so I took him there. Well, he didn't, so I found a lawyer and a judge. Turns out they'd long been concerned about the boy, given who his only parent was. When I told them the story and showed them the paper the man had signed, they let me adopt him right there."

From out in the back, Missy heard Muff and Little Blue playing. One laughed and the other yipped. She could love that child, without a doubt she could.

"I took him and rode away fast, just in case his pop sobered up and wanted to fight me for him, because at that point I would have. I stopped in Still Water the next day because Little Blue was sicker than the day before. I couldn't drag him about in the rain so we stayed there for more than a week until he recovered.

"I sent a wire to Raymond, to explain everything."

And that is where Zane Coldridge lost her. "Do you know, if it hadn't been for that wire, I'd believe your story?" She turned to her brother. "Grab our bags, Edwin, it's time to go."

Zane clutched her arm and pulled her out from the midst of her family who had turned, about to industriously gather up bags.

"I don't understand," Zane whispered, letting go of her arm. "If you read the wire, then—"

"I read it, all right!" Missy spun away from him, her lacy skirt brushed his muddy boots. "I see it in my sleep, it eats at me every minute of every day, Zane Coldridge. There's nothing you can say to change what you wrote."

"And exactly what is it about that wire that has you so fired up?"

"I'm finished talking to you. Let's go home, everyone."

She had only taken two steps toward the door when Mother's touch on her back halted her.

"Listen to him," she whispered close to Missy's ear. "There are decisions too important for hurt and pride to decide, and I think you know what I mean." Mother glanced at her belly. "Listen hard to what the man has to say."

Mother walked away, leaving her face-to-face with Zane and an ocean of hurt roiling between them. It seemed like they were alone in the world, even though the others had not left the room but stood near the door with valises in hand.

"What was so all-fired wrong with that telegram?" To his credit, Zane truly did look perplexed.

"You asked Raymond to forgive you for a sin!" She couldn't help it, she poked him in the chest, forcing him back a step. "You said that I was a mistake and a burden! Really, is that what I was to you? A quick buck? A sordid night and a good reward? If you took the time to read the small print, you'd see that you weren't even entitled to the money."

Edwin groaned, or cursed, it was hard to tell.

Zane looked stunned. "I'd like to see that telegram, it sure isn't what I noted it to say."

"It said what it said, Zane." If she stood here one more second, she knew her heart would burst. She spun about, heading for the door.

"'Forgive me, Raymond,'" Zane called out, clearly reciting his version of the infamous wire.

Let him make up quotes until forever, for all the difference it would make. Lies that seemed to be the truth rolled so easily off his tongue. She didn't pause in the long walk toward the door.

"'Forgive me Raymond,'" he repeated while everyone moved toward the door, silent as stones. "'Tell Missy, even if she can't hear you, that I'm on my way. Forgive me for leaving the burden of her care on you. It's a sin to delay but it would be a grave mistake to rush home at present.'"

She stopped, looking out the open door with her new life's path stretching away. It looked to be a cold and lonely road. If only she could believe that is what the smears on the telegram said, she would turn around, throw her arms about his neck and never let him go.

She didn't even try to contain her tears now. The sob that had been trapped in her chest for days finally escaped.

A few more steps toward the door and it would be over. The decision that sliced her heart into bitter pieces would be made. She wiped her sleeve across her face.

"I've seen the butterfly moon." Zane's words cut her at the knees; they nearly buckled. If a voice could ache, his surely did.

"Drop the bags, Edwin," Mother ordered.

Valises hit the floor in a chorus of thuds.

Zane slipped up behind her, so close that she could feel the warmth of him, smell prairie and wood smoke on his clothes. He put his hands on her shoulders and turned her.

She looked into his eyes and knew the truth. It gazed out at her, clear and honest.

"I've seen it and there's no going back for me. If you walk out that door I will follow you." Suddenly, her new path had another traveler on it. He'd turned the road around, curved it back so that she was exactly where she wanted to be. "As a former bounty hunter, I've got tracking skills. You'll never be free of me. You know that's true?"

She nodded, then cupped his face, running her fingertips over two weeks of unshaved stubble. Oh, yes, the West still rode wild in those smoky brown eyes. Her bounty hunter—former, that is—had not been tamed by the sight of the butterfly moon and that suited her just fine.

"I'm going to begin a new book," Missy murmured. "It's probably going to start off with a little surprise."

"Should I keep Ace at the ready?"

She shook her head. While the seeds of adventure had, once again, taken root, they would hold her to this spot and this man forever.

He lifted her off the purple rug and kissed her, smearing her tears on his cheeks and lips.

Gradually she became aware of sounds other than Zane whispering in her ear that he loved her.

When he set her on her feet she looked about and saw Mother weeping, Suzie clapping in delight, Hortense sniffling into Edwin's shirt and the reverend praising God. Desmond and Maybelle stood, arm-in-arm, grinning.

The last thing she wanted to do was let go of Zane, but he held her at arm's length, then bent on one knee.

"Darlin', when a man has seen the magic, there's nothing left to do. As I recall we've missed our wedding day. Marry me now, marry me and Little Blue."

She nodded her head because she couldn't speak. Magic must have robbed her of her voice.

Luckily, Raymond Gilroy knew what to do. He marched forward with Cupid sitting on his shoulder and a great grin on his face.

Christmas Eve 1881

Missy Lenore Coldridge leaned toward the fireplace in the foyer of the Luminary School of Proper Deportment for Ladies of Social Change. She opened her coat to fill it with warmth before she made the short walk to Maybelle's.

Through the window next to the hearth she watched icy-looking clouds press down upon Luminary.

"It looks like snow for Christmas," she called out to her mother.

Footsteps tapped across the wood floor. Mother's head popped into view around the door frame.

"How utterly romantic." Mother's face blushed with pleasure.

"Will the ladies be ready for the party tonight, do you think?"

"Oh, yes indeed!" Mother glanced back into the room, smiling brilliantly. "Most of them, anyway."

Emily, looking sweet and stylish in a modest gown, came out of the room and stood next to Missy, reaching her fingers toward the heat of the flames. Mother joined them.

"How do you do, Mrs. Coldridge?" Emily nodded her head, her posture polished, her smile genteel. "It is a pleasure to see you again."

"Well done, Emily!" Mother clapped her hands. "You are a most becoming woman. You'll certainly gain the favor of the right sort of gentlemen tonight."

Emily blushed, which must have pleased Mother to no end. It was common knowledge that the only gentleman Emily had in mind was the reverend.

"If I do it will be because of you, Mrs. Devlin." Emily shook off her proper posture for a moment to wrap Mother in a great hug. "Some of the whores—ladies, that is—" she corrected, seeing mother's sudden frown "—we'd be dead or worse if you hadn't remained here to teach us a better way. To think of the life you left behind in Boston…well, we're all as grateful as can be."

"Oh, posh, Emily. Boston will hardly be the worse for the loss of one stuffy old matron. Now go back inside and help the others practice their diction."

"I'd better get going, too." Missy hugged her mother. "It can't be easy preparing the hotel for the Christmas Eve party with Edwin Blue and Muff underfoot."

"I can't imagine that your brother would ever feel his namesake was in the way. Let me get my coat, I'll walk with you."

"You don't have to. It's only a few blocks."

"Don't set a foot outside this building without me, young lady. Your husband would never forgive me if I allowed you to slip belly-first off the boardwalk." Mother shrugged on her coat and tapped down her hat. "Besides, I need to stop by the *Gazette* and borrow a hat from Suzie. Poor Miss Adele turned up at my door with barely a stitch to her name."

"Suzie might have a hat, or ten, to spare." Missy looped her arm through her mother's as they walked out the front door. "Since she and Desmond took over the paper it's selling like blazes."

"Really, Missy, I'd never allow my students to use such an expression." Mother shot her the arch look that Missy had grown accustomed to over the years.

"Hot cakes, then, selling like hot cakes."

"That's so much better on the ears, dear."

The short stroll down Ballico Street was pleasant. The town had changed. It scarcely resembled the wicked place that Missy had first seen while sitting upon Ace and snuggled between the safety of Zane's thighs. Back then, her eyes had been wide with astonishment and delight. But really, all along, she had been naive.

Cold air nipped at her nose, smelling wet with the coming snow. Once in a while the scent of pine garlands strung over store windows filled her lungs. Merry-looking candles burned in the windows of the bakery and Newton's Steak House.

Under the freshly painted sign that read Maybelle's Inn for the Gentle Travler, Missy bade her mother goodbye.

It took only a moment to collect Edwin Blue, but rounding up Muff meant a trip up and down the stairs, then a romp through the kitchen where she finally cornered him in the pantry.

Edwin, Hortense and Maybelle, bustling about in preparation for the Christmas and Coming Out Party, spared a quick good-bye when she went out the front door with Blue's little fist gripped in hers and Muff riding her mostly vanished waist.

Her destination, the marshal's office, was across the street and only a block down.

All of a sudden, the wind picked up and the temperature seemed to fall by half. On the other side of the street Mother rushed past with a hatbox tucked under her arm. She waved and watched until Missy opened the marshal's door and went inside.

Missy hung up her coat, set her hat on the desk then led Blue toward the woodstove in the center of the room. She took off his small coat and turned him in circles, evenly warming him.

"Papa must have just stepped out." Half a cup of coffee sat beside her hat with steam curling up and away. "Now, it's nap time for you, young man."

"No nap, Mama!" Blue frowned up at her while rubbing his sleepy eyes.

"You'll need your rest." She picked him up and carried him to the cot behind the desk. She tucked a blanket around him and knelt down to kiss his forehead. "We're going to the Christmas party at Uncle Edwin's hotel. And later, after you go to bed…Santa's coming!"

Maybe he heard the last part of what she said, but already he was asleep, sucking on his thumb as though it were a candy cane.

"Sweet dreams, Blue," she whispered. And he would have sweet dreams, now that he had a family. She tucked in the blanket once again, shuddering when she wondered where he would be this very moment if Zane hadn't won him. Out in the cold with no one to care, more than likely. Certainly, Santa wouldn't have a clue where to find him.

Getting up wasn't as easy as it used to be. She held on to the edge of the cot to push to her feet. With several weeks to go before the baby's birth, she'd likely get so big she'd have to catch a ride with Suzie in her chair in order to get about.

Beautiful, blessed silence settled over every corner of the room. Until lately, she'd never appreciated the wonder of it. With an hour or so to herself, it was the perfect time to begin her new project.

The very bottom drawer of Marshal Coldridge's desk belonged to her. She sat down, moved Zane's abandoned coffee aside, then opened the drawer and drew out her writing supplies. She flipped open the pristine pages of her new journal and dipped her pen in fresh ink.

She paused for a moment to look out the window and listen to a chunk of wood fall to coals in the stove. Just now, while she watched, snow began to blow past the glass.

Lovely! Life was lovely, marriage was lovely and the little one tumbling in her belly was lovely.

She smoothed a knee, or an elbow, away from her ribs. "Merry Christmas, little one."

Nothing could mar the peace of the moment.

Except an angry voice out on the boardwalk and the front door flinging open to let in a blast of frigid air.

Zane marched inside with a handcuffed prisoner secured in front of him.

The marshal appeared more than pleased. His prisoner, however, looked as if he might be choking on a putrid fish.

The string of foul sentiments pouring out of

his mouth dried up, his pale face grew ever more pasty as he stared at her.

"You!" he squealed, sounding like a cornered piglet.

"You remember my very valuable wife, Mr. Wage." Zane's grin cut across his face. Clearly, he took more than professional pleasure in this arrest. "Good thing for you, really, that her bounty went uncollected, at least by you. She's wicked with a hat pin, you might recall."

Missy stood up but kept the desk between her belly and the prisoner. Wage would not get away from Zane this time, but if she moved an inch closer, her husband would give her a scolding.

She wouldn't smudge this moment for him for all the ink in Ink Town.

"Up to no good again, Mr. Wage?" Missy shook her head and frowned. "I wouldn't mind a moment alone with your prisoner, Zane."

Zane would never allow that, of course, but the look of horror in Wage's heavy-lidded eyes and the sweat breaking out on his flaccid cheeks when she reached for her hat was all the setting-straight she needed.

"Lock me up, Marshal, I demand my rights."

Zane shrugged his shoulders, melting her with a wink and a grin. "Sorry, darlin'. The prisoner does have a right to be kept safe until trial."

Missy sighed with a good bit of drama and set

the headpiece back on the desk. "You are such a one to go by the books."

Wesley Wage all but dragged Zane back into the holding area behind the office.

"Merry Christmas, Mr. Wage!" she called after him.

A moment later the cell door clanked closed and the key grated in the lock.

Lovely! Merry Christmas one and all. Snow fell silently beyond the window. She picked up her pen and began to write.

She listened to the heavy oak door between the cells and the office close. A moment later the stove door squealed on its hinges and Zane tossed in another log.

He came up behind her and laid his big, cold hands on her shoulders. He bent to kiss her head.

"Well, partner, you finally got him," she said, turning her face up to capture his kiss.

"No reward, though."

"How ever will we console ourselves?"

He bent over, drew a strand of hair away from her neck, sniffed her skin then kissed the very spot.

"We'll come up with something, I suppose." He popped open ten inches of buttons on her bodice and slipped his fingers inside. "Blue asleep?"

"Sweet dreams of Santa."

He glanced down to see what his explorations had uncovered. "Ho, Ho, Ho."

She set her pen down.

"You writing another dime novel, darlin'?" He leaned over her shoulder, peering at the page.

"The Domestic Adventures of Missy Lenore Coldridge and her Intrepid Husband, Zane," she quoted.

"Heaven help us all," he murmured close to her ear, but she felt his smile tickle her cheek.

* * * * *

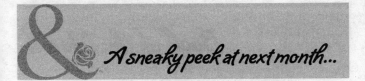

HISTORICAL

IGNITE YOUR IMAGINATION, STEP INTO THE PAST...

My wish list for next month's titles...

In stores from 1st February 2013:

☐ Never Trust a Rake – Annie Burrows

☐ Dicing with the Dangerous Lord – Margaret McPhee

☐ Haunted by the Earl's Touch – Ann Lethbridge

☐ The Last de Burgh – Deborah Simmons

☐ A Daring Liaison – Gail Ranstrom

☐ The Texas Ranger's Daughter – Jenna Kernan

Available at WHSmith, Tesco, Asda, Eason, Amazon and Apple

Just can't wait?

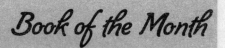

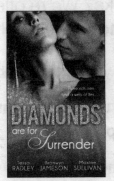
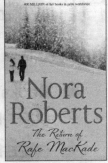

*What will you treat
yourself to next?*

*Ignite your imagination,
step into the past...*
6 new stories every month

INTRIGUE...

Breathtaking romantic suspense
Up to 8 new stories every month

*Captivating medical drama –
with heart*
6 new stories every month

MODERN™

*International affairs,
seduction & passion guaranteed*
9 new stories every month

nocturne™

*Deliciously wicked
paranormal romance*
Up to 4 new stories every month

RIVA™

*Live life to the full –
give in to temptation*
3 new stories every month available
exclusively via our Book Club